ROGUE

By John R. Monteith

Braveship Books

# Table of Contents

# CHAPTER 1

Dmitry Volkov raised his head and pressed his palms into the navigation table. His back straightening, he felt shards of shame.

"How long until our weapon hits?" he asked in Russian.

"Almost thirteen minutes," the sonar operator said.

"This doesn't feel right."

"Trust the plan, Dmitry."

"An elaborate plan of vandalism," Volkov said. "Three ships. Three phases. Three commanders. This is the opposite of what we stood for in the Russian Navy."

"We're not in the Russian Navy anymore. We work for Pierre Renard and his mercenary fleet."

"He seems trustworthy, but I don't know him well enough yet to know if this is proper."

"Nor him, us," the sonar operator said. "Which is why you're managing only phase one, and that on the other side of the Suez Canal from his other ships."

"You noticed that detail."

"You pay me to notice things."

Volkov realized he preferred the use of first names and the wearing of white dress shirts and beige dress pants to the staunch formalities of the Russian Navy.

"I'm glad you joined me in this mercenary life, Anatoly. I needed a sonar operator I could trust."

"You pay me a salary more than I had ever imagined," Anatoly said.

"You can thank our French boss for that. He pays us all well."

"That explains how he stole the complete crew for this ship from the Russian Navy."

"It's more than his money," Volkov said. "He has a certain charisma about him. I find it hard to reject his propositions."

"Even when he tells you to start a war?"

Volkov reflected upon the Frenchman's plan. Vandalism followed by naval skirmishes followed by more vandalism and then greater battles at sea. All to drive a NATO nation to the brink of revolution.

"Combat will ensue, men will die, and the fate of at least one nation will be sealed."

"Greece," Anatoly said. "Forced succession from the European Union."

"They brought it upon themselves through corruption. Their so-called leaders must be punished, but the hands of those who are funding this mission are tied. They cannot risk overt hostilities. So they pay us instead."

"Who's paying? The Germans? The French?"

"Yes. Probably both, I mean. And possibly other nations that are suffering from the Greek economic disaster. I'm sure Turkey is involved, if I understand the way Renard captures payment from those to whom he offers benefits."

"If so many are behind this, why do you seem so... despondent?

"I know it's necessary for change and growth," Volkov said, "but I dislike that innocent people will suffer."

"I assume the Frenchman has thought it through. He seems like the type of man to leave nothing to chance."

"His success speaks for itself. However, I must admit that I preferred our prior vessel to this French designed *Scorpène*-class. The submarines are comparable, but I still prefer the *Krasnodar* over the *Wraith*."

"But you appreciate our new ship, don't you?"

Volkov smirked.

"Yes, I do. The *Wraith* is up to the task."

"Then why do you seem concerned?"

"It's not the task that concerns me. It's the reaction."

Anatoly pointed to his headset.

"I'm sorry, Dmitry, but you've reminded me that I need to listen to the sea. I need to make sure the reaction doesn't catch us by surprise."

"Right."

Volkov turned and stepped upon the *Wraith's* elevated conning platform. The deck tilted as the submarine rocked in the swells, and he extended his hands to balance his descent into a bulkhead-mounted foldout chair. Beside him, a monitor showed an overhead view of bulbous tanks protruding upward from the liquefied natural gas vessel steaming towards his torpedo.

The video feed from a satellite made the targeting trivial.

"How much time until detonation?" he asked.

"Nine minutes," Anatoly said.

Volkov tapped keys and lifted his chin towards the upper monitor where crow's feet framed the piercing blue eyes of his French employer. Sharp features under silvery hair stared at him.

Leaning on the polished rail encircling the conning platform, one of Volkov's translators awaited orders. Though his boss understood simple Russian, he used the translator to assure impeccable communications.

"Let's talk to him," Volkov said.

"I'm ready," the translator said.

Volkov spoke in small phrases, letting the two-way translations become a drone in his mind.

"Nine minutes to detonation," he said.

"Very good," Renard said in English through the translator. "Have patience."

"Patience, yes. It's the shame that's bothering me."

"Shame?" Renard asked. "What shame?"

"Attacking commercial shipping during a time of peace."

"It may be a time of peace, but it's also a time of corruption that can no longer be tolerated."

"I feel like a pirate."

"Mercenaries apply pressure where it must be applied in places where the navies of nations dare not risk exposure."

"I'm starting a war with Iran or Greece or both," Volkov said. "I can't be sure."

"You're no coward. You proved this when I fought against you in the Black Sea. Nor are you prone to second-guess yourself. Why the hesitation?"

Volkov tested his learning by answering Renard in English.

"I am ready," he said. "I am talking to eat time."

"You mean you're talking to kill time, to make it pass faster while you await your detonation."

"Yes."

"Hold on a moment."

The Frenchman's face tightened as he looked aside.

"You should release your dolphins."

Volkov switched back to Russian and reliance upon his translator.

"Why?" he asked.

"I've just received word that an Iranian submarine is submerged within one hundred miles of you and heading in your direction."

"How could you know this?"

"I pay for such intelligence–at a premium, just as I paid for your dolphins. They, too, were quite costly."

Volkov assumed an American submarine provided the information through Renard's link to the CIA. Given that he was destroying a ship carrying Iranian natural gas bound for Greece, he expected trouble.

"I'll make the preparations to deal with this submerged threat," he said.

"I expect that you'll need to secure your electronic transmissions before we speak again."

"Then this is good bye, at least from my end of the conversation, until I'm safe again."

"I hope the good fortune that surrounded you in the Black Sea continues for you now."

Volkov nodded to the monitor and then walked away. He passed behind the backs of technical experts seated at consoles of the *Wraith's* Subtics tactical system. He then left the control room and headed forward into the torpedo room where a man as lithe and graceful as the animals he trained hovered over a makeshift aquarium in the compartment's center passageway.

"Vasily?" Volkov asked.

The trainer kept his hand on a broached dorsal fin as he looked up. His face appeared strained.

"They hate this, Dmitry. This is their prison."

"My torpedo technicians have grown fond of them, despite having to crawl over and around their tank."

"They can barely turn around in this."

"There was no other way to get them this far from home," Volkov said. "But I have good news. It's time to deploy them."

The trainer smiled but then furrowed his brow.

"Why?"

"There's an Iranian *Kilo*-class submarine within one hundred miles of us."

"What do you want them to do?"

"Just monitor its position for now and keep an eye out for other contacts."

"But combat is possible for them?"

"Yes, Vasily, I'm putting your babies at risk again. That's what you trained them for."

The trainer stiffened his back.

"Mikhail and Andrei are prepared to return to the battle-field."

"Good. Get them suited up and into tube three as soon as possible. I'll send torpedo technicians to handle the procedure."

The *Wraith's* commanding officer returned to the control room and stooped beside his sonar operator.

"Less than a minute to detonation," Anatoly said.

"Are you recording the video feed?" Volkov asked.

The sonar operator nodded towards the man seated beside him, where a feed ran on the upper of two Subtics displays showing the ship carrying Iranian liquefied natural gas bound for Greece.

"He's verified it," Anatoly said.

"Good," Volkov said. "Though I'm not sure how many times I'll want to analyze a video recording of me attacking an unsuspecting merchant ship."

Volkov walked towards the elevated conning platform, sat in his foldout chair, and watched the targeted vessel on his monitor.

"Our torpedo is range-gating," Anatoly said.

"Very well," Volkov said.

"Ten seconds," Anatoly said. "Five seconds. Detonation."

The overhead view showed the ocean erupting through the tanker, splitting it in half. The bulk of the heavyweight Black Shark torpedo's warhead vaporized water under the keel, cracking it with its own weight, but enough of the energy rose upward into two of the super-cooled tanks to burn a bright ball of gas into the sky.

Volkov knew that the unburned gas would either be contained or float into the atmosphere, avoiding the environmental blemish and backlash that could roust negative public sentiment. And though few would protest unwarranted aggression against an Iranian ship, he hoped that most crewmen survived his attack. The huge ship's superstructure appeared intact, giving the sailors a chance at survival.

"Should we go deep, Dmitry?"

Volkov glanced at the gray-bearded mechanical technician seated at the panel that controlled his ship's propulsion, depth, and steering systems.

"Not yet," he said. "I want to hear Renard's final words."

Seconds later, the Frenchman's lips moved in the screen, and the translator spoke in Russian.

"So far, no reaction... Now there are distress calls... And now a response. The tanker's captain is unsure if he was torpedoed or hit a mine, but he has declared his ship lost and is requesting rescue assistance from the Yemeni authorities. You have time, but not much."

Volkov looked at his executive officer, a man in his late twenties who had been a junior officer on a Russian *Kilo*-class submarine.

"Sergei."

"Yes."

"I'll be in the torpedo room. Listen to Renard and contact me immediately if he mentions any threat that approaches within counter-detection range of our periscope."

When he reached the weapons racks, he saw four sailors lifting a dolphin from the tank with a tarp. The animal exposed its long rows of small teeth, and Volkov saw the back of its tongue flutter while it released a staccato cackling whine.

"Be calm, Mikhail," the trainer said. "Don't resist them."

The dolphin obeyed, remaining stationary as the men cradled it between them. As they aimed the animal towards the opened breach door, Volkov saw the blue harness wrapped forward of the dorsal fin. He recognized a camera, a sonic communications transceiver, and a small explosive device.

"Slide him in gently behind Andrei," the trainer said.

Two sailors pushed the dolphin's fluke as two others slipped the tarp from under the animal.

"Close the breach," the trainer said. "Good. Now equalize air pressure in the tube with sea pressure. Slowly... take your time. Yes. That's it. Now flood the tube and start the clock. I don't want them in there for more than four minutes."

"Don't worry, I'll release them as soon as you're ready," Volkov said.

"As soon as the tube is flooded."

Volkov got his indication of the tube's preparedness from a torpedo technician and then ordered the muzzle door opened.

"Fly, my babies," the trainer said.

"I trust they will," Volkov said.

"They'll swim out immediately and sprint straight ahead for thirty seconds."

"God willing, if they remember their training. I'd hate to deafen or even cook them if they remain too close to our bow sonar."

"You'll be using minimum transmission power, won't you?"

"Of course," Volkov said. "But I hope to never find out what happens if they remain too close to the ship."

He returned to the control room and stood over his sonar

leader's shoulder.

"Send them a transmission. Minimum transmit power. Hail them for a response."

"You're sure they're far enough away?"

"No. I can only trust their training, as I always have."

Anatoly called up the screen of recorded dolphin sounds and pressed the icon that invoked the chirps and whistles the cetacean duo would recognize as a request for an immediate response. Volkov heard nothing but saw his sonar guru nod.

"They responded immediately. Range, two hundred yards, based upon the roundtrip speed of sound."

"Good. Now send them out at ten o'clock relative to our position."

"Towards the Iranian submarine?"

"Indeed. If we need to fight our way out of here, I'd prefer to avoid tangling with a *Kilo*-class submarine."

"I've just sent them a command to swim at ten o'clock relative to our position of twelve o'clock, and they've acknowledged."

The translator called Volkov to the conning platform where Renard's face appeared silent and stern on the monitor.

"I think you need to hear this," the translator said.

"What did he say?"

"Let me replay it and translate it word-for-word while you watch for effect. Much can be said with facial features and intonations that I cannot replicate with mere words."

"Go ahead."

Volkov watched the Frenchman speak as the Russian meanings droned in his ear.

"I hope you're listening," Renard said. "The Iranians are vectoring their submarine towards you, and at least three nations are committing to a coordinated search with their patrol craft and helicopters for the submarine they suspect is behind the attack against the tanker."

"Shit," Volkov said.

As if listening, Renard replied.

"I can't give you a detailed analysis yet of the threat, but I recommend that you evade on course one-two-zero."

Volkov checked his chart and agreed.

"Make haste, my friend," Renard said. "A larger response than I had expected is brewing, and they're coming for vengeance."

## CHAPTER 2

The *Wraith* rolled into the turn.

"Any sign of that helicopter?" Volkov asked.

"We've lost the one to the south, for the moment," Anatoly said. "But the one to the west is still pinging with active dipping sonar. There's been no sign of the others for at least ten minutes."

"A helicopter can disappear for ten minutes and drop a torpedo in the eleventh. We're far from safety."

"You need to take matters into your own hands. You need to fight back."

"I don't trust the anti-air weapon, and it would reveal our location if used. But I'll prepare it as a last resort."

"Where the hell are all these helicopters coming from?" Anatoly asked.

"Yemen, Oman, and Saudi Arabia," Volkov said. "At least that was what Pierre's last report said. The more interesting concern is where they're going to land when they run out of fuel."

The sonar technician raised his finger and bowed his head. The *Wraith's* commander folded his arms and waited while Anatoly tapped his screen and assigned a tag in the Subtics system to the new sound. An outline of a surface combatant appeared on the screen above the technician's head, showing the threatening vessel's tactical data.

"Warship," Anatoly said. "A modern corvette."

"Within weapons range?"

"No, barely audible. But it's the answer to your question. I've classified it as an Omani *Kareef*-class corvette, based upon twin, five-bladed screws. It's making flank speed and is capable of helicopter operations."

Volkov stooped and glared at the corvette's information.

"It's incapable of anti-submarine warfare, but it can refuel these accursed shore-based anti-submarine helicopters that hunt us. The local nations have united to use it as a floating airport against us, and they deployed it awfully damned fast."

For a fleeting moment, Volkov succumbed to doubts that Pierre Renard had recruited him and a Russian crew for the sole purpose of sacrificing them to an Arabian Gulf nation. Though unable to fathom a reason for such a sacrifice, he lacked complete trust in the Frenchman and knew his skill of navigating complex schemes. But he regained his foothold on reason by reminding himself of his boss' emotional attachment to the *Wraith*, which escaped consideration as a bargaining chip.

"Do you want to target it with a torpedo?"

"No."

"Not even a slow-kill weapon? Just to cripple it?"

"If you can get me a targeting solution, perhaps. Let Sergei know if you get one. I'm heading to the torpedo room to verify loading of the anti-air drone."

"Will do."

"Sergei!" Volkov said.

The young executive officer looked up from the room's central plotting table.

"Yes, sir."

Volkov allowed the formality when his men felt like calling him "sir".

"Keep us at eight knots on course for the shoals north of Socotra. Don't change course, speed, or depth unless Anatoly tells you a torpedo has been dropped and is a threat to hit us."

"Understood, sir. And if a torpedo is a threat?"

"Then deploy countermeasures, get us to flank speed as fast as possible, and pray."

Standing in the torpedo room, Volkov glared at the weapon's casing that reminded him more of an empty shotgun shell than a torpedo. He grabbed a flashlight from his technician's hands and aimed it down the cylinder's open nose. The warhead of a Sidewinder missile stared back at him, and in the shadows he saw tail fins touching the hollowed launch system's inner diameter.

"Install the cover," he said.

A second technician joined the first and helped him slide

a cap over the missile. The housing shared dimensions with a Black Shark torpedo but perplexed Volkov with its unlikely existence.

"It will remain waterproof to the surface?" he asked.

"Yes," the elder of the two technicians said.

"How many times has it been tested?"

"Mister Renard said three, sir. All against drones."

"Did they all succeed?"

"Two out of three. In the second test, the missile began too far off course, and the drone was too close to hit."

"Meaning that the more dangerous a helicopter is due to its proximity atop us, the less chance I have of hitting it?"

"Yes, sir. I'm afraid so. The angular control of the launch system is crude in azimuth and negligible in altitude. The missile has to compensate on its own with the heat seeker."

"Remind me why."

"The sensors here give a good idea of the altitude and the azimuth."

As the technician pointed to infrared sensors on the cover, Volkov recalled the limitations of the weapon he remained unsure he'd use.

"Then the limits are in the aiming of the launch?" he asked.

"Yes. The weapon bobs like a cork when it hits the surface. When air opens the seawater-sensing circuits and the infrared sensors detect a heat source, or the strongest heat source among many, the bolts explode to eject the cover and free the missile for launch."

"But not straight up."

"No. The low-pressure air tank under the missile will inflate selected sections of the annular bladder around the tail section, causing the tail to rise and tilt the missile toward the target."

"For a two-thirds chance of hitting."

"At least it gives a chance of hitting a helicopter whereas we'd otherwise be challenged to fight back."

Volkov grunted and placed his finger on the plastic cover.

"And fortunately we have four of them. I have an option for a timer, should I wish to risk wasting one, do I not?"

"Up to two hours, yes."

"Set the delay to one hour and load it in tube three," Volkov said. "Then load two others without delays into tubes four and five."

"You'd have me backhaul torpedoes from tubes four and five?"

"Torpedoes don't help me with helicopters, and our dolphins are dealing with the only other vessel within range of threatening us."

In the control room, Volkov briefed his team.

"Attention, everyone. I'm loading Sidewinder missiles into tubes three, four, and five. I'm going to launch tube three with a one-hour delay. The others have zero delay. I'm going to hold tubes four and five until I need them. God willing, I won't."

"Tube three indicates that the breach door was just closed, but I don't have any wire connection," a technician said.

"Very well, you won't have a connection since you can't control the weapon. It's armed by an accelerometer when pushed from the tube. After that, it's all automatic except for the timer."

"Then tube three is ready, sir."

"Launch tube three."

The pneumatic torpedo impulsion system beyond sight in the ship's forward compartment thrust a weapon into the sea while sucking air into its piping. The rapid pressure change popped Volkov's ears.

"Tube three is launched," the technician said.

"I hear it," Anatoly said. "It just breached the surface."

"And the helicopters?"

"Only two at great distance. Nothing close within the last ten minutes."

"And the dolphins?" Volkov asked.

"Their last report was the detection of a submerged contact greater than ten miles from their location, bearing eight o'clock relative to our position of twelve o'clock."

He looked at the room's central chart and noticed icons of the mammals approaching the best interpretation of the Iranian *Kilo* submarine's position. Natural sonar painted perfect hologram images of the hostile vessel in the minds of the dolphin duo, but communication barriers left Volkov with a crude understanding of their insights.

Seated at a Subtics console, the trainer turned his nose towards him.

"You could have them plant their charges on the Iranian *Kilo* whenever you want," he said. "But I can't guarantee that you're close enough for your detonation command to reach."

Volkov recalled that the detonation signal mimicked crackling shrimp, a sound beyond the cetaceans' ability to emanate. He made note to have the charges' acoustic trigger signal changed and to have the trainer condition his babies to detonate the explosives themselves for future missions.

"Fortunately, there's no need for action against the Iranians until they're close enough to attack," Volkov said. "Have the dolphins mirror our track."

Mirroring was the new trick he'd ask the trainer to teach them since they'd last seen combat. The animals would match the *Wraith's* course and speed until commanded otherwise.

With the sonar system piped through overhead speakers, Volkov heard the pre-recorded chirps and whistles that represented orders to the dolphins. The response then came from the duo.

"They've acknowledged the mirroring order," the trainer said.

Then, the shrill dissonance of high-frequency pinging filled the room. Volkov cringed and looked to his sonar expert.

"Dipping sonar," Anatoly said. "Strong, but still less than fifty percent chance of detection."

"What would you say the chance of detection is?" Volkov asked.

"Thirty-five percent. Guessing."

"Very well. We'll maintain course, speed, and depth."

Volkov awaited the splash of an air-dropped torpedo that failed to materialize. Then the sonar of a second helicopter rang throughout the compartment.

"Less than fifty percent chance of detection," Anatoly said. "Twenty-five percent, if I had to guess."

"It sounded as loud as the last one," Volkov said.

"But it was farther astern. We gave it a low sonar cross section for the return."

"Understood."

The thought that his crude Sidewinder launch system gave him a means of fighting back comforted him, but he resisted the urge to shoot.

He remained patient.

Thirty minutes later, the seas became quieter with the helicopter dipping systems drifting into the distance. He looked to the screen that had held Renard's face, but while he floated a low-frequency antenna on the water's surface, bandwidth constraints prevented a video feed.

Data from the Frenchman came as a series of numbers representing the coordinates of the ships and aircraft that pursued him, but with the helicopters' frequent repositioning, the icons representing their locations blended into streaks on Volkov's tactical display.

Then a loud ping startled him.

"Forty percent chance," Anatoly said.

"Very well."

Then the ping came again from the same direction.

"Forty percent again," Anatoly said. "They've stayed in the same place."

Renard's data feeding the Subtics system, the icon of the closest helicopter stabilized on the chart.

"Four miles," Volkov said.

"Why aren't they moving, Dmitry?" Anatoly asked.

"Damn," Volkov said. "They're resolving our course and speed. They've got us–for the moment. Helm, come left, steer course one-eight-zero."

The mechanic acknowledged the order, and the deck took a gentle roll.

"I see what you're doing," Anatoly said. "You've given them a complete stern aspect. Their return off our hull will be minimal."

"Precisely."

Ten minutes later, the ping came from the west.

"Weak," Anatoly said. "Maybe ten, at most fifteen percent chance of detection."

"Very well. Stay alert. I suspect this helicopter has vectored in another after detecting us."

Then a haunting shrillness rose in the control room to a crescendo that electrified Volkov's skin.

"From the east," Anatoly said. "Greater than fifty percent chance of detection. Maybe seventy. That one was close."

"Very well," Volkov said. "Come right to course two-eight-zero. All ahead standard, make turns for fifteen knots."

He grabbed the railing as the deck dipped and rolled.

"The stern aspect may not save us this time," Anatoly said.

"Let's see."

A horrifying ping filled the room again.

"Damn it, that's enough," Volkov said. "Shoot tube four."

His ears popped.

"Tube four is away," a technician said.

"I hear it," Anatoly said. "It breached the surface. Missile ignition!"

Volkov held his breath.

"Well?" he asked.

"Nothing. No sound of a hit. No sound of a fuselage splashing."

Volkov spoke to the technician beside Anatoly.

"Backhaul tube four and load our final Sidewinder into it."

"The torpedo room acknowledges the order."

He then raised his voice towards his gray-bearded mechanic.

"Have the Stinger missile team lay to the control room in preparation to climb to the bridge."

The mechanic relayed the order.

"The Stinger team is en route to the control room."

"Torpedo in the water!" Anatoly said. "Bearing zero-nine-five."

"Assign a tracker to it," Volkov said. "It's a helical search weapon. I need to see its bearings."

"Done. It's behind us–for the moment."

Lines fanned out on the chart, showing the torpedo cutting circles of increasing depth behind him. The air-dropped weapon needed to be atop or in front of him to matter, and fortune had favored him.

"A narrow escape," he said. "But now they know we can shoot back. Let's see how their courage holds."

"You only have two anti-air weapons left, Dmitry," Anatoly said. "And now they're developing a good idea of our position, due to the missile that just missed them."

Volkov checked the clock.

"Eight minutes," he said.

"What about it?"

"We need to evade for eight more minutes."

"That's a long time."

"Have faith," Volkov said. "If they're smart, they're adjusting their tactics to account for our newfound ability to shoot back at them. If I were them, I'd now try to detect us from as far away as possible, predict our path, and drop the torpedo well ahead of us."

Two panting men carrying a shoulder-mounted missile arrived and looked to Volkov.

"Do you need us to climb the conning tower?" one man asked.

"No," Volkov said. "Wait. The risk of you giving away our position by clanging metal against metal is too great. Stand by."

The pinging continued, but the helicopters remained out of detection range.

"I think you're right, Dmitry," Anatoly said. "They're keeping their distance. They're scared."

"Fear is a great motivator."

"I hear a missile. Your delayed Sidewinder, nine miles away."

"Indeed."

"Low-altitude explosion! That's a hit! Impact on the water's surface. You got one!"

"The weapon must have had time to adjust in flight over the longer range. I should remember this tactic. I was only using it for misdirection, but I'll take the good luck."

Minutes later, the messages from the Frenchman proclaimed the departure of the defeated search party.

Volkov had succeeded, and the *Wraith* had survived.

## CHAPTER 3

Captain Nicos Floros slammed the secure telephone's receiver into its cradle.

"Damn them," he said in Greek.

"What's wrong, sir?" the *Hydra's* commanding officer asked.

"The vice admiral just told me we have no air cover because we never will. Apparently, the entire Hellenic Air Force is on strike."

"You can't be serious."

A wave swallowed the prow of the Hellenic Ship *Hydra*, and Floros grabbed an overhead grip as the frigate pitched.

"Apparently, the generals have already backed a candidate for a replacement government and have turned their backs on the prime minister."

"They want him to fail?"

"The entire world wants him to fail. He's corrupt. His entire cabinet is corrupt. That's why our economy is in shambles."

"Then why are we carrying out his orders?"

"Because they make sense," Floros said. "We need to protect this oil rig's deployment. We need the oil to give our economy a chance to grow, whether he remains in power or not."

The commanding officer, a man in his early thirties with a youthful exuberance, appeared satiated with the simple explanation, but Floros knew Greece faced a long road to political stability and economic prosperity.

He lifted night vision glasses to his face and looked through the bridge window at the floating edifice on the horizon. Working since dusk, crews had towed the semi-submersible oil rig into place, and divers raced to moor it to the floor of the Aegean Sea before dawn.

"Since the Air Force has abandoned us, should I have the task force take control of the sky, sir?"

"Wait until sunrise," Floros said. "Right now, we're just blips on radar that look like merchant vessels. No need to give the Turks advanced warning of our presence."

"Maybe the Turks won't come at all, sir. Technically, we're just announcing our adherence to accepted international standards."

"Technically, yes. But we're also grabbing an oil field in formerly international waters while claiming the twelve-mile extension from our islands' coastlines. This will be noticed."

"Noticed, yes. Protested, likely. But challenged? The Turks don't want a war any more than we do."

"Maintaining peace through deterrence is our mission," Floros said. "If this becomes a hostile encounter, we will have failed."

As dawn's early redness crested the horizon, the phone beside him squawked. Seated in the captain's chair, he reached over its arm and lifted the receiver to his ear.

"Task force commander," Floros said.

"This is Vice Admiral Agathocleous. The twelve-mile national boundary has been officially declared."

"I understand, sir."

"Be on your guard, captain. None of us know how the Turks will react, but do everything in your power to avoid escalation."

"Of course, sir. I will."

"Good. That's all."

Fifteen minutes passed as Floros watched the cresting red turn yellow across the horizon. After the *Hydra's* commanding officer ordered the frigate to cut back towards the island of Lesbos, the deck tilted, and the sun rolled across the bridge windows.

As the warship's bow pointed at the oil rig, an animated voice issued from a loudspeaker and filled the frigate's bridge.

"Bridge, operations center. I have a Thales AMASCOS maritime radar, bearing zero-four-eight. The other ships in the task force report that they also detect the radar on their electronic sensory measures systems. Given the triangulated location, I'm assuming that's a Turkish fixed-wing maritime patrol craft from the Cengiz Topel Naval Air Station."

The *Hydra's* commander acknowledged the report and turned to Floros.

"Sir, there's a Turkish Airborne Maritime Situation and Control System radar painting the entire task force. I request permission to energize the task force's radar systems."

"Denied, commander," Floros said. "Be patient. Keep the adversary uncertain of which ships among the fishermen and merchants are our combatants as long as you can."

"I understand, sir. However, would you allow my helicopter to transmit active radar?"

Floros grabbed a tablet and lifted it to his lap. The icon of the *Hydra's* SH-60 Sea Hawk helicopter hovered northwest of Lesbos, forty miles from the nearest task force combatant.

"Very well, transmit active from the helicopter."

A dozen icons representing aircraft appeared over western Turkey. With all traffic moving at subsonic speeds, any military aircraft keeping its radar systems off blended in with commercial flights.

Then two more radar systems sprang to life in the northeast.

"There's a total of three Turkish maritime patrol craft fanning out to explore the Aegean Sea, sir," the *Hydra's* commander said. "They're reacting to our proclamation. With the sun risen, it's only a matter of time until they see what we're doing."

"Let them figure it out," Floros said. "No need to help them. Keep your radars dark. We have many islands, and they have a lot of water to search."

"They'll see the oil rig within minutes, sir. It's only fifty nautical miles off their coast."

"It's not a matter of when, but of how, they discover us," Floros said. "More important, is how we react."

The *Hydra's* commander glared at a tactical display.

"We'll find out soon. A maritime aircraft is in visual range of the *Ritsos*. The *Ritsos* is requesting permission to energize its search and fire control radar systems."

"Denied," Floros said.

"These maritime aircraft carry anti-ship missiles, sir."

"They won't launch them."

Reports of sightings of the Turkish aircraft came from the lookout sailors posted on the bridge wings.

"I hope you're right, sir."

"I am right. Keep all ships' radars dark."

He reached for his secure phone and rang the naval air boss, who controlled the scant air resources at Floros' disposal from an island naval air base one hundred nautical miles away.

"Get the anti-submarine warfare helicopters on station patrolling around the oil rig. Turkey has two *Type-209* submarines on patrol at the moment. They could be anywhere."

The air boss acknowledged. As he hung up the phone, Floros craned his neck to look through a window. The Turkish patrol craft passed over the task force that surrounded the oil rig, and it continued into the sea.

"No reaction, sir," the *Hydra's* commander said. "They didn't even dive for a closer look."

"But I'm sure they saw us, and they reported our situation. The information is filtering through military channels and will culminate in a diplomatic message. There will be a warning before there would be hostility."

"Agreed, sir."

"There's still more I must do," Floros said.

He reached for an internal phone and rang the anti-submarine warfare boss, a former commanding officer of a *Type-209* submarine, in the *Hydra's* operations center.

"Commander, take control of all anti-submarine assets. You have helicopters one through four, the sonar systems of the *Hydra*, and the oil rig. You have permission to transmit active on all sonar systems of the task force and the oil rig."

As the anti-submarine boss obeyed, Floros suspected he was the first naval officer in history to order an oil rig to energize its military sonar apparatus. The rig had been built with a low-frequency system to deter would-be diver-saboteurs with bone-crushing acoustic energy and to rid the seas of Turkish submarines with the threat of sonic reflections bouncing off their hulls.

"That's it," he said. "We've done all we can do."

"Is there a chance of getting our own submarines to assist us?" the *Hydra's* commander asked. "With the Air Force abandoning us, the added support would allow me to dedicate the *Hydra* to the air defense instead of multi-tasking."

"Negative, commander. We have the undersea defenses optimized, and we can hold the air."

"I understand, sir."

Tapping his finger on a console, the ship's commanding officer seemed nervous. Floros leaned over his chair's arm and lowered his voice.

"Are you okay?"

"Of course, sir."

"I mean are you nervous?"

The officer lowered and clasped his hands.

"My courage will stand the test, as will that of my crew."

"I'm sure," Floros said. "I wanted to make sure you were aware enough of your situation to know that you needed your courage. Otherwise, I would be concerned."

"Well, sir, we extended our Aegean Sea national boundary to twelve miles, which Turkey said would be considered an act of war. We've sneaked in an oil rig beyond the old boundary of Lesbos and into our newly declared boundary to emphasize our commitment. They've seen it, and something hostile must be coming our way, but all we can do is wait."

"Yes, commander, we wait."

The *Hydra's* commanding officer grunted.

"This is the worst part of a military operation."

"Indeed," Floros said. "Waiting makes you think about everything that can go wrong, despite thorough preparations."

"Forget I brought it up, sir. Neither of us can afford to overthink things, or we'll go mad."

"This operation's well planned."

"It was, sir, before that liquefied natural gas tanker was blown up last week in the Arabian Sea. Since then the widespread panic about our energy sources makes us look vulnerable. It makes this rig look vulnerable."

"Perhaps," Floros said. "But one random act of terrorism limited to international waters can also be forgotten. Let it slip into the past while we focus on our present."

"Haven't you been following the financial markets? The pundits are blaming the attack for the downward spike."

"I have no concern for such news."

"I'm just trying to talk about something other than what the Turks might do next."

The phone beside Floros chirped, and he lifted it to hear his boss.

"The Turks have rejected our declaration of the twelve-mile boundary," the vice admiral said. "They will not honor it, and they're protesting our deployment of the oil rig in waters to which they believe they have joint rights."

"That's expected, sir," Floros said.

"The only good news is that NATO forces at Izmir won't interfere. NATO has agreed to view this as a bilateral affair between us and our neighbors."

"That's good to know, sir. Also, it's expected."

"Regardless, be on your guard. Despite our good relations over recent years, the Turks can't ignore this. They'll have to make a show of strength–somehow."

His boss signed off, and Floros returned the phone to its cradle.

Uneventful minutes passed, and he teased himself with hope that the Turks would remain silent.

Then, the helicopter reported two air contacts accelerating to supersonic speeds.

"They're heading right towards us, sir," the *Hydra's* commander said. "Two F-16 Fighting Falcons. We detect their search and fire control radars now, too."

"Very well," Floros said. "Let them come right for us. That's why we're the closest ship to the Turkish coast."

"I request permission to energize the task force's radar systems."

"Not yet. Hail them and warn them their flight path shows them flying over Greek airspace without permission and threatening a Hellenic combatant vessel."

Floros overheard the translator speaking into a radio. After several attempts, a Turkish retort came.

"They say they're flying in international airspace," the translator said.

"Warn them again," Floros said. "Refer to today's proclamation and state that we consider their flying in our national airspace a hostile act."

The translator obeyed, but the Turkish pilots ignored him.

"Very well," Floros said. "From here on, we speak with our ship."

"May I energize the task force's radars?" the *Hydra's* commander asked.

"How far away are they?"

"Nineteen nautical miles. Our lookout just spotted them."

"Not yet. At ten miles, energize your Phalanx point defense systems and your point defense systems only. Hold your fire until I say otherwise."

"Fifteen miles, sir. Low and fast."

"You know what to do at ten miles."

The *Hydra's* commander nodded and then raised a microphone to his mouth.

"Ten miles," he said. "Energize Phalanx systems!"

"They're not turning away, are they?" Floros asked.

"No, sir. I request permission to energize all radars and weapons systems."

"Not yet. Light them up at one mile."

"That will be hardly less than five seconds before they overfly us."

"I know."

"Five miles," the commander said. "Four miles. Three miles."

Floros slid his shoes to the deck plates and glared through the bridge windows. He saw the sun reflecting off the incoming cockpits.

"Two miles," the commander said. "One mile. Energize all radars and weapon systems!"

Three seconds later, the pilots veered away, and the sonic boom shook the windows.

"That did it, sir. We called their bluff."

"Their first bluff was a quick reaction to test our mettle," Floros said. "But we need the oil under that rig, and the Turks know it. They'll be back, and they'll come with something more than a bluff next time."

## CHAPTER 4

Jake Slate raised his head and pressed his palms into the navigation table. As he mustered the mettle to play God, he surprised himself by wondering how his newest teammate, Dmitry Volkov, had fared in his earlier, similar situation.

"How long until our weapon hits?" he asked in English.

"What? Almost thirteen minutes, Antoine?" Henri asked.

Seated at the Subtics station, Antoine Remy, Jake's sonar operator, nodded his toad-shaped head. At the *Specter's* control station, the silver-haired Henri Lanier shrugged.

"Twelve minutes, Jake," he said. "The data's right there on the display for you."

"Heck, I know where to see the data," Jake said. "I just wanted to say and hear the words out loud. This doesn't feel right."

"Trust the plan," Henri said.

"It's vandalism all over again," Jake said. "Just like our last mission. I'm afraid Pierre's turned us into nothing more than hired guns."

"That's all we've ever been. The shame is yours if you think more highly of yourself."

As of a week ago, Jake considered himself a fledgling Christian. Humility was a requisite virtue in his new belief system, and he expected to struggle. He lowered and shook his head.

"I don't get it," he said. "I joined Pierre twelve years ago because I was desperate. But I stayed with him and you guys because we were doing the right things. We were fighting just wars, stopping terrorists, and even doing rescue missions."

"That's our legacy, Jake," Henri said. "It always will be."

"But three months ago, he had us blowing up the links between Russia and Crimea, and now he's got us blowing up natural gas heading to Greece. What happened to fighting the bad guys? Now we are the bad guys."

"No, Jake," Henri said. "The governments of those whom we strike are the bad guys."

"Then why aren't the governments who pay us doing this

themselves?"

He knew the answer but wanted the comfort of Henri saying it. The elder Frenchman's counsel soothed his nerves.

"Germany, France, and Italy cannot risk overtly attacking Greece, but they can pay us to do it and force them out of the European Union."

"But if it doesn't work, then we're just vandals."

"If it doesn't work, it's not our fault. It will be the fault of diplomats who made erroneous predictions and movements."

Jake sighed.

"Maybe. I'm not so sure."

"We're fighting the right fight, Jake. Whether the damage creates a coup, an exit from the European Union, or both will be up to Greek politicians. But creating pressure for the coup is all we can do with our meager resources."

Jake raised his gaze to Henri.

"Did you just call my submarine 'meager'?"

"Why, yes. Yes, I did."

"Well played, challenging my pride."

"I was growing weary of your whining."

"Fine. I was just killing time to avoid thinking about how guilty I feel sinking a helpless tanker. Let's get it done and see what the Greek Navy has to say about it."

"I believe it's called the Hellenic Navy."

"Whatever. After I turn this tanker into a flash of flame, I'm going to have a respectable fleet steaming across the Aegean Sea for my ass. And somehow I'm going to turn it away with–how should we characterize our slow-kill weapons?"

"Less-than-lethal?"

"Maybe. Or semi-lethal. Or quasi-humane. But trying not to kill anyone while fighting naval battles is bizarre."

"It was your idea to invent such weapons."

"Yeah, it was. I don't think I could stomach these missions without them."

"And I doubt that people would hire us without them," Henri said. "If you cripple a warship with a weapon that can spare the crew, it's a quite different affair from cracking a keel and sending the crew to their graves."

Jake grabbed the elevated conning platform's polished railing for balance as the *Scorpène*-class submarine, *Specter*, rolled under the swells at periscope depth. He swung his buttocks into the bulkhead-mounted foldout chair, looked to his display screen, and saw a satellite view of his target—an Iranian tanker bound for Greece's Revithoussa Liquefied Natural Gas Terminal. He reached for the touchpad and unmuted his microphone as the steel blue eyes of his boss and mentor blinked on the screen.

"I can only assume you were talking about me whilst on mute?" Renard asked.

"There's no fooling you," Jake said.

"I hope it wasn't all bad."

"Not all of it, but it was all accurate."

The Frenchman grunted.

"Much as I'd enjoy comparing notes on my character flaws, my commanders have weapons in the water."

"Dmitry launched already?"

"Five minutes before you," Renard said. "I want his weapon to hit first, since he'll have to run from helicopters again."

"They almost got him last time, and the Iranians learned their lesson, if I remember right."

"You remember correctly. Their tankers are getting helicopter escorts all the way from the Arabian Sea to the Suez Canal. Two helicopters are attempting to protect Dmitry's target now."

"But you think Dmitry's getting away this time without any problems?"

"We waited just long enough for the Iranians to become complacent. They're getting comfortable after a week of quiet. And Dmitry has also learned his lesson. On his present attack, he cut the guidance wire to his torpedo and left the area already. He's probably halfway to Socotra."

"Good thinking. I'd hate to lose my newest buddy."

The Frenchman frowned.

"That sounded sarcastic."

"Well, shit, Pierre. You knew I liked Terry before you invited him to join us, but Dmitry's spent more time trying to kill me than getting to know me."

"This opportunity against Greece came upon me rapidly, and our ships were well placed in France after the Crimea mission. I couldn't refuse it, despite the challenging timing. The *Wraith* was in Taiwan and close enough to reach the Arabian Sea to be useful."

Jake recalled flashes of his self-proclaimed maverick heroism when he stole the Russian commander's submarine from the Malaysian Navy.

"I'm more worried about the *Wraith* than Dmitry and his band of Russian recruits. I'm very fond of that submarine, having stolen it for you."

"I have a small contingent of Frenchmen on the *Wraith* to render technical expertise."

"Technical, huh? Do you mean technology like knives and small arms for hand-to-hand combat, if needed?"

"Four of them have commando training, should the need arise for internal security."

"And you have a bunch of translators, I assume?"

"Four of them, each fluent in three languages covering Russian, English, French, and Arabic."

Jake studied Renard's face for signs of doubt and saw none. But he probed.

"This is your least planned mission ever, isn't it?"

"Perhaps. What of it?"

Searching for an argument, Jake clenched his jaw and came up empty.

"I just don't like the concept of vandalizing and running. It's like a 'smash and grab' without the 'grab'. It didn't work so well in the Black Sea, and you planned that out for months."

"I did plan it for months, and it worked out just fine. If I recall, we earned our pay and netted our greatest profit ever."

"Only because your deepest contingency plans bailed us out

of a stalemate at the last second."

"And such contingency plans would avail us in this scenario as well, I assure you."

"What plans? It sounds like you had three days to plan this one out."

"Ye of little faith. Have I ever failed you in planning?"

"Yes! In Argentina!"

Renard blushed.

"Not entirely did I fail you there. And even after my client turned his back on me, I was able to adjust the plan to work out in our favor. Why are you so damned worried, man?"

"You didn't need to bring Dmitry into our gang so fast," Jake said. "You could've let me and Terry handle it. You could've kept the *Wraith* out of this."

"I may not have stolen the *Wraith*, but it is mine, and you know how attached I am to my possessions."

"I still don't think you needed it attacking tankers in the Arabian Sea."

"Subtlety, my friend. You're thinking in terms of pure military goals. I'm thinking in terms of political fallout and social panic. We need to flex our muscle on both sides of the Suez to create the full impact. And it will also focus the Hellenic fleet on the tankers and away from Terry's ultimate aim."

"Maybe."

"Regardless, it's a perfect opportunity to bring Dmitry into the fold and test his commitment to our mercenary life."

"Terry and I have risked our lives for each other. Dmitry will still be a wildcard after this mission's over."

"We'll cross that bridge of trust at the appropriate time."

Renard's face angled away from the screen.

"Take a look at the aerial footage," he said. "The Americans were kind enough to follow Dmitry's tanker with an unmanned aerial vehicle."

Jake toggled his screen in time to see a ball of flaming gas rising from a severed ship. The sea around the tanker whitened as Volkov's torpedo vaporized the water below the keel, lifting it and then cracking it.

"Dang," he said. "That's a lot of rapid destruction."

"Indeed. And your weapon will be next."

"Right. Can I expect to be chased down after it happens?"

"No, you're in the clear. You'll face quite a different threat than Dmitry."

"You still see no military assets within fifty miles of me?"

"No, and you'll clear the area before any new ones could deploy. You needn't worry about a thing."

"If you say so."

Jake watched his screen in silence as the icon of his torpedo crept up on the unsuspecting tanker. He felt the air move, and he craned his neck over his shoulder.

Henri stood over him.

"You said you've become a Christian."

"Yeah," Jake said. "I guess."

"Guessing is good enough. The desire to make an effort is an acceptable start."

"Okay. What's on your mind?"

"We should pray."

"Now?"

"Yes, now. Today's torpedo isn't semi-lethal or quasi-humane. It's a heavyweight, and you're about to kill people."

"Maybe. Probably. Okay, you're right. Dmitry killed four people with his torpedo last week. I don't want to get touchy feely and hold hands or anything. I have a submarine to command."

"Just bow your head for a moment and listen to me. I normally do this silently when we're launching weapons, but this is the calmest attack we've ever conducted. So I took the opportunity to join you."

"Fine. Go ahead."

Jake quieted himself and listened to the Frenchman recite gracious words on the behalf of the souls his weapon would cause to perish. They provided him minimal hope that the burden of dealing death could be borne by a power greater than himself.

"I'm not sure that worked," he said.

"A single prayer rarely does," Henri said. "It may take years to see an effect."

As Henri returned to the control panel, a technician announced the *Specter's* torpedo's detection of a target. Seconds later, the weapon's telemetry data to its future victim aligned with the location of a liquefied natural gas tanker that steamed north of Crete.

Jake watched the satellite view showing the ocean erupting through the severed tanker. Residual heat from the Black Shark torpedo's warhead rose upward into two of the super-cooled tanks and sent a ball of fiery gas into the sky.

"Should we go deep, Jake?" Henri asked.

"Normally, I would. But in this case, I'll refer to my boss."

He toggled the satellite image to Renard's face.

"Should I just stay here at periscope depth?" Jake asked.

"Best that you do. I believe that maintaining high-bandwidth communications with me is more prudent than running from ghosts. You face a different fate than Dmitry. I reassure you that nobody will come for you except the Greeks themselves."

"I know that's the plan, but it sounds too good to be true."

"All other local players are either in direct support of your actions or complacent to spectate. All forces that will come for you, including the submarines, are coming from Greece."

Jake toggled his console to bring up an overhead view of his waters. He tapped keys to highlight the Hellenic fleet. Eleven submarines, thirteen frigates, and countless gunboats and helicopters dotted the Aegean Sea. Most were in ports, but a significant force steamed within a day's travel from him.

"Okay, Pierre," he said. "Let me know what's coming for me as soon as you can."

"Of course," Renard said.

"I guess you have plenty of time to warn me. They're two hundred miles away, and I've got a half-day head start."

"Indeed."

Thirty minutes passed before Renard offered his first political update.

"Interesting, but not completely unexpected."

"What?" Jake asked.

"The Greek prime minister has made an announcement about our tanker attacks. He's blaming the Turks."

"Everyone mocked him last week when he blamed the Turks for destroying the first tanker."

"The international community did, but the people of Greece are being fed enough lies about possible sabotage or air-dropped mines to cast doubt on the situation. He's now claiming that early evidence of our coordinated attacks on the tankers today points to Turkish doing."

"Why?" Jake asked. "What does making up such a crazy story get him?"

On the screen, the Frenchman's eyes narrowed.

"It turns the ire of the Greek people away from his corruption and focuses it on a common enemy. It's also far better for him to blame a nation than to admit to being outflanked by a small band of vandals."

"But we'll prove him wrong with Terry's phase of the attack."

"Indeed we will, but not yet," Renard said. "Actually, his adherence to the Turks as the instigators plays into our plans. Head east now, and prepare to attack any Greek tankers that may have the courage to steam towards the Aegean Sea. There's one coming from Cyprus that will make for a perfect target, should it maintain its course and speed."

"They won't possibly risk it after we've sunk three tankers inbound for Revithoussa."

"Don't underestimate pride or desperation. The news of our attacks today have already hit the energy markets. Prices are irrational. Panic is escalating about the viability of Greece's energy supply."

"That's part of our plan, right?"

"Indeed. But remember that the Greek military reaction will

include ruthless retaliation. Whether it's a solitary ship or the entirety of the Hellenic forces, be ready to keep them occupied and away from Terry."

"Will do."

"And for God's sake, stay alive. You're impossible to replace."

## CHAPTER 5

Volkov stooped over the central plotting table and marked the crude distance between himself and the dolphins' report of the Iranian submarine that chased him.

"If I believe the dolphins," he said, "the Iranians sense where we are and where we're going."

"It illogical," Anatoly said. "The dolphins can only say they're beyond ten nautical miles. Based upon the geometry, I would guess at least fifteen. But I cannot hear them, and there's no possible way they hear us. They must be guessing about our direction or guided by divine power."

"Agreed. I'd like to rid ourselves of this nuisance."

"You could send a slow-kill weapon at them," Anatoly said.

"With the uncertain information we have from the dolphins, the chance of hitting is questionable. I'd be announcing our location with a tracer bullet they could use in reverse."

Volkov looked to the dolphin trainer, who sat and tapped nervous fingers on the console beside the sonar expert.

"Vasily?"

"It's hard to tell," the trainer said.

"I haven't asked my question yet."

"You want to know if my babies can attack the Iranian submarine. They can plant the charges, but with the uncertain range, I can't tell you if your detonation signal would reach."

"I'm willing to have them plant the charges and then take my chances on the detonation signal," Volkov said. "If the Iranians ever come close enough to threaten us, they'll be close enough for our detonation signal to reach."

The trainer's tight eyes betrayed his pain.

"If you send them beyond the reach of our communications, they may become lost."

"Is a two-step order possible? Order them to plant the charges and then to immediately return to us?"

"I've never taught them sequential orders. It would only confuse them."

Volkov rethought his tactics. Having fled the scene of his attack at twelve knots, he saw several advantages in slowing. He could preserve his battery, listen for the Iranians, and give his mammalian weapons a chance to return.

"How close are they to their feeding and sleeping window?"

"They're already in it. By nature, they'd be eating and then resting now. But they're conditioned to push themselves."

"Get a location check on them."

"Of course," the trainer said. "Right away."

Three sequences of chirps whistled from the *Wraith's* sonar system, over loudspeakers, and into the control room. The cetaceans sent three sequences of responses, verifying their distance and bearing from the submarine.

"Eight miles away, bearing zero-five-two," the trainer said.

"Can you have them sprint home?"

The trainer furrowed his brow in thought.

"No, that's too far to sprint. They could average, I'd say, fourteen knots over the distance."

"Can you command them to swim at fourteen knots?"

"Nature equipped them to know their optimum speeds to intercept submerged objects. I'll tell them to come back, and they'll know. If they swim too fast or too slow, I can send them commands to accelerate or decelerate. They'll also send me a distress call if they fear they're fatiguing and incapable of catching us."

"Really?

"I trained them to be safe and to come back to me."

"Then I'll slow the ship, and they'll be home in an hour."

As the trainer's lithe body relaxed in relief, Volkov looked to the gray beard.

"Slow us to six knots."

With the *Wraith's* speed halved and its self-generated flow noise reduced, Volkov walked to the conning platform and studied the enhanced crispness of the sea's sounds on the sonar display.

Everything looked like natural sounds, but an elder sonar

technician seated to Anatoly's side became animated and pointed to his screen. The younger guru leaned and studied the elder's display before glancing at Volkov.

"Helicopter."

"This far from the Yemeni coast?"

"They must be getting flight operations support from a combatant like last time."

"Agreed. How far away?"

"Far enough," Anatoly said. "At best a ten percent chance of detection. I believe anyone who's pursuing us assumed that we stuck around to guide our weapon in like last time. Firing and cutting the wire instead of waiting to guide the weapon has given us a five-mile head start against their assumptions."

"We'll need to snorkel soon, and they know it."

"We can maintain six knots for a long time with the MESMA system."

Volkov considered the French *Module d'Energie Sous-Marine Autonome* air-independent propulsion system inferior to that which he'd known in his Russian *Kilo* submarine, but it provided him a crucial long-lasting energy source while submerged.

"I prefer not to conduct the remainder of this evasion at six knots," he said. "Or at five or four knots as our battery empties. Once you can assure me I'm safe from nearby listeners, I'll come shallow to snorkel."

"I've been listening for that Iranian *Kilo* submarine, and there's nothing," Anatoly said. "I hear nothing out there. Even that helicopter is gone now."

Volkov looked to the gray beard.

"Bring us to snorkel depth and prepare to snorkel."

The deck rose, leveled, and rocked in the shallows.

"Take three minutes to search for threats, Anatoly."

While his sonar expert listened, Volkov sought visual information. He announced his intentions as he tapped an icon.

"Raising the periscope for a full panoramic sweep."

Above him, hydraulic valves clicked. When the optics broke the surface, they sent daylight images to his screen, and then the valves clicked again to lower the periscope. The three-hundred-and-sixty-degree view of the waves showed emptiness.

After his sonar expert claimed silent waters, Volkov risked concluding his relative solitude and keeping a piece of the *Wraith* exposed above the water.

"Raise the induction mast," he said.

Hydraulic valves clicked.

"The induction mast is raised," the gray beard said.

"Commence snorkeling."

A gentle rumble filled the compartment.

"Let's risk a transmission to Pierre," Volkov said.

"What message to send?" the gray beard asked.

"Text only. Give him our coordinates, tell him we're retrieving the dolphins, and the dolphins have been tracking a submerged contact, which I believe is an Iranian *Kilo*, at long range behind us. The *Kilo* has been following us for at least six hours."

A technician verified the message and entered it into the system.

"Raise the radio mast and synchronize with the satellite."

Valves clicked.

"The radio mast is raised," the gray beard said. "Seeking the satellite, and linked."

"Send the message."

"The message is sent, receipt by the satellite is confirmed."

"Very well," Volkov said. "Lower the radio mast."

A low-frequency update from Renard confirmed receipt of Volkov's message and updated the location of threats with respect to his precise location. The nearest helicopter flew twenty-five miles behind him, and except for the undersea world that eluded Renard's borrowed reconnaissance tools, the Frenchman's perspective concluded Volkov was alone.

But the report indicated that one of the remaining two Iranian *Kilo*-class submarines had deployed, hidden itself within the sea, and joined its twin in hunting the *Wraith*.

Volkov noted the irony of his homeland having built the submarines that chased him. He also decided his ship was superior to the older vessels and his skills outpaced those of his pursuers.

But he diverted himself from hubris by thinking about tactics. His secret weapons came to mind, and he aimed his voice at his sonar expert.

"Remember to keep our active sonar silent to prevent hurting the dolphins. Inform the torpedo room immediately when they request entry."

In the torpedo room, Volkov watched the trainer return a sound-powered phone to a torpedo technician.

"The dolphins are requesting entry," the trainer said.

"You're sure they can do this at six knots?"

"Yes, Dmitry. They're quite quick and agile. They're just waiting for you to open the door."

"Very well. Open it."

A technician verified shut the breech door and then opened the muzzle. A green light indicated that the tube opened to the sea.

"How can you tell if they're in there?" Volkov asked.

"You can't, but I can," the trainer said.

"How?

"A mother just knows."

"Aren't you scared about their flukes getting caught in the door?"

"Yes, I was when I trained them in this maneuver. So I taught them to swim all the way in."

"Very well," Volkov said. "Are they in yet?"

"Yes. I think so. You can close the muzzle door now and drain the tube."

Volkov looked to a technician.

"Well, you heard him. A mother knows. Close the muzzle door and drain the tube."

With the tube drained, Volkov ordered the breech door opened and was greeted by a pair of chirping cetaceans.

"There your babies are," he said.

The trainer stepped in front of him and aimed a flashlight into the open circle.

"Ah, yes. Andrei entered first. He's the brave one. Mikhail always follows. Get that cradle underneath him. He looks exhausted. Get their dinner ready. They need to eat quickly and then sleep."

"How long do they need?" Volkov asked.

"Six hours, please, Dmitry."

"Very well. Six hours."

Volkov climbed over the edge of the makeshift aquarium and walked away. As he reached the end of the compartment, the pungent odor of an opened tub of mackerel turned his head, and he saw the first dolphin being lowered into its tank.

He reached the control room and looked to the gray beard.

"Secure snorkeling. Take us to fifty meters. Make turns for ten knots."

The rumble stopped, hydraulic valves clicked, and the deck plates tilted downward.

For three hours, Volkov monitored his tactical team monitoring the seas for solitude. Accepting his safety, he allowed himself to rest his cheek in his hand, and he drifted to sleep.

"Dmitry!"

He stirred and opened his eyes. The tense, silent bodies in the control room verified his lucid nightmare had been real.

"Say that again," he said.

"Torpedo in the water," Anatoly said.

"Bearing and bearing rate?"

"I don't have a bearing rate yet. Bearing three-five-two."

"Bearing drift?"

"Perhaps slight right, but not much. It's almost coming straight at us, but with a slight leading trajectory. I'm hearing the active seeker at low signal strength."

Volkov's movement and adrenaline stretched his legs as he stood and placed his hands on the polished rail.

"What should we do?" the gray beard asked.

"Slow to three knots," Volkov said.

"Slow? With a torpedo coming for us?"

"Yes. And Anatoly will watch the bearing rate as if his life depends upon it."

The speed display ticked down to three knots.

"What do you have, Anatoly?"

"You're right. The torpedo is drawing ahead of us. The bearing rate is now half a degree per minute to the right."

"Can you hear the shooting platform?"

"No. I'm unable to get even a sniff. But I have confirmed that the torpedo is a USET-80, most likely from an Iranian *Kilo*."

"It's a second *Kilo*," Volkov said. "The first one the dolphins were tracking couldn't have moved to our flank so quickly from so far behind us."

"Unless the dolphins were wrong," Anatoly said.

Volkov assessed his options. If he commanded the hostile launch platform, he would have turned into the *Wraith's* baffled sector to make a possible counter-fire weapon inaccurate. Any counterstrike with his submarine's torpedoes would be foolish.

But he had another option.

"I imagine it's possible they're wrong," he said. "But let's see what they have to say about it."

He reached for a sound-powered phone, rang the torpedo room, and called upon the trainer.

"Dmitry?"

"Can you get them into the water in ten minutes?"

"They haven't had their full rest."

"It will be a quick strike. A second Iranian *Kilo* just launched a weapon at us. Thankfully, Anatoly heard it from far enough away that I could avoid the intercept course, but I think your babies can catch them."

"How far is the swim?"

"Probably five miles. We can't hear them, but they were close enough to hear us when I was snorkeling and going faster. My guess is they're in our baffles now, crossing to our right side very slowly."

"I don't know, Dmitry."

"I'll be right down there."

Volkov looked at the dolphin that faced him. One eye froze

in an enduring wink as the mammal rested half its brain while keeping the other half alert. The soft, bright blue harness stretched around the torso forward of the dorsal fin, holding a camera, its communication transceiver, and a small shaped charge.

"It sounds to me like you could shoot a torpedo at them," the trainer said.

"I could. It would be a mediocre shot with much guesswork, but it might hit. However, it might miss and give the adversary a better idea of our position. At the moment, I believe they've lost track of us."

"How could you know?"

"Because when I slowed, they didn't steer their torpedo at us. It's drifting safely ahead."

"Maybe the wire broke and they can't steer it."

"On Russian-built military hardware? We have good enough quality on our military weapons. And also keep in mind we are on a mission where money matters. Why waste a torpedo when I can use inexpensive explosives from your little assassins?"

The trainer smiled and caressed his nearest child.

"My little assassins," he said. "What a morbid title for my little angels."

"I'm sorry, but that's their job."

"Yes, yes, it is. I think you should pet them."

"Me? Why?"

"They can sense human emotions, and they can tell you're the one feeling the stress of making decisions. You would calm them if you petted them and reassured them."

"Very well."

Volkov lowered his hand to the watery, reflective sheen of the closest dolphin's head. His fingertips made contact, and the sensation reminded him of wet rubber. He then reached and extended his fingers to the second animal.

He spoke in the most soothing voice he could muster.

"I hope that makes your little angels feel a little better."

"My little angels. My little assassins. I'll send them immediately."

In the control room, Volkov verified the Iranian torpedo vectored into oblivion and then hovered over his sonar expert.

"Still nothing?" he asked.

"It's quiet. It's a good Russian-built submarine, and the crew is showing discipline in its operation. We were lucky... well, everyone else here was lucky that my ears are so good and I heard the torpedo's seeker wake up from so far away."

"If you're so good, why can't you hear any Iranian submarines? At last count, there were two out there."

"If I can't hear them, they can't be heard."

"I'll bet you a bottle of top-shelf vodka of the winner's choice that I'll detonate the dolphins' charges on the Iranian hull before you even hear the submarine."

"I have expensive tastes," Anatoly said.

"I have battle-tested dolphins."

The trainer entered the compartment and told Volkov his dolphins were deployed. Without concern for his shipmate's rights, the trainer bumped shoulders with the sonar technician seated beside Anatoly and nudged him from the seat.

Seemingly aware of the trainer's crude habits, the technician moved to a new console and let the dolphins' master sit.

"May I transmit the acknowledgment message?" the trainer asked.

"Very well, transmit."

Volkov twisted a knob above his head to increase the volume of sound passing through the compartment's loudspeakers. He listened as the *Wraith* simulated an aquatic animal by broadcasting a recorded dolphin's message.

The series of whistles meant nothing to him, but the relaxed features on the trainer's face affirmed their intended significance.

"It always calms them to know we're in communication," the trainer said.

The natural incoming chirps and whistles filled the compartment.

"They already see a new submerged contact," the trainer said. "I recognize the signal."

"Excellent," Volkov said. "Now I want information. Bearing and range to the contact."

The trainer tapped his screen, and a new series of recorded whistles from the *Wraith's* hydrophones filled the room. Moments later, Volkov heard a dolphin's high-pitched response.

"They've echolocated the contact," the trainer said. "I'll query for the bearing."

Volkov forced himself to incorporate the bottlenose dolphins' perspectives into his mind. He accepted their view of the undersea world as a sonic painting that would elude his understanding. Though useful, the data they could provide him frustrated him with its limits.

"Go ahead," he said.

Another exchange of chirps and whistles.

"Andrei says the submerged contact is at six o'clock."

"Very well," Volkov said. "Passing through our baffles almost exactly, if not exactly. Now get the range"

More chirps.

"In between," the trainer said. "Not near, not far."

"Call it five nautical miles and send it to the plot," Volkov said. "Give it a radius of uncertainty of three nautical miles."

The sonar operator nodded and obeyed.

"Now, order the dolphins to approach the target."

Recorded whistles. Mammalian response.

"Andrei has confirmed," the trainer said. "They're accelerating towards the target."

"Excellent," Volkov said. "I don't suppose you hear our adversary yet, Anatoly?"

"No, and I won't if you keep asking."

"I only asked once. You have a crude bearing and range to guide you. I thought you might want your free vodka."

"Their data is no less crude than I could have guessed."

Beside the frustrated Anatoly, the trainer displayed his habitual agitation as his children entered battle.

"Remember that I trained them to announce when they pass a distance boundary," he said, "either from long range to medium range or medium range to short. They'll tell us when they've closed within a mile."

The unsolicited chirp arrived.

"They're within a mile of the target," the trainer said.

"Prepare them for explosives deployment." Volkov said.

He envisioned one dolphin sliding its snout into the carrying strap of the bomb attached forward of the dorsal fin of its partner as a chirp announced completion of each animal's arming.

"They're ready to lay explosives," the trainer said.

"Very well, deploy the explosives."

Six minutes later, a chirp came.

"The explosives are applied to the target," the trainer said. "And the dolphins have swum to a safe distance for detonation."

"Detonate."

The trainer tapped buttons on the console, and recorded shrimp-like sounds rang from the *Wraith*.

"Nothing," Anatoly said. "They may be too far away."

"Nonsense. Increase power to one-half and verify that the acoustic beam is aimed at the target."

"We may be heard at half power."

"So what? An abnormally active bed of shrimp is heard by a submarine that's about to enjoy a flooding casualty in–where, its control room?"

"For submerged targets," the trainer said, "I trained them to deploy from above and in the middle of the vessel so they avoid sonar and seawater systems."

"Okay, fine," Anatoly said. "I've increased power to half power, verified aimed at the target."

"Very well, detonate."

The two pops reminded Volkov of an assassin's bullets.

"Those were the detonations," Anatoly said. "I hear flooding. Now emergency air. Now hull popping. Yes, they are shooting to the surface. They're going to make it."

"Of course, they'll make it," Volkov said. "Those are small

warheads. Just enough to motivate the correct behavior of surfacing and leaving us alone."

"My babies succeeded."

"Indeed, they did," Volkov said. "Now give the order to bring
them home."

"Andrei has confirmed the order," the trainer said. "They're
coming back."

He leaned in close to his sonar expert's ear and pulled back
one of his muffs to whisper.

"I believe you owe me a bottle of vodka, Anatoly," he said. "A
ridiculously expensive one."

## CHAPTER 6

In disbelief, Floros listened to his vice admiral's voice over the secure phone line.

"The prime minister is publicly blaming the Turks for the attacks."

"All three tankers?" Floros asked. "The two today and the one last week?"

"Yes."

"That's impossible. Perhaps the one north of Crete was within their reach, but no Turkish submarines are in the Arabian Sea, unless one went the long way around Africa. We would have noticed if one passed through the Suez."

"No Turkish submarines are in the Arabian Sea. Each one has been accounted for in recent weeks, and as you said, none of them went through the Suez Canal or had time to go the long way."

"Is anyone believing him?" Floros asked.

"Only those that already fear him, which is unfortunately a large enough percentage of the population to matter."

"Even if the Turks could, why would they? The only recent animosity between us is this oil rig, and they would have had to plan the attacks against the tanker days, if not weeks ago."

"I know this. Every rational person knows this. But that's irrelevant to the sentiment I'm seeing here on dry land. You've seen the market's hysteria, have you not?"

"I have, sir," Floros said. "Even in a national crisis, it's challenging to serve a man who makes such wild accusations."

"You don't serve him. You serve Greece."

Floros looked out the *Hydra's* bridge windows at the setting sun. Then he glanced to the north at the oil rig and its high blinking lights. With his nation's energy markets in wild fluctuation after the tanker attacks, he knew his need to protect the rig had become vital.

"He's going to announce this at an upcoming press conference," the vice admiral said. "But he's already released a statement. The Turks will be furious."

"And the easiest target for their frustrations is this oil rig."

"It's going to get worse before it gets better. I have a change to your rules of engagement. You may now fire upon any Turkish asset you perceive as a threat to the rig or the task force. You don't have to wait until you're fired upon."

"Dear God, sir, I'm tracking a dozen Turkish assets, and each one is a threat. Any one of them could launch weapons at any time. The distances between us are too small."

"I know. Use your judgment and contact me if you're unsure. This is a bad situation, but with the prime minister's attitude, you'd be best to explain yourself afterwards for being too assertive as opposed to being too cautious. He won't tolerate anything that could be construed as signs of weakness."

"This is dangerous," Floros said. "The prime minister's igniting a fire."

"It gets worse. You also need to engage any Turkish combatant that enters our territorial waters or airspace."

"Then I'll have no choice but to start a war."

"Use your weapons wisely and minimize escalations. That's unfortunately the best advice I can give you."

After digesting the severity of the order, Floros returned the plastic receiver to its cradle.

"What news, sir?" the *Hydra's* commander asked.

"Brace yourself," Floros said. "It's about to get nasty. I now have permission to engage Turkish combatants without having to be fired upon first, and I have orders to engage any Turkish combatant that enters our air or water."

The *Hydra's* commander's face became pale.

"Those are dangerous rules of engagement, sir."

"And the prime minister just blamed the Turks for the attacks on the three liquefied natural gas tankers that were destroyed," Floros said.

"That's impossible. They couldn't have done it."

"People are panicked back home and want to believe we know who to retaliate against."

"Well, who do you think it is, sir?"

Floros reflected about the intelligence he'd learned about a mercenary fleet's latest escapades in the Black Sea.

"The vice admiral hasn't told me yet, but I'm sure he would agree it's that private band of pirates that took on the Russians a few months ago. Someone has hired them to be vandals, or they're operating against us for their own agenda."

"We'll know soon enough, sir. Half the fleet is chasing the submarine that attacked the last tanker."

"I don't envy our hunting party against a team that frustrated the Russians, but that's not our concern. We have our own problems. Take a look at the display. Our helicopters are moving erratically."

"Let me look, sir."

Floros followed the *Hydra's* commander to a display table where icons showed the sea of Greek and Turkish war machines in a dance around Lesbos.

"Find out what they're doing," Floros said.

The commander picked up a phone and gathered information from an officer inside his ship who was in communication with the helicopters.

"They're prosecuting a possible submerged target."

"Have all surface combatants begin anti-submarine defensive maneuvers immediately. Bring all ships to general quarters."

As the *Hydra* rolled out of its first turn designed to complicate the targeting of a hostile torpedo, a sailor handed Floros a helmet. The chinstrap irritated his neck as he donned it. Red lights pulsated, and an alarm blared while another sailor dogged shut the watertight door to the bridge.

"Confirmed, sir," the *Hydra's* commander said. "It's a submarine. We have two helicopters over it. Its position is on the display now."

"Very well," Floros said.

"The pilot is requesting orders, sir. He wants to know if he should drop a torpedo."

Floros glared at the display and noticed the undersea vessel inside Greece's expanded national boundary and within torpedo strike range of the oil rig and two of his ships, including the *Hydra*. The crisis he feared and foresaw had reached him, and he sought a humane solution.

"Denied. Track it, blast it with active sonar, and drive it out of our waters. All assets are ordered to keep vigilant for the sounds of a torpedo launch from the submarine."

"You said your orders were to engage any combatant within our waters or air, sir."

"My orders are to engage, yes," Floros said. "But engaging doesn't require destroying. Once a helicopter has a submarine, it's like a lion's jaws. With two helicopters engaged, it won't get away. Be patient."

"We may not be able to hear an incoming torpedo."

"It won't fire," Floros said. "Not while our helicopters remain a deterrent."

"If the submarine escapes our helicopters?"

"It won't. Not as long as they're flying over it."

Floros reflected upon his own words.

"And let's make sure they remain flying over it. Have the *Ritsos* take station on the helicopters to protect them."

Through the bridge windows, Floros saw darkness crawl over the island of Lesbos. The silhouette of the missile boat, *Ritsos*, became a spec backlit by the island's shore life.

Then an animated voice issued from a loudspeaker and filled the frigate's bridge.

"Bridge, operations center. I hold a surface combatant breaking away from the Turkish surface fleet and heading towards Lesbos."

A task force of Turkish surface combatants patrolled the outskirts of the extended twelve-mile boundary off the Greek island's southern coast. Floros had excused the short-lived challenges when a Turkish combatant would slip a hundred yards inside Greek waters and slip back out again.

But a solitary ship aimed itself on a trajectory that implied enduring defiance, and he noted its velocity vector on the tactical display taking it within gun range of the helicopters that hovered over the Turk's submerged vessel.

"Which ship is it?" he asked.

"The frigate *Yavuz*, sir."

"Their oldest and least capable ship. It's not a threat. It's a test of our resolve."

"Which we'll fail if we look weak by ignoring it or fail if we respond too harshly by destroying it."

Floros agreed and felt trapped between restraint and his prime minister's orders to engage challenging forces. He forced his mind to generate an answer.

"We'll do neither," he said. "Patch me through to the commanding officer of the *Kanaris*."

He grabbed a secure phone from its cradle and spoke to the old frigate's captain.

"Have all your guns ready but keep them pointed forward. You're going to take station on the *Yavuz*, turn yourself into an unavoidable tugboat, and force it off course by pushing its bow."

"Shall I give it a warning shot across its bow, sir?"

"Negative. It's an old ship, but it has the largest cannon out here. Keep this to a contest of seamanship and gross tonnage. Don't invite a gun fight."

The lights in the bridge shifted from white to soft red as the dusk settled into night. Floros lifted night vision optics to his face and saw the greenish outline of the Turkish frigate slicing across the horizon.

"Perhaps we should be ready to lend gunfire support," the *Hydra's* commander said.

"Right," Floros said. "Energize all gunfire control radars and maneuver to within range of your ship's cannon against the *Yavuz*."

The *Hydra* rolled out of the turn as the Turkish frigate slid forward across the bridge windows.

"We're chasing the *Yavuz* but cannot intercept it at its present speed," the *Hydra's* commander said. "It would run into the island before we could. However, the *Kanaris* will take station on the *Yavuz* in twelve minutes."

"Very well," Floros said. "Hail the *Yavuz*, inform it that its presence in our waters is an act of war, and order it to leave Greek waters immediately."

The translator spoke into his handset but received no response. He repeated himself to no avail.

Minutes later, the commander of the *Kanaris* rang Floros.

"Task force commander," he said.

"Sir, I'm getting no response from my hails to the *Yavuz*, but I have a visual. It's only five miles away now."

"What do you see?" Floros asked. "Running lights? Guns being aimed? Anything?"

"It's actually got its running lights on per international laws, and the deck lights are illuminated, too. All its guns and fire control radars are secured. It's making no attempt to hide or provoke me."

"Other than by steaming at flank speed in our waters."

"No, sir, it just slowed to ten knots."

Floros glanced at the chart.

"That's because it's approaching the six-mile boundary that the Turks have always honored."

"I'll reach the intercept point eight miles from our coast."

"Good. Turn back the *Yavuz* the second you can."

Through his optics, Floros watched the frigates collide on a glancing angle as the Greek vessel nudged the Turkish warship off course. The laws of physics precluded one ship overpowering another of comparable size, and the battle become a test of wills.

Seven miles from the Lesbos coast, the Turkish combatant relented and reversed course.

"Well done, commander," Floros said. "Stay two hundred yards off its port flank until it's outside our twelve-mile boundary."

Declaring the encounter a draw in his mind as the Turkish

frigate returned to international waters, Floros reflected upon how he might address a future similar challenge, but his mind remained an overworked morass.

"That could have gone far worse," the *Hydra's* commander said. "But it's hardly a victory."

"No, it's not. But it's over, and we'd be better positioned elsewhere now. Make flank speed towards our helicopters to assist them in prosecuting the submarine."

"Understood, sir. They're approaching international waters as the submarine retreats."

"The advantage shifts to the submarine as it approaches Turkish waters." Floros said.

"Agreed. We can only protect the helicopters so far."

"If there was ever an argument for a weapon that could force a submarine to surface without sinking it, this is it. Without such a weapon, it needs to only run to the safety of its waters, reposition, and then start its hostile work against us again."

"Someone should mass produce such a weapon," the *Hydra's* commander said. "But today, we can only drive it away."

"It forces me to consider sinking that damned submarine."

"Are you, sir?"

"Considering it? Yes, unfortunately."

The loudspeaker startled Floros.

"Bridge, operations center. I have two air contacts accelerating to supersonic speeds. Two F-16 Fighting Falcons."

Icons appeared on the display.

"They're heading south to bypass the island," the *Hydra's* commander said. "I expect they'll turn west and attempt to overfly us to engage the helicopters."

"That's an astute estimation," Floros said. "They must have noticed that we have their submarine under duress. Hail them and warn them to avoid Greek airspace or that I personally promise to shoot them down."

An eerie look of surprise covered the commander's face.

"Do it," Floros said.

He overheard the translator speaking into a radio, followed

by the Turkish reply.

"They say they're free to fly in international airspace," the translator said.

"Warn them again that our airspace now extends twelve miles into open waters south of Lesbos."

The translator obeyed, but the Turkish pilots ignored him as they veered west towards the *Hydra*.

"How far away are they from us?" Floros asked.

"Nineteen nautical miles. Our lookout just spotted them with night vision googles."

"How far from our airspace?"

"Sixteen miles."

"Tell them we track them sixteen miles from our airspace and that I'll launch weapons at them if they enter it."

"Sir, the helicopter pilot requests permission to launch a torpedo," the *Hydra's* commander said. "He's concerned that the F-16s will shoot him down."

"Denied. But enter a targeting solution against the submarine into two of your ship's torpedoes and warm them up."

"Understood, sir. Also, the Turkish pilots say they're free to fly in international airspace outside of the six-mile boundary around Lesbos."

"Get ready to shoot them down."

"Understood, sir. I'll assign one missile to each F16."

"Very well. Assign the missiles."

As the *Hydra's* commander prepared his ship for battle, Floros walked to the translator and glared at him.

"Do I look serious to you?" he asked.

"Yes, sir," the translator said.

"Good. Now make the pilots understand that."

The translator lifted a handset and shot his harried voice into it. He repeated his gesture twice, earning silence.

"Five miles from our airspace," the *Hydra's* commander said. "Four. Three."

"They're not turning away, are they?" Floros asked.

"No, sir. I request permission to release weapons."

A pit formed in Floros' stomach.

"Granted," he said. "Shoot them down."

The commander pulled a key from his pocket and slid it into a lock on a console. He turned it, and a red light pulsated. Then, reaching to press a button, he yelled.

"Launching missiles!"

A distant hiss echoed through the frigate's steel, and bright streaks of reddish orange sliced the darkness. The evolved Sea Sparrow missiles climbed into the night and then exploded.

Every free pair of eyes on the bridge sought the outcome with night optics, but Floros averted his gaze from the carnage he knew he'd inflicted.

The voice from the *Hydra's* operations center confirmed his expectations.

"Bridge, operations center, splash two bogeys."

"Good job, commander," Floros said. "Do you see any parachutes?"

"One, sir. Just one."

"Over which waters?"

"Ours, sir. About nine miles from Lesbos."

"Good enough," Floros said. "Those are our waters, and no matter what the Turks say, it's at worst international waters. Have the *Ritsos* send a skiff to rescue the downed pilot."

"Understood, sir."

"And while you do that," Floros said, "I'll let the vice admiral know that I've killed a Turkish aviator and started a war."

## CHAPTER 7

Terrance Cahill pressed his palms into the console behind him, leaned backwards, and craned his neck upward. Through the *Goliath's* domed bridge windows, he watched the white-washed water from the propellers of a Greek gunboat churn the moonlight above him.

"Don't make a peep, Liam," he said.

"You mean like telling me not to make a peep," Liam Walker, his executive officer, said. "I wouldn't worry. That thing hasn't got a sonar system."

"Unless they thought far ahead enough to mount a towed system," Cahill said.

"They didn't. They have no idea we're here and not even a concept of our plans against them."

"Right," Cahill said. "Maybe I'm just paranoid with old habits, mate."

"With all the Greek warships moving about, just be thankful that's the only one that found its way anywhere near us."

"Pierre's data feed is magical, telling me without a doubt that there's no sonar on that gunboat. Without it, we'd be running from the damned thing now, and God knows whose attention that might have caught."

"Nobody's, mate," Walker said. "We're submerged and undetected, just how you submarine types like it. It still gives me the willies being underwater."

Cahill moved to the corner of the bridge that jutted from the ship's starboard bow. Through the polycarbonate windows that interlaced steel bars backed and reinforced, he watched the undersea darkness while his eyes teased his mind with the phantom silhouette of the Greek warship's sleek body fifty meters above him.

He blinked, cleared his mind, and realized the moon backlit the gunboat but failed to penetrate the depths' darkness that enshrouded him.

"Stop torturing yourself," Walker said. "They can't see us or hear us."

"Sure, mate."

"You should be the one reassuring me. I'm still the newbie to this underwater life."

"You're the one who knows how truly deaf a gunboat can be," Cahill said. "I can't fathom the concept of a warship without ears. The deafness is just a bizarre concept to me."

"Stone deaf, mate. Not a single sonar system."

Cahill lowered his gaze to a display, noticed smudges, and then reached for a spray bottle. He aimed the nozzle and wetted the screen. While he wiped it, he glanced at Walker.

"How long until we can take action?"

"Huh?" Walker asked.

"Until that thing's fifty miles away and we can shoot?"

Beside Cahill, Walker tapped his screen.

"About three hours."

Cahill dropped the moist wipe into a trash can.

"You have the bridge," he said. "I'm going to tour me ship."

Walking off his anxiety, he passed through a door, latched it behind him, and descended a steep stairway to a tight, odd-shaped compartment under which welds held the bridge and rakish bow upon which it rested to the cylindrical, submarine-based section.

As he reached for a watertight door, a peek in the bilge revealed the inverted triangular keel section, which provided stability and added buoyancy, continuing underneath the ship. Swinging the door open, he stepped through its machined frame and into the familiar, circular-ribbed world of a submarine.

Lacking a torpedo room, the *Goliath* presented Cahill its tactical control room as its first cylindrical compartment. Two of his four-man tactical team staffed the space, with one seated before a console and a supervisor sitting beside him.

"Good afternoon, sir," the supervisor said.

The young leader had been an officer aboard Cahill's submarine prior to quitting the Australian Navy for lucrative mercenary adventures. Like all of Renard's commanders, Cahill let his crew address him by name or retain the habit of addressing the officers as 'sir'.

"What's on sonar?" Cahill asked.

"Half the Aegean Sea, sir."

"Keep listening for warships, and make sure the one over us keeps driving the hell out of here."

He continued his sternward walk, passing electronic cabinets that appeared where he would have expected a conning platform and additional display consoles on Pierre Renard's other warships, the *Specter* and the *Wraith*.

With the elevated bridge pod atop the starboard bow and with cameras mounted atop the weapons bays in the sterns providing external views, the *Goliath's* design omitted half the standard submarine control room. Renard had instead allowed for a larger crew's accommodation area, which he extended into the control room, to add both crew comfort and extra buoyancy for carrying the *Goliath's* heavy cargo.

A high-powered, unique ship designed to transport the *Specter* or the *Wraith* to distant operations theaters, the *Goliath* had shown Cahill its value as a standalone combatant. While walking into its elongated berthing area, he reflected upon the hybrid transport-submarine-gunship's rise in Renard's pecking order to center stage against the Greeks that relegated the two *Scorpène*-class submarines to the distracting roles of attacking liquefied natural gas tankers. As its commander, he felt privileged.

Placing his weight onto the balls of his tennis shoes, he crept into the ghost-silent scullery and then continued to the mess hall, where two men played dominoes. He nodded and continued to the first ethanol-liquid-oxygen propulsion plant MESMA section. The hiss of steam filled the room, and heat wafted over him.

With his jumpsuit's torso flopped over his waist, a technician exposed a sweat-marked tee-shirt. He was examining gauges on a control panel when he looked up and winked. Since the man had proved himself on two combat missions, Cahill agreed he'd earned the right to affirm his readiness with a solitary eyelid.

Twenty-five meters and two MESMA plants later, Cahill ran an industrial-strength paper towel across his face and then dropped it into a waste bin. He turned athwartships towards the tunnel that connected the halves of his ship. Reaching through the opened circular doorway, he hoisted his torso into the cramped space and began crawling.

The confines bothered him. Difficult to clean, the intra-hull tunnel smelled stale, and the air tasted thick. Bowing his head to avoid the air-intake cross-connect, he watched his multiple shadows stretch under the thin grating that served as a floor. His labored breathing echoed off the bilge, where condensation reflected light from the twin rows of LED bulbs that ran beside the crossing air duct. He abraded his knuckles on a hydraulic isolation valve to the giant stern planes, to which the controller and lever arms loomed ahead.

"Bloody hell."

He licked blood and swallowed before continuing his crawl and followed hydraulic lines to an oversized block of metal. With algorithms sending electronic commands to the controller, its arms glided with grace across a small range of their full motion. Cahill craned his neck and watched them move outward through grease-coated holes into an invisible nook that shaped the hydrodynamic rear of the ship and housed the rocker that transferred the arms' piston-like movement into the arcing swing of the stern planes.

Scrunching his shoulders to his ears, he slipped past the controller and raised his gaze to the tunnel's end. His blood pressure rose.

"Dumb bastards."

Three stacked crates of spare rounds for the port railgun blocked his egress. He thought about muscling the top one to the grated flooring but realized his kneeling leverage was nil. Instead, he leaned into the tunnel's curved metal wall and felt its coolness through his shirt.

Habit preventing him yelling, he cast his raised voice through the crawlspace's port hatch.

"Who the hell's on watch in MESMA plant six?"

He listened for a response to rise above the steaming hiss but heard none. He risked a louder attempt.

"This is the captain. Who the hell's on watch in MESMA plant six?"

Again, no response.

As he pondered giving up and backtracking to the tunnel's sound-powered phone, the desired response arrived.

"Oh shit! Sorry, Terry. Hold on. I'll get this out of your way."

"Be quiet about it, for God's sake," Cahill said.

"Right."

The man slid the top rack through the portal, causing the rounds to rattle. As he reached for the next crate, Cahill saw his face.

"Johnson."

"Yes, sir."

"Who put these here?"

"Do I really have to answer?"

"I'll find out eventually."

"It was Brown, sir."

"Do you know why he did it?"

"He said he was getting tired of moving them around during his workouts. They were in the way of the exercise machines."

"This isn't a storage area. How the bloody hell do you guys expect to travel between hulls with this pile of metal in the way?"

"That's the problem, Terry. We don't have much chance to move between hulls. We have all we need in the port hull. We don't get to the starboard side much."

Cahill suspected he may have been leading independent crews on either side of his ship.

"But I have the MESMA plant supervisors switch sides every three days."

"We just move two of the three crates and then put them

back after they're through the door."

Cahill took the hint and crawled over the remaining crate, and Johnson stepped back.

As his head emerged in the port hull, Cahill twisted his torso and grabbed a bar attached above the door. He pulled his shoulders through the portal and then reached for a higher bar. With his waist freed, he walked his heels out and pushed his buttocks free. He drove his haunches backwards, making space for his legs and feet to back into the compartment and transfer his weight to rungs mounted below the door.

He felt free as he stood and gathered his bearings.

"Well, what about food?" he asked. "You're not eating the emergency rations are you? I see food being carried back through the starboard MESMA spaces to you guys every meal."

"Right, again, Terry. The main meals come sealed in cellophane. We turn them sideways and slide them around the spare rounds. We do the same for the soups and drinks."

"You do that for all ten meals, three times a day?"

"All ten, three times a day. Plus snacks and beverage runs a couple times in between. Whoever's the most junior guy on watch on the starboard MESMA plants is the poor bastard who gets to bring it all over to us. Everyone is fed and happy."

"Agreed that everyone is fed. But I'm not happy."

"Right. I'll have these moved back where they belong."

Cahill moved forward through MESMA plants four and two, reaching the open space that paralleled the starboard side's galley and mess. The quiet compartment had dining tables, housed spare parts, and served as the recreational space for the crew—rather, for less than half his crew, as he realized the port hull team monopolized it.

Hundreds of spare railgun rounds covered the free spaces between pieces of exercise equipment. Some crates formed short walls around a treadmill, and others concealed the lower half of a Bowflex machine. The three crates in front of the resistance-training equipment dipped low to allow a man to step over them, and he understood why Brown had removed the additional three that blocked his access to his workout.

But life on a warship required sacrifices, and Brown would need to move the crates into the passageway and then return them to their rightful place each time he exercised.

Cahill continued to the port hull's berthing area, and he heard snoring. A quick mental count told him three men slept while the other seven tended to the port hull's systems. After gaining trust in the French-designed MESMA systems, he had relaxed the watch team for each hull's three plants from seven sailors to five. He also had a man in the propulsion plant and a solitary gunner in the weapons bay.

He crept through the space and reached the abandoned tactical control room that served as a redundant brain of the *Goliath*. A final door led him to the port bow module, where instead of stairs leading to a bridge, he saw the hydraulic hoist to the retracted Phalanx close-in weapon system.

"All's quiet up here," he said.

Retracing his steps, he reached the aft MESMA plant and then entered the port engine room. He walked under the wide air ducts to the gas turbine engine that allowed direct feeding of the ship's motors for speed while surfaced.

"How are we doing back here?" he asked.

A man in coveralls seated before a control panel looked up and then nodded towards the electric motor at the tapering cylindrical stern.

"Everything's fine. Purring like a kitten."

Cahill glanced aft and saw the top of the motor, which the ship's Taiwanese builders had sunk into a custom recess. He then opened a hatch on the engine room's angled slope, reached upward to handles, and pulled himself through. Closing the hatch, he noticed the quietness of the weapons bay. He climbed a ladder and entered his ship's aft space.

The railgun was unimposing, impressing Cahill with its compact size. The greatest mass rose behind the breach to absorb recoil, and as he walked deeper into the bay, he stood on his tiptoes to reach the top of the cannon. Withdrawing his fingertips to his face, he saw the right amount of dust to suggest that his crew followed the railgun's proper cleaning schedule.

He saw a lanky man reclining in a cot reading a magazine under a recessed curve in the hull.

"What brings you this far from the bridge?"

"I was taking a tour to get me mind off the Greek warship that just passed over us," Cahill said.

The man stirred, as if expecting action. Cahill had his propulsion and weapon technicians trained to back each other up to operate the railgun, propulsion plant, and the MESMA systems. He recognized this watch stander as a neophyte in the weapons bay, and he knew a senior gunner would replace him before his attack on Greece would begin.

"I need to be ready for action."

"No need," Cahill said. "It's a small gunboat. No sonar. No clue that we're below it, and I plan to keep it that way."

"Oh. Right. I don't imagine you'd be back here if we were getting ready for battle."

"Right, mate."

A light source flashed by one of the polycarbonate windows that offered a thin panoramic view out the weapons bay. He recognized it as some form of biological life and ignored it.

A sound-powered phone chirped by the man's head. He reached, tore it from its cradle, and lifted it to his cheek.

"Port weapons bay," he said.

He extended the phone, and Cahill took the handset.

"Captain," he said.

"Terry, it's the bridge," Walker said. "I've got an update from Renard. He says the gunboat that just passed over us is the last ship of concern. All engines of Greek warships in port remain cold, and all other deployed ships are far away. He wants us to attack when the gunboat is out of reaction range."

"Excellent," Cahill said. "How long until the gunboat is fifty miles away?"

"Two and a half hours."

"Schedule the tactical briefing in an hour, and have the weapons bays load the explosive rounds."

"Will do, Terry. Explosive rounds. This will be interesting."

"New levels of vandalism," Cahill said. "I feel like a mongrel for ambushing a friendly nation, but I know it's exactly what we need to do."

## CHAPTER 8

Jake Slate leaned over the navigation table.

"I can't believe that tanker's crew is testing me," he said.

"The prime minister must have ordered them to," Henri said.

"I know," Jake said. "I still can't believe a man can be that arrogant. Or that stupid."

"His arrogance–or his stupidity–has allowed him to succeed in something. He's forcing us into a difficult decision. The outpouring of Hellenic warships has exceeded our expectations, and if we give away our position by attacking the tanker, there's true risk that we're discovered."

"We wouldn't give ourselves away entirely. There's plenty of water around that tanker from where we could be attacking."

"But our hunters know we're attacking from the west since they know our maximum speed and the rough location of our prior attack north of Crete."

"I was trying to be optimistic."

"It doesn't become you."

Jake smirked.

"True."

"It's your call," Henri said. "This is why I presume Pierre pays you a captain's share of the bounty."

Jake restrained a smile as he considered his multi-million-dollar commission for each mission.

As Renard's first recruited commanding officer, he knew his mentor appreciated competent commanders and found ways to support their handsome payments by squeezing money from his clients. His French boss could smell desperation and extract maximum pricing from those who needed his services. He wondered how many Euro Renard had negotiated from the French, Germans, Italians, and Turks.

"He pays me to think things through rationally."

"Yes, he does. But you have that look in your eye like you're getting ready to blow something up."

"The ultimate intent of our mission is to force a new

regime," Jake said. "I can't let the prime minister get away with stating that tankers bound for Greece are safe. One torpedo undermines his credibility. So let's do it."

From the control station, Henri turned his nose at Jake.

"Does Pierre have an opinion?" he asked.

"I suppose I should check. I can be cavalier about our lives but not about his precious submarine."

"He cares about our lives, too," Henri said. "And more so than just for our value to him as a crew. Ask him."

Jake walked to the conning platform and leaned into his console. Where he expected Renard, he saw an empty chair.

"He's not there. He's probably taking a leak."

"Or indulging in a cigarette," Henri said.

Frowning, Jake twisted his neck to look at the Frenchman.

"What?" Henri asked. "Didn't you notice that he's not been smoking in front of you?"

"I guess. It wasn't near the top of my thoughts."

"Well, our boss is losing his battle to stop smoking, and the Toulon command center doesn't allow smoking indoors."

"Sucks to be Pierre, then."

"Why?" Renard asked.

Jake looked back to the screen.

"Having to run outside to smoke."

"Nonsense. I was using the facilities."

"Then why do I smell nicotine on your breath?"

The Frenchman laughed through his nostrils.

"Funny. What's on your mind?"

"I want to attack the LNG tanker that's in transit from Cyprus to Revithoussa."

"Always the daredevil," Renard said. "It's still forty nautical miles away from you, and Hellenic warships will be near you before you could get off a close-range shot."

"But I'm not taking a close-range shot. I'll hit it from seventeen miles away and evade long before anyone finds me."

"Possibly, if the tanker maintains course and speed."

"It will. They always do."

Renard turned his face towards an off-screen monitor and then returned his gaze towards Jake.

"Apparently, it's taking a direct route to Revithoussa. Interesting. The prime minister all but dares you to attack his tankers, yet he gives no instruction to have them drive defensively. Not the slightest hint of zigzag anti-submarine legs."

"Makes my life easier," Jake said.

"Aren't you the slightest bit concerned about the legitimate threat? Half the Hellenic fleet is barreling down upon you."

"We expected that."

"Not this many ships," Renard said. "Not this many helicopters. You even inspired fixed-wing maritime aircraft to pursue you. I fear for your safety if you attack this tanker."

Jake checked his bravado and tapped his wisdom to grant himself a broader view of the danger.

"I've got a question," he said. "Is there anything protecting the tanker?"

"I don't see anything."

"That's foolish of them, don't you think?"

"I suspect the admiralty has advised the prime minister to use all available assets to hunt you, and I've got the best satellite and aerial radar coverage that the European Union can provide."

Jake tasted the irony that the regime change he desired to impart upon Greece included nudging it out of the European Union.

"Seems like a stab in the back to the Greeks, using assets against them that are technically allied with them."

"It is," Renard said. "And for good reason, because it is one enormous stab in the back, which is the mission you seem to struggle to accept. Stay focused."

"I am focused. So you think the tanker is a free shot, albeit a difficult one?"

"Free? Hardly. Though it has no escort of its own, you'll have to commit to getting within the reach of Greek helicopters to complete your attack. I have half a mind to forbid you."

"But half a mind to consider me a coward if I don't."

"You're no coward."

"But I know how you think. You see this as a calculated risk in our favor that boosts the odds of our mission's success, and you believe I'm charmed enough to still be invulnerable."

"Indeed. Do you still feel charmed?"

Jake halted his tactical mind and allotted a moment to assess himself. His emotional state was stable, and his body felt strong.

He reflected upon a new central focus in his life–Jesus Christ–but his mind served as a prison for the connection with his savior. Mental machinations had stymied the relationship Christians suggested would form with the central person of the religion, and Jake lacked any real-world experiential benefit from his new beliefs.

His mind believed, his heart resisted, and any charm he'd once enjoyed by self-aggrandizement had lapsed while he wrestled with the selflessness of his adopted doctrine.

If arrogance had once been his strength, his efforts towards humility left him groping for new ground.

"Shit, Pierre. I have no idea. I just know I can get it done."

"So be it, my friend," Renard said. "Prove the prime minister a fool and sink one more of his tankers."

"I need to go deep to do it."

"I'll contact you on low-frequency if I must. Make me proud."

Jake nodded and then lowered the periscope.

"Henri," he said, "take us to fifty meters."

The deck dipped and then leveled.

"Steady at fifty meters," Henri said.

"Very well," Jake said. "Empty tubes three, four, and five and reload with Sidewinders."

Thirty minutes later, Jake stood by the central plotting table, sensing opportunity and risk.

"We're within launch range," he said.

"Are you sure you want to do this?" Henri asked.

"This is the big one. It's Greek flagged, it started its journey in Greek Cyprus, and it's on its way to the Revythousa re-gasification terminal in Greece. No Iranian involvement. Just Greece, Greece, and Greece to get the message across to the Greek prime minister. We have to."

"Tube one is ready," Remy said.

"Presets?"

"Slow speed run to maximize range. Anti-surface mode. Active seeker."

"Very well. Shoot tube one."

The soft whine and pressure change hit Jake's ears.

"Tube one indicates normal launch," Remy said. "I have wire control. I hear its propeller."

"How long is the expected run?"

"Twenty-three minutes," Remy said.

"Shall we cut the wire and evade?" Henri asked.

Jake raised his finger to pause the conversation while he studied the chart. Icons shifted with the slow data feed from Renard's intelligence sources. With an armada approaching, he understood Henri's concern. Self-preservation dictated he should turn and flee.

But he noticed dense shipping near his targeted liquefied natural gas tanker, and prudence dictated he should stay put to assure he could guide an accurate shot.

"Not yet. There's too much shipping around the tanker. Our torpedo could hit any one of them."

"A small mistake to risk in exchange for assuring our survival by evading now."

"We don't need to evade. And it would be a huge mistake. Imagine the prime minister's gloating if he scares us into sinking the wrong ship."

Fifteen minutes later, Jake dared to hope his attack would succeed unimpeded.

Then Remy's toad-head rolled down, and the sonar guru's hands clasped his earpieces.

"Helicopter," Remy said.

"How close?"

"Medium range. Fifty percent chance of detecting us."

"Are you shitting me?" Jake asked. "Just like that? No warning?"

"Helicopters can get lucky and start new searches near us."

"Then we can get lucky and not be heard."

"Would you like to cut the wire now?" Henri asked.

"No."

"Then how about shooting down that accursed helicopter?"

"And give away our position? Be patient, my friend. Remember your nerves of steel."

"I'm getting too old for this," Henri said.

"That's no excuse. You were too old for this when I met you. A man your age should be running out of breath playing with his grandkids."

"Well, I'm instead underwater with you running out of breath worrying about dying."

Jake twisted his neck to lock eyes with the Frenchman. Reading his friend's face, he said nothing.

"What?" Henri asked.

"Is there anything else you'd rather be doing than this while you die?"

A smile broke out on Henri's face.

"No," he said. "I imagine not."

"The helicopter's gone," Remy said. "But I hear another one, farther away, different frequency."

"Shit," Jake said. "This could get ugly."

"Depends where the first helicopter repositions," Henri said.

"How long until our weapon hits?" Jake asked.

He watched his sonar expert lower his toad-shaped head towards his Subtics station.

"Still seven minutes," Remy said. "It was a very long shot."

"But the tanker's running into it face-first?"

"Yes," Remy said. "The geometry's trivial with Pierre's data, but perfect geometry doesn't guarantee perfect targeting if another ship gets in the way."

Jake took the subconscious hint and glared at the chart.

A subtle gift appeared.

Where updates had been arriving every five minutes for all ships in his vicinity, the data now came every thirty seconds for assets of highest interest—helicopters and ships near the tanker.

"Pierre gets it," he said. "He always gets it. He remembers how to command a submarine."

"What do you mean?" Henri asked.

"He's figured out that we're at the critical point. He knows we have a weapon close to hitting, and he knows we have helicopters hounding us. He filtered out the ships that aren't an immediate danger, and he's sending data every thirty seconds for the helicopters and ships around the tanker."

At the control station, the silver-haired Henri shrugged.

"What's that mean? Tactically?"

"It means I can see the helicopters with enough detail to know if they're a threat, at least while they're stopped and pinging. And it means I can see the ships around the tanker well enough to see if they're a risk of distracting our torpedo."

"And?"

"Hold on," Jake said. "Let it update again."

He tapped the screen to zoom in on the tanker. A cruise ship was passing it going the other way, en route to Cyprus.

"How many lives are on that ship? A hundred? A thousand?"

"What's wrong Jake?" Henri asked.

"A cruise ship, according to Pierre. He highlighted it."

A silent prayer to his new god entered Jake's mind. He feared murdering droves of innocents, and his heart sought solace in avoiding the weighty guilt.

"How close is it to our weapon?" Henri asked.

"Close enough that our weapon just acquired it," Remy said. "I'm steering our weapon ten degrees to the left to avoid it."

"Five degrees," Jake said. "Not ten. Five."

"Five degrees to the left," Remy said. "That's still very close to keeping the cruise ship in our weapon's seeker field. If the wire breaks after the steer–"

"It will still miss the cruise ship. Barely. But it will miss.

Hand off control of the weapon and keep listening for helicopters."

Remy tapped his screen, and the technician beside him did the same to take control of the torpedo. Jake burned his eyes dry watching the icon of his weapon skirt the stern of the passenger vessel.

"Good enough," he said. "Steer the weapon back to the right five degrees."

"Helicopter," Remy said. "Fifty percent risk of detection. Bearing two-two-one."

"Damn it," Jake said. "We need to run."

"Do you want to cut the wire?" Henri asked.

"No. We'll keep it until it breaks. Come right to course zero-six-five. Make turns for ten knots."

The deck tilted into the turn.

"How about shooting down the helicopter?" Henri asked.

Jake shook his head while watching the torpedo's icon pass behind the cruise ship.

"We'll slip away the old fashioned way."

On the display, the tanker's icon moved into the area in which its keel fell prey to the seeker's acoustic acquisition. Jake held his breath as the torpedo's feed evaporated, leaving its fate in the hands of its automated systems and physics.

The technician beside Remy announced the loss of the guidance wire.

The final minutes passed in slow, anxious moments as Jake awaited a distant explosion while praying for the airborne threats above him to disappear.

"Loud explosion, bearing three-five-two," Remy said. "That's the bearing of the tanker."

"We'll wait for Pierre to confirm," Jake said.

A minute later, Renard's data feed confirmed the destruction of the correct target. Jake exhaled and offered silent thanks to his new god for the success of his attack.

"Any sign of the helicopters?" he asked.

"I hear one far away," Remy said. "The sea's large size is finally working in our favor."

"Good," Jake said. "We'll head towards Haifa. Our sanctuary is Israeli waters, and God willing, we'll make it there alive."

# CHAPTER 9

Cahill watched moonlight glimmer in the shallow waves.

"Verify through visual inspection that rounds one through ten in each cannon are explosive rounds," he said.

"I'm verifying with both gunners," Walker said.

Cahill glanced at a chart showing him the distance to his target equaling ninety percent of his railguns' ability. The explosive shells contained guidance programming to spread them across lengths of a pipeline feeding compressed natural gas to Greece's people.

"The visual verification is complete," Walker said. "Rounds one through ten in each cannon are explosive rounds. The rounds are loaded in the proper sequence to land from west to east across the pipeline in their firing order."

"Very well, Liam," Cahill said. "I'm bringing us to minimum cannon depth."

He tapped a key that set the *Goliath* into its routine of pumping water from trim tanks to the sea. A depth gauge counted the ship's imperceptible rise while the deck tilted downward to raise the stern-mounted weapons bays above the waves.

"The weapons bays report being clear to raise the cannons," Walker said.

"Very well," Cahill said. "Raising the cannons."

He tapped two icons on his screen, ordering hydraulic fluid to lift the railguns above the waterline.

"Cannons are raised," Walker said.

"Prepare to shoot ten rounds from each cannon at the Interconnector Pipeline."

Walker touched keys at his console.

"Each cannon is aimed at the Interconnector Pipeline, ready to fire with pre-programmed target coordinates."

"Fire."

The boom from the starboard railgun preceded the port weapon's supersonic crack that echoed throughout the hull and reverberated in the water above the domed bridge.

"Raise the radio mast but maintain emissions control," Cahill said.

"Raising the radio mast."

A screen before Cahill turned from darkness to the image of his weary boss. Renard's face angled downward while the Frenchman examined a screen at his desk.

Steel blue eyes then turned and faced Cahill.

"I see your rounds on radar now," Renard said.

The Frenchman waited.

"Can you hear me, Terry?" Renard asked. "Rather, will you respond?"

His boss waited again while Cahill stayed in listening mode.

"No need to contact me if you wish to maintain emissions control," Renard said. "I know you've risked your position with your attack, but no need to simplify life for the Greeks by risking a radio broadcast. I'll make sure your rounds have GPS augmentation for targeting."

"Thanks, mate," Cahill said.

"He can't hear you unless you transmit," Walker said.

"I know, but it's comforting to talk to him."

Five seconds separated each round, and as the minute passed, Cahill waited for his tactical team to announce a hostile helicopter's presence above him. But silence from his crew and Renard's farewell quieted his paranoia and suggested his desired isolation.

"I'll keep you updated with the low-rate updates in case you aren't listening to my video feed," Renard said. "But the information I have is favorable in that no Greek assets are within twenty minutes of you. Jake succeeded in pulling them away."

"The final round is away," Walker said.

"Lowering the cannons," Cahill said.

He tapped icons and waited for a red ring around his weapons bay hatch symbols to signal their closure.

"Diving to thirty meters," he said. "Coming to twelve knots."

The *Goliath's* automated ease allowed him quick finger strokes on a capacitive touchscreen to maneuver its mass, and the ship steadied on its undersea evasion.

Once concealed below the waves, he tapped another icon to invoke preset coordinates for his next launch point, twenty-one miles away, and the ship glided through a gentle southerly turn while angling downward to fifty meters.

"Just under two hours until we can attack the Revythousa regasification terminal," he said. "That's a long time."

"Half the fleet is chasing Jake, except for that small task force that's defending the oil rig," Walker said. "What's left won't be able to reach us before we've unloaded and are long gone."

"True, for the ships we can see. But there are submarines out there that worry me, and there must be extra helicopters getting ready to search for us after what we just did."

"Technically, we haven't done it yet."

Cahill looked at the display that showed the estimated flights of his railguns' shells arcing towards the Greek pipeline.

"I assume the Greeks will notice projectiles moving at Mach 7 on someone's radar."

"Probably," Walker said. "But their air force is still on strike. It would have to be a naval system."

"The ships protecting the oil rig near Lesbos will notice. Keep watchful of Pierre's incoming feed for their movement, or movement of assets from the shore. I'm sure we were noticed."

"Will do, Terry. Nothing yet, though."

The trickle of characters on Cahill's screen changed as Renard's feed offered a simple update.

He had destroyed the pipeline–many times over, across a mile of its length, condemning any future repair crew to weeks of effort to reinstate the flow.

"The first target is destroyed," he said.

"Roger that, mate," Walker said.

"Spread the word to the crew, quietly. No loudspeakers. Let them know we've already accomplished half our mission."

"Will do, Terry."

Walker lifted a sound-powered phone to his cheek and updated several men with instructions to pass the word to all compartments.

Cahill's satisfaction in his success waned as time eroded his patience approaching his second target. As he hoped he might continue his assault unnoticed, Renard's update highlighted two helicopters leaving the Greek mainland and heading towards his last surfaced location. Then the coordinates came, and automated updates generated figures on his chart.

"Just two," Cahill said. "Maybe this is our lucky day."

"They appear to be flying behind us, if we can trust the data," Walker said. "It's stale before it reaches us, at this baud rate."

"But useful. I think they're going to start where we were and expand their search from there."

"I'm sure they'll figure out that we're running to the south. It's not like we could run to the north, unless we intended to ground ourselves on the Greek shoreline and surrender."

"Good point, mate," Cahill said. "I have an idea."

"I'm listening."

"Load five splintering rounds into each cannon followed by ten explosive rounds."

"Right. I see your point."

Walker lifted the sound-powered phone again and relayed the command to the weapons bays.

"Five splintering rounds are loaded in each cannon followed by ten explosive rounds each," he said.

"Very well."

"When do you want to attack the helicopters?" Walker asked.

"I'm not sure I want to."

"But you've just committed the rounds."

"If we're lucky enough that they don't become an issue, I'll decide what to do with the rounds when we attack Revythousa."

Below Cahill's chin, Renard's data shifted, giving him faster updates on the helicopters' positions in exchange for lagging data on the rest of the Aegean Sea's activity.

Standing beside him, Walker scanned similar news.

"There's one getting close to us."

"Close, yes," Cahill said. "But no worries yet, mate."

He sighed in relief as the helicopter veered to the west, but then its partner leapfrogged ahead of the *Goliath's* track.

"Damn," he said.

"Fight or flight," Walker said.

"Flight. We're too far from our launch point to get distracted in a battle. Coming right to course two-two-five."

He tapped keys, and while the deck angled into the turn, his sonar supervisor's voice issued from a loudspeaker.

"Dipping sonar. Less than fifty percent chance of detection."

Cahill raised his voice towards a microphone.

"Less than fifty percent even while showing our broadsides?"

"Yes, sir. It's a low signal strength."

"Very well."

Renard's data showed the airborne threat moving away.

"Coming left to course one-eight-zero," Cahill said.

"How long do you expect our luck to last?" Walker asked.

"I never expect luck," Cahill said. "I hope for the best and prepare for the worst."

The executive officer's voice rose half an octave.

"Here's the worst of it, mate."

"Shit," Cahill said. "Coming to all stop. Ascending to minimum cannon depth."

He tapped a key that set the *Goliath* into its automated rise routine. The deck tilted downward to raise the weapons bays.

"The weapons bays report being clear to raise the cannons."

"Very well," Cahill said. "Raising the cannons."

"Cannons are raised," Walker said.

"Bringing the phased array radar online."

Cahill touched an icon that energized the elements spread across the flat, exterior edges of his sterns' twin elevated superstructures.

"Phased array shows online," Walker said. "We have the closest helicopter on radar."

"Prepare to shoot five rounds from each cannon, target the

closest helicopter."

Walker touched keys at his console.

"Closest helicopter is targeted."

"Fire."

Sonic booms reverberated in the hull and echoed through the water. Twenty seconds later, the airborne threat disappeared from the screen.

"Hit!" Walker said.

"Cease fire." Cahill said.

He watched Walker tap his screen and silence the railguns with five total splintering rounds remaining.

The sonar supervisor offered an enthusiastic report.

"The helicopter has splashed!"

"I can't find the other helicopter," Walker said. "It's beyond the horizon. We're too low in the water."

"Damn it. I'm surfacing the ship."

Cahill tapped an icon commanding pumps to spew water from the *Goliath's* trim tanks to the sea, and the combat transport ship became a cork.

Seconds later, radar energy painted the other airborne threat.

"I got it, Terry."

"Fire."

The railguns expelled their combined five rounds.

"It's a hit!" Walker said. "The helicopter's losing altitude and slipping laterally."

"Very well. I'm taking us down. Coming to thirty meters."

He tapped keys to secure the radar, lower the railguns, and inhale water into the *Goliath's* tanks.

"That was close," Walker said.

"Too close. Let's get to our launch point and get out of here without further drama."

After an uninterrupted submerged transit to his launch point against the solitary regasification plant that could convert incoming cooled liquid into compressed natural gas for dissemination to the Greek economy, Cahill slowed his ship and ascended to the minimum cannon depth.

"Verify ten rounds in each cannon are loaded, sequenced from south to north against the Revythousa regasification plant."

"Verifying," Walker said.

Cahill heard muffled reports from his weapons bay technicians squawking from Walker's sound-powered phone.

"The sequence is verified."

"Fire."

Sonic booms echoed as Cahill watched the Frenchman's face appear on his monitor.

"Your attack on the pipeline and the helicopters has stirred the hornets' nest," Renard said. "I see propulsion systems warming up on harbored Hellenic warships."

"Hopefully it won't matter," Cahill said.

"Do you want to risk talking back to him?" Walker asked.

"Not yet. I've got nothing to tell him that would help matters. He knows what to do."

"Right."

As his ship unloaded its arsenal at the distant regasification plant, Cahill sensed an ugly premonition–the type he'd developed after years of warfare.

"What's wrong, Terry?"

"I thought I heard a click over the loudspeaker."

While fears and potential reactions to phantom threats flooded Cahill's mind, Walker frowned, tapped an icon, and spoke.

"Sonar supervisor, is there something on your mind?"

"Yeah, maybe. We're analyzing something."

Cahill aimed his jaw towards the microphone on his console.

"Spit it out, mate."

"Possible launch transients."

"From a submerged contact?"

"Yes. Pneumatic whining. Very faint. Very far away."

Cahill shifted into reactive mode.

"Give me a bearing," he said. "Now."

"Two-two-three or one-three-seven."

The long line of hydrophones he towed behind the *Goliath* sensed low-frequency sounds and distant noises, providing him his first warning of danger. But exposed to the water without any mechanical backstop, his towed array was helpless to tell its left from its right.

"I can't maneuver for you yet, mate," he said. "We'll have to live with the ambiguity for now."

"How would maneuvering help ambiguity?" the supervisor asked. "It was a transient noise. It's gone."

"In case there's a torpedo on the same bearing."

"If it's on the same bearing, it's coming right for us."

"That's me point," Cahill said. "Do you hear anything on the hull arrays?"

"No. Nothing."

The proximity to the *Goliath's* self-noise condemned the hydrophones that spanned the hull's skin to a weaker sensitivity than the sensors towed behind the ship. Cahill wanted to dive, turn, and accelerate to dissect the details of any new sounds coming from the direction of the possible launch, but his mission precluded it.

Rhythmic sonic booms hammered the water as he glanced at cutaway graphics of his railguns and counted four shells remaining in each. Twenty seconds left of shooting. Twenty seconds left of walking face-first at four knots into the fury of a potential torpedo.

He looked to the image of the Frenchman for hope.

"Your rounds are looking good," Renard said. "All are thus far headed on proper trajectories towards their targets. I'm also tracking the Hellenic ships that may prosecute you. Fortunately, no additional helicopters yet. One gunboat has just gotten underway, but it has no sonar system to threaten you if you can stay submerged during your egress."

The railguns stopped.

"I'm taking us down," Cahill said. "Coming to thirty meters. Accelerating to ten knots. Turning left to course one-zero-zero to resolve ambiguity on the towed array."

He tapped keys to lower the railguns, inhale water into the *Goliath's* tanks, and maneuver the ship. The deck angled and rolled, and he grabbed a railing for balance.

"You mean we're only resolving ambiguity if we hear another sound while on the new course?" Walker asked. "Either another transient noise, machinery noise from a launching submarine, or a torpedo."

"Right."

"I hope you're just being pessimistic."

After the deck steadied, the half-octave increase in the supervisor's voice over the loudspeaker heralded the danger.

"High-speed screws! Torpedo in the water!"

"Bearing!" Cahill said.

"Two-two-three or three-three-seven. Ambiguity is resolved to two-two-three correlating to the prior launch transients."

"Shit," Walker said. "We were sitting ducks. This is a perfect shot against us."

"Surfacing the ship," Cahill said.

He tapped keys, and the deck lifted his stomach into his throat. Blackness yielded to translucent shimmering, yielded to a starry, moonlit sky. He then instructed Walker to invoke his strengths as a surface warfare officer and transform the *Goliath* into its best impersonation of a destroyer.

"Shift propulsion to the gas turbines, energize all radar systems, and elevate all weapon systems."

After his executive officer obeyed the commands, Cahill tapped keys to triple the behemoth's speed.

"Coming to all ahead flank. Coming left to course one-zero-three to place the torpedo off our port flank."

As the ship undulated over the swells, Cahill committed to a two-way conversation with his boss.

"Damn," Renard said. "I see you on the surface. I assume you're running from a torpedo."

Cahill forced a cavalier response to calm his nerves.

"Not the first time, mate."

"Well, I have some good news. An Italian maritime patrol craft intercepted a transmission from the submarine that shot at you. It was an encrypted message that's not been broken, but at least the patrol craft was able to geo-locate the submarine for you. I'm sending the coordinates. It was far away when it attacked you."

"It probably broke off from the pursuit of Jake after I attacked the pipeline."

"Indeed. I'm calculating now," Renard said. "And I think you can just barely outrun the torpedo. You have a sixteen-knot speed disadvantage, and I estimate the torpedo is six miles from you. It should run out of fuel if you can maintain your top speed."

"Thanks for the propulsion upgrades you gave me in Toulon," Cahill said. "The extra knot makes a difference. I'm coming left to zero-four-three to put the torpedo right in me stern."

Renard's jaw tightened as he turned his face from the screen.

"Away from one danger and into another."

"Shit," Cahill said. "You're right. I'm heading right into that bloody mess near Lesbos."

"Your attacker was wiser than he appears with his long-range shot," Renard said. "He's forced you to either deal with his torpedo or deal with the Hellenic task force at the oil rig."

"I'll take the task force. I know how to disable their propulsion systems and keep their helicopters away from me ship."

"You do, but the Hellenic forces are likely aware of the countermeasures the Russians used against you in the Black Sea. Keep your wits about you and remember the counters to the counters."

"I will."

"If nothing else, let me at least assure you of your mission's success. I'm sending the satellite videos now."

A screen above Renard's face showed huge compressed natural gas tanks exploding in Revythousa as the *Goliath's* shells peppered the facility. Then a ball of fire engulfed the industrial complex that converted incoming liquefied fuel into its useable gaseous form.

"So I'm running from a torpedo and into a hostile task force that rightfully has reason to hate me."

"I can't help that, but rest assured that the intended consequences of our effort have been taking shape since you struck the pipeline."

"How so?"

"A coup," Renard said. "The man we expected to take power under the duress of our attacks is preparing to announce his control of the government and invoke temporary martial law to restore order to the chaos that's already erupting."

The Frenchman's access to intelligence impressed Cahill by reaching farther and wider than his imagination could consider.

"Do I dare ask how you know this?"

"Best that you don't, my friend. Just keep the *Goliath* in one piece and find a way out of this mess alive."

## CHAPTER 10

Nicos Floros jammed the secure telephone's receiver into its cradle. He'd spent ten minutes developing a plan with his boss, and as he freed his mind from tactics, the day's emotions escaped.

"Incredible," he said.

"What's the news, sir?" the *Hydra's* commander asked.

"Both the Revythousa re-gasification terminal and the Interconnector Pipeline are destroyed."

"Obviously coordinated with the attacks against the tankers."

"It gets worse," Floros said.

Then he reconsidered the epic speed at which his nation underwent transformation.

"Or it gets better, depending on your political perspective," he said. "Senator Daskalakis is claiming rule over the nation."

The *Hydra's* commander scoffed.

"The speaker of our parliament? I can't say I dislike the man when compared to the countless worse politicians, and the fortitude to boldly claim rule is admirable."

The gravity of his nation's victimhood sank into his being as Floros reflected upon the news Vice Admiral Agathocleous had conveyed a minute earlier.

"You may consider him bold, but the evidence suggests puppetry," he said. "This attack on our natural gas infrastructure... it appears backed by our so-called allies."

"Conspiracy theories are always enticing to believe, but what's the evidence?"

"The ship that attacked the homeland is the same that attacked the Russians in Crimea–the mercenary vessel, *Goliath*."

"The *Goliath*?" he asked. "You're certain?"

"Based upon the intelligence, who else could it be? The only other ship capable of a sea-based railgun attack is an American *Zumwalt*-class destroyer."

"I had half-considered the *Goliath* a myth, despite the reconnaissance photos. It just doesn't look like a proper warship. It's a vigilante abomination."

Implications of the mercenary attack sloshed throughout Floros' mind–those that the vice admiral had shared and the hauntings of his imagination.

"That abomination is changing your life and mine," he said. "For starters, Daskalakis is calling for a diplomatic solution to this oil rig we've been defending. He's offering to pay the Turks for letting us use it unchallenged."

"After all we've been through defending it?"

"We'll retain the task force, but the rules of engagement will be tightened on both sides to preclude hostility."

"He's already giving orders? Daskalakis?"

"Apparently so."

"And our admirals are obeying?"

"Yes," Floros said. "As are the army generals, enforcing his call for martial law. Troops are moving to protect the people and to keep our new energy shortage from escalating into a civil war."

"All this because of kinks in our natural gas supply."

Floros turned his head, scolded, and lowered his gaze at the *Hydra's* commander.

"We get twenty percent of our total energy from gas, and a solitary ship just choked out half of that in two hours. Emergency repairs will take weeks. Make no mistake. This is a crisis."

"And Daskalakis is our supposed savior?"

"He's being well received by many heads of state," Floros said. "Too quickly and too enthusiastically to be random."

"I see what you mean by puppetry, but who's pulling the strings?"

"Germany. Italy. France. Turkey. Any mix of them. I don't give a damn who it is, but I'm sure it's a conspiracy. The tanker attacks draw our assets away from the Aegean to free up the *Goliath* against the pipeline and Revythousa, and then an ambitious senator with a readymade reaction plan steps in with international backing to dethrone our prime minister."

"It does stink of conspiracy. But why?"

"Regime change. Pushing us out of the European Union. I'm no diplomat, but I assume such talks will take place in immediate response to this crisis."

"But since you're no diplomat, you don't care."

"No, I don't. Not at all. Putting the *Goliath's* cracked hull on the bottom of the Aegean is my new purpose."

The *Hydra* commander squinted.

"You're supposed to be defending the oil rig."

Floros slid his buttocks down the captain's seat and placed his boots on the deck plates.

"Not anymore," he said. "The *Salamis* will replace the *Hydra* as the flagship of Task Force October Eighteen One in eight hours," Floros said. "Since peace has supposedly broken out around the oil rig, according to Daskalakis, we can use a less seasoned captain to take my place and let a frigate with a more junior crew be his flagship."

"Then I assume we're taking my ship after the *Goliath*, sir. I'll ready a battle plan."

"It's already done. I hashed it out with the vice admiral. I'm taking the *Hydra* and four of the helicopters with us."

The commander swallowed.

"Four, sir? That would leave the oil rig at risk. Part of maintaining peace is deterrence."

"The Turks will stay at bay while Senator Daskalakis preaches appeasement. Task Force October Eighteen One can get by with what I'm leaving it. Yes, we're taking four."

"You intend to take a solitary frigate and four helicopters against a warship that gave the Russians fits?"

"Initially, but I'll get us some help."

"From our air force?"

Floros scoffed as he considered his nation's turmoil.

"Allowing this attack was a naval failure," he said. "We should've been protecting our home, but we became vengeful against a submarine that sank our tankers. In retrospect, we walked into a trap by following a diversion."

"Still, the defense of the nation is on the shoulders of every military professional."

"Yes, and our ground forces are doing their duty by preserving the peace at home. We're doing our duty of hunting those who attacked us. But our air force apparently sees no need to intervene while its generals jockey for favor with Daskalakis."

The *Hydra's* commander shrugged.

"Then we're facing difficult odds. The *Goliath* can strike us before our helicopters could reach it."

"The *Goliath* can strike us right now where we stand," Floros said. "I respect that ship as much as I hate it, which is why I'm going to use numbers to defeat it. I'm recalling the surface combatants from Task Force October Eighteen Two."

"You're giving up on the submarine that sank our tanker?"

"Nobody gives a damn about a tanker anymore compared against crippling explosions on our home soil."

"I keep forgetting that nobody respects violence at sea except those who live at sea."

"Right," Floros said. "And here's the order from Vice Admiral Agathocleous."

He lifted a tablet from a pouch beside his chair and extended it. The *Hydra's* commander's eyes skimmed the screen.

"Task Force October Eighteen Two is disbanded," the *Hydra's* commander said. "We're taking its surface combatants as we become the flagship of newly created Task Force October Eighteen Three. Our sole purpose is to destroy the *Goliath*."

Floros eyed the *Hydra's* commander as the man aimed his receding hairline towards the moon's reflection on the waves.

"What of Task Force October Eighteen Two's submarines?"

"Astute question," Floros said. "They'll remain on station with patrol areas that I think you'll appreciate. Come."

He walked to a plotting table and touched its capacitive touchscreen, invoking icons on the Aegean Sea.

"Here," he said. "This is where the *Goliath* is now, pinned to the surface by a torpedo and running right for us."

"The *Pipinos* got off a good shot."

"Its torpedo would already have hit ninety-nine percent of

the ships on the planet," Floros said. "Only a ship capable of more than thirty knots had a chance to evade."

"It's only thirty-five miles from us. Well within range of its cannons. Why are they not attacking us yet?"

"We've been within it cannons' range for hours, if not days. Why provoke us now? We're maneuvering as if we have no interest in it, and our best play is to feign disinterest as long as possible."

"Conflict is inevitable, sir. It has to end up inside our cannon's range to escape the *Pipinos'* torpedo."

"And we'll be ready to exchange blows when it does. I'll take our explosive ordnance over its high-speed bullets."

Floros watched a new icon appear on the map, showing the appearance of a friendly aircraft.

"And here's how we're going to do it," he said.

"I thought the aviators were sitting this one out."

"One general was kind enough to lend us the electronic warfare support of an early warning and control craft," Floros said. "No danger to any pilot, but an immense help to us."

"Jamming of railgun rounds."

"Our best chance to overcome that damned ship."

The *Hydra's* commander pointed between islands."

"The *Pipinos* seals off the southwest. We come from the northeast. The combatants of the old task force seal off exits to the south and southeast, using their helicopters. Our shoreline bounds the north and northwest. It's trapped, sir. The *Goliath* is ours."

Careful to stifle hubris' temptation, Floros clenched his jaw and nodded.

"But what about the old task force's submarines?"

"Right," Floros said. "They'll patrol the waters here, here, here, and here."

"That doesn't make sense, sir. Those axes are already sealed off by the surface combatants and their helicopters."

"Think harder."

The man's face tightened as he shifted his buttocks backwards and leaned his thin frame over the chart.

"These positions mean nothing with respect to attacking the *Goliath*. Sorry, sir. I don't see it."

"Well, then. Think broader."

The *Hydra's* commander brooded, and then color filled his face with the onset of realization.

"Ah. The mercenary submarine. Whatever its name is, it's part of this mercenary band of pirates, and its commander may have the courage to think he can help the *Goliath*."

"Right," Floros said. "But I won't credit him with the courage. He's just arrogant and thinks himself invincible. Therefore, we'll humble him with a trap."

"He'll see our combatants attacking the *Goliath*, and he'll want to sneak up behind them. But our submarines will kill him."

"Kill him indeed. Since his fate is in the hands of our submarines, I'm not commanding that effort. But I sure hope they're as successful as we'll be against the *Goliath*."

A voice from a loudspeaker startled Floros.

"Incoming gunfire from the *Goliath*!"

"Take your ship to all ahead flank," Floros said. "Head towards the *Goliath*. Use erratic maneuvering to evade its rounds and place your ship within range of your cannons."

The deck rolled as the frigate turned and accelerated, and a sailor appeared with a helmet and lifejacket to assist Floros' equipping for general quarters.

He grabbed a secure phone and hailed his boss.

"We're under attack," he said. "I need jamming, and I need it now, sir."

"You should already have it," the vice admiral said. "Can you see it on your sensors?"

Floros placed the receiver against his clavicle and looked at the frigate's commanding officer.

"Where's our jamming?"

The *Hydra's* commander lowered the sound-powered phone that connected him with his frigate's enclosed combat team.

"Confirmed, sir. We've got our electronic warfare support."

Knowing chunks of Mach 7 metal raced towards him in ballistic flight, Floros impressed himself with the calmness in his voice. Air friction was slowing the projectiles below Mach 6, but his knowledge of the *Goliath's* attack on Russian warships portended horror. The *Hydra's* steel walls were paper against railgun shots, and every hit would be a guaranteed puncture wound.

Floros lifted his phone.

"Jamming's confirmed, sir," he said. "I'm going to get us within cannon range of the *Goliath.*"

"God speed, captain," the vice admiral said.

Floros hung up and looked to the frigate's commander.

"I recommend you station your best ship handler on the bridge as the conning officer. Maneuvering is now a crucial job."

"He's already stationed, sir. Our best. I placed him there after the *Goliath* surfaced."

"Well done, commander."

From the corner of his eye, Floros watched a young lieutenant aiming night vision glasses at bridge windows. He held his breath as he trusted the man's instinct, training, and luck to dodge death.

"Right full rudder!" the lieutenant said.

The ship rolled out of the turn, and a pair of sonic booms cracked off the port beam.

"Left full rudder!" the lieutenant said.

Five seconds later, two booms rocked the night beside the frigate, and then five more seconds brought new sonic shrieks.

"I can see the newly launched rounds rising over the horizon," the lieutenant said. "They're compensating now, trying to predict our course."

Three more pairs of ballistic metallic demons howled.

"The jamming's working," the *Hydra's* commander said. "Our tactical team is tracking perfect and near-perfect incoming ballistic flight paths. The *Goliath* can't guide its rounds. Keep us dodging them, and we'll be in cannon range in twenty minutes."

"That's a long twenty minutes," Floros said. "The lieutenant is only human. So make sure your ship's ready for damage control, commander, and get the close-in weapon systems online to shoot down the incoming rounds."

The young officer's strained reply unveiled his trepidation.

"I'll keep us safe as long as I can, sir. Left full rudder!"

The ship rolled, and two booms cracked to the starboard.

"Right full rudder!"

Roll, settle, and booms to the right side of the ship.

"Rudder amidships!"

The sonic cracking continued but seemed to walk closer to the bridge. A sailor extended soft ear plugs and hardened hearing protection muffs that Floros donned.

The world became muted auditory chaos.

Before the next shots arrived, the *Hydra's* Phalanx close-in weapon offered its chainsaw protest of staccato hellfire. Then came the twin cracking booms.

He looked to a display that showed the readiness of aircraft to fly towards the *Goliath*. Lifting a phone, he barked.

"Send helicopters one through four to sink the *Goliath*!"

The order acknowledged, Floros hung up and watched icons fly towards the vigilante abomination.

Chainsaw protest. Cracking boom. Cracking boom.

"Left full rudder!"

The lieutenant's order kept the howling metal hail off the *Hydra's* starboard side–for twenty seconds.

Then flying steel found its mark.

The *Hydra* screeched like a banshee with a blood-curdling wail, forcing Floros to cringe. When he recovered his senses, he forced himself courageous.

"Keep it up, lieutenant," he said. "You won't dodge them all, but you're doing well."

Beside Floros, the frigate's commander held a phone to his ear and then lowered it to its cradle. He lifted a microphone to transmit his news and orders throughout the *Hydra*.

"We've taken one round in the port engine room," he said.

"The Phalanx was able to bring down one round in the salvo, but not both. This is consistent with our adversary's expected tactics. They missed vital equipment, but they'll continue to target our propulsion. All non-essential personnel are ordered to leave the engine rooms."

He then moved close to Floros.

"Sir, we're not going to remain so lucky for twenty minutes. I want to use anti-ship missiles."

"I've been considering it," Floros said. "But how? A saturation attack would allow the *Goliath's* crew a single dive to escape all our weapons. A series of one-off missiles would give them the choice of using their point defense system as opposed to diving and slowing."

"Agreed, sir. I'm considering either approach."

"Contact the *Pipinos* to find out the torpedo's position."

The *Hydra's* commander nodded and grabbed a phone. After a ten-second conversation, he hung up.

"I spoke to the *Pipinos*. Its torpedo is four miles from the *Goliath*, predicted to run out of fuel one mile from the target."

Floros assumed he could slow the *Goliath* by twenty knots by forcing it to dive below the *Hydra's* anti-ship missiles. To cost the targeted ship a mile of transit, he needed to keep it underwater for three minutes.

"Let's test their courage with a single Harpoon."

The *Hydra's* commander locked eyes with Floros to verify his sincerity as the conning officer dodged another salvo.

"Right full rudder!"

The deck tilted and settled as Phalanx machineguns' staccato protests preceded sonic cracks.

"Rudder amidships!"

"I understand I have permission to launch one Harpoon missile at the *Goliath*," the *Hydra's* commander said.

"Correct," Floros said.

The commander slid a key into a lock and turned it, causing a pulsating red light. Then, reaching to press a button, he yelled.

"Launching one missile!"

A distant hiss echoed through the frigate, and a streak of reddish orange sliced the darkness as the missile's exhaust howled.

Metal screeched, and Floros cringed. He looked to the frigate's commander, who absorbed news through a phone receiver and then lifted a microphone.

"We've taken one hit in the port auxiliary machinery room. The port main refrigeration unit is offline."

The *Hydra's* deck shifted and supersonic salvos shrieked as Floros watched the icon of the Harpoon streak towards the *Goliath*. Five minutes and two puncture wounds later, the frigate maintained full propulsion, and a missile merged with the mercenary on his tactical display.

"Our Harpoon is destroyed," the *Hydra's* commander said. "They used their point defense system."

"I don't think they'll be so brave against three missiles," Floros said. "Unload your first quad canister."

As three streaks painted the sky, Floros expected a trio of flying warheads to quiet the mercenary menace.

# CHAPTER 11

Cahill glared at his display.

"We survived one," he said. "But we can't take down three."

"Time to impact, three and a half minutes," Walker said.

"That gives me time to think."

"You're not going to trust the Phalanx system to take down three, are you?"

Submerging and slowing with a torpedo three miles behind him worried him, but a close-in weapon system against three simultaneous missiles offered poor odds.

Through his domed bridge, he watched moonlight transform the Vulcan Phalanx system on the *Goliath's* port bow into a cylindrical silhouette. He pictured its radar system targeting the nosecone of each incoming Harpoon and likened the task to shooting down dinner plates a mile away.

One, yes. Two, maybe. Three, unlikely.

The seconds required to shoot, track, and adjust the Phalanx' sabots were precious, and Cahill refused to risk his ship on a blend of perfect performance and luck.

"We're going to crash dive," he said. "But not too soon, or we'll give up too much ground on the torpedo."

"You know how to turn this ship into a porpoise."

"Indeed I do, mate," Cahill said. "But I don't like the looks of those helicopters, and those mongrels on the *Hydra* still have four Harpoons left onboard. We're sprinting into a bind."

"You'll target the helicopters next, when they're in range of our phased array?"

"Of course, but not before I have to dive us. They're flying low below our horizon."

The Frenchman's voice issued from the console.

"I wish I could present you targeting information," Renard said. "But I have nothing available that can overpower the jamming of that Hellenic early warning and control aircraft."

"Helicopters aren't me biggest problem yet, Pierre. I'm getting ready to crash dive below the Harpoons, unless you have a better idea."

"I do not. You have no choice."

"Liam, prepare to crash dive."

Walker tapped keys, and Cahill watched multiple graphics pop up and coalesce into a group of systems to be lowered and secured upon the touch of a single key.

The induction mast, the turbines, the phased array radar system, and the railguns. All mounted toward the rear of the ship. All ready to submit to the undersea world.

"One minute to missile arrival, Terry."

"Very well. Flooding the forward trim tank and securing the Phalanx close-in weapon system."

Cahill tapped an image that ordered huge centrifugal pumps to inhale the sea and drive water towards the forward-most internal tanks. He then repeated the motion and watched the cylindrical silhouette recede into its stowage compartment within the port bow.

"Placing full rise on the stern planes."

He tapped another graphic that drove the sterns downward to counterbalance the heaviness of the bows. The added weight increased drag on the *Goliath's* hulls and sapped three knots of speed. He pressed a button to send his voice throughout the ship.

"Prepare to crash dive. Crash diving in five seconds. Four. Three. Two. One. Crash Dive!"

He stabbed his finger against a graphic that ordered the preselected group of systems to shift to their undersea states, and then he walked his hand across the screen to command the stern planes to their opposite extreme.

"Hold on, Liam."

He grabbed a railing and took a wide stance as the rising rear drove the prows into the waves. Speed pushed the rakish bows under tons of water, and a glide factor consumed the ship.

Water rushed to the domed bridge and engulfed it, and Cahill cringed as he trusted the transparent plastic windows. The rapid thirty-degree down angle tugged the *Goliath* below the waves and created a fulcrum that lifted the propellers above the water. Momentum carried the hulls under.

"The ship's submerged," Walker said.

"No shit, mate. Bring us back up to twenty meters. Make us light but keep a ten-degree down angle to hold us under."

Walker tapped keys that commanded pumps to thrust water weight throughout the trim tanks. The ship rose, and Cahill saw moonlight shimmering above the dome.

"Propulsion is on the MESMA systems," Walker said. "All plants running normally. We're at seventeen knots, drifting towards a maximum sustained submerged speed of twelve knots."

Cahill spoke to a microphone.

"Sonar supervisor, listen for Harpoons passing overhead."

"I hear them already. They'll pass in ten seconds."

"Get a fix on the torpedo, too, if you can hear it."

"I've got it faintly on our hull array. It's still behind us. Hard to give you any better fix on it when the bearing rate is zero."

"Understood," Cahill said.

"Those Harpoons will circle back if they miss," Walker said. "They had us targeted dead to rights."

"Damn it," Cahill said. "You're right."

As he rebalanced his stance against the deck's lessening angle, he shifted his eyes to a two-dimensional overhead view of the *Goliath* and its surroundings. The submarine-launched torpedo trailed two and a half miles behind him.

"We can't stay down here forever."

"But it takes the Harpoons a minute to circle back," Walker said. "They're most vulnerable when they expose their broadsides."

"To the cannons, you mean?"

"Why not? Splintering rounds, guided by our phased array. Those missiles present decent cross sections when they're turning."

Cahill heard the Harpoons' echoing howl with his naked ears, and he craned his neck to see blurry plumes overhead.

"I'm taking us back up, Liam. Prepare to bring everything

back online for surface combat. Target the Harpoons with the cannons and the Phalanx."

"I'm ready."

"Here we go."

Cahill released the stern planes to their neutral position and pumped water off the ship. The artificial wind of the *Goliath's* motion walked sheets of water across the dome.

"We're up," he said. "Bring everything online. Get us back on the gas turbines and flank speed. Take down the Harpoons."

The whine of compressed air reached the bridge as hungry gas turbines fed. Wind swept glimmering droplets off the windows above Cahill's head.

"Targeting the Harpoons with the cannons," Walker said.

"Prepare to fire splintering rounds at will."

"Ready."

"Fire."

Cahill saw Walker lift night vision goggles to his face and aim them off the *Goliath's* quarter as the first duo of sonic booms cracked.

"Get those Harpoons off me ass," he said. "I'm tracking the helicopters now, and I'm going to need the cannons on them soon."

"The shots are looking good," Walker said. "At this range, Mach 7 gives us only three to four seconds of travel. We're going to hit them. We're going to bring them down."

"Hurry."

"Splash one!" Walker said. "I see it toppling."

An announcement over the loudspeaker confirmed it.

"Take down the other two," Cahill said.

"They're circling around. The shots will get harder. You need to think about diving again, Terry."

"We lost nearly half a mile against the torpedo by submerging. No, mate, we can't go under again."

"One more hit!" Walker said. "The second Harpoon is veering off course. Wait. It's recovering. Must've only grazed it."

"Hit it again."

"I need the Phalanx."

Cahill glanced to his left at a display that showed the close-in weapon's firing arc and azimuthal limits.

"You're clear. Use it."

"The second Harpoon is down!" Cahill said. "The last one is coming for us."

The Phalanx spat a staccato chainsaw line of metal across the *Goliath*, and Walker's shoulders went limp as he lowered his goggles.

"The third Harpoon is splashed."

"Very well," Cahill said. "Now target the helicopters. The first is showing up on our radar."

Red pulsating icons caught his attention.

"More Harpoons," he said. "Pierre's sending us the data."

"They've unloaded on us," Walker said.

"And well timed to make us deal with missiles and helicopters all at once. Target the first helicopter with splintering rounds from the cannons."

"The first helicopter is targeted."

"Fire."

Sonic cracks overflew Cahill.

"The four Harpoons are only two minutes away," Walker said. "The *Hydra* is twenty miles away, empty of Harpoons but seven minutes from cannon range against us."

"Understood, mate. That's two minutes to shoot down helicopters. Use them well."

"Splash one helicopter!"

"Target the next helicopter. I see it on our radar now."

"Targeting the second helicopter."

More cracks rocked the night.

"I think we damaged it," Walker said. "It looks to have turned back."

The Frenchman's face moved on the once-dark screen.

"Indeed you did," Renard said. "I have one on satellite that's leaving a trail of smoke on infrared camera and heading back towards the *Hydra*."

"Two left," Walker said. "Still outside our radar's range."

"But also outside of their torpedo range," Cahill said. "We still have a chance."

"We need to dive under those Harpoons."

Cahill felt his blood pressure rising.

"Damn it, I know. Not yet. Shoot down those helicopters."

"I don't envy our chances until I have them on our phased array."

A helicopter's icon shifted from an outline to an opaque figure, followed by that of the last rotary-winged threat.

"You have them both on phased array now," Cahill said. "Shoot them down."

Multiple sonic cracks.

"I think I just nicked one," Walker said. "And now, it's splashed. The third helicopter is down."

"Damn it, we're out of time," Cahill said. "I'm flooding the forward trim tank, placing full rise on the stern planes, and securing the Phalanx close-in weapon system."

He aimed his voice towards his console's microphone.

"Prepare to crash dive. Crash diving in five seconds. Four. Three. Two. One. Crash Dive!"

He stabbed his finger against a graphic that ordered systems to their undersea states, and then he commanded the stern planes to their opposite extreme. Tightening his grip on the railing, he watched the prows plow into the sea. Water engulfed the bridge and then swallowed the ship.

"The ship's submerged," Walker said.

"Take us back up to twenty meters, light and with a ten-degree down angle."

The bow rose, and Cahill saw moonlight shimmering above the dome as the ship began slowing. Bright exhaust plumes lit the sky as the Harpoons passed overhead, but Cahill held his breath and looked to his sonar information.

"That torpedo's sound level is growing," he said.

"It's getting dangerously close," the sonar supervisor said. "We can't stay down here at twelve knots."

"We can't surface under four Harpoons," Walker said. "They're going to circle back like the others."

Having thought he'd survived every conceivable danger on the *Goliath*, Cahill sought a solution to his unique dilemma.

Inspiration struck.

"How fast do you think we can go on the gas turbines while submerged?" he asked.

"No idea," Walker said. "Twenty knots. Maybe twenty-two."

"Sonar, does twenty knots get me away from the torpedo?"

"It'll be close, depending on the accuracy of our estimate of its fuel state."

"Let's raise our induction masts and snorkel," Cahill said.

"And run the gas turbines underwater?" Walker asked.

"You have a better idea?"

The executive officer shook his head.

"I'll make it happen," he said.

The deck rolled and pitched in the shallows, and the whine of inhaled air echoed in the hull.

"We're on the gas turbines," Walker said.

"All ahead flank."

"Can you give me a quick turn?" the sonar supervisor asked. "I want to get a fix on the torpedo."

Cahill aimed his voice at the microphone.

"I'll give you thirty degrees to the right for thirty seconds."

"I'll take it," the supervisor said.

"You heard me, Liam. Make it happen."

During the turn, the damning clunk of a head valve shutting as a swell sucked an induction mast underwater alarmed Cahill, but he heard the cross-connected air system feeding his gas turbines from the solitary valve that remained open. Then the waves released the ship back to its dual-intake feed.

A minute later, the *Goliath* steadied with the pursuing weapon in its baffles.

"It's crude, but I have a fix on the incoming torpedo of less than a mile," the supervisor said. "Nineteen hundred yards."

"Are we going to make it?"

"I don't know. It'll be close, but even if we outrun it, they could command-detonate it and give us a hell of a beating. I'd feel better if you'd get us back to thirty-four knots on the surface."

Having circled back, the missile quartet traced translucent brightness above Cahill's head.

"The timing needs to be perfect," Cahill said. "We'll surface after the Harpoons make their next pass."

Walker stared forward into the sea's nothingness.

"You scared?" Cahill asked.

"Yeah. You?"

"Yeah. I'm taking us back up. Prepare to bring everything back online for surface combat. Target the helicopter with the cannons and target the Harpoons with the Phalanx."

Walker glared at him.

"I don't expect to need the Phalanx," Cahill said. "But have it ready."

"Harpoons are approaching," the supervisor said. "I hear them. They're passing behind us, giving me enough bearing rate to track them. You can see them on the system."

Cahill looked to his display.

"You think we're outside their seekers' swaths?"

"Probably," Walker said. "Now's as good a time as any."

"Here we go."

Cahill set the stern planes to neutral and pumped off water. Artificial wind walked sheets of water across the dome's windows.

"Bring everything online. Take down the last helicopter."

"Targeting the helicopter with the cannons," Walker said.

"Prepare to fire splintering rounds at will."

"Ready."

"Fire."

"Loud splash from the direction of the helicopter," the supervisor said.

Cahill found the voice behind the expected positive news unsettling.

"Was that the helicopter splashing?" he asked.

"Shit. No! High-speed screws. Torpedo in the water, bearing zero-two-five."

"Keep shooting, Liam. Take down that helicopter."

With the high-frequency link reestablished, the Frenchman's face appeared on Cahill's screen.

"I see a fire broken out on the helicopter on infrared imagery," Renard said. "You hit it, and it's running back towards the *Hydra*, but you still need to get under the Harpoons. They're circling back in roughly forty seconds."

"I've also got an air-dropped weapon from the helicopter," Cahill said. "It must've launched before we hit it."

"And the submarine-launched torpedo?" Renard asked.

The answer came as thunder, and a shockwave threw Cahill against his console. The handrail punched his belly, and then his head and chest smacked displays.

He staggered, palpated his forehead, and extended blood-covered fingertips. A glance across the small room showed his companion lying unconscious against the deck.

"The torpedo was command-detonated," the supervisor said. "We've taken the shockwave, but we evaded it."

"You sound none the worst for it," Cahill said.

"We were all strapped in here. I'm not sure how the rest of the ship is, though."

Having survived a heavyweight blast from the trailing fuel-exhausted torpedo, Cahill looked at a monitor and saw that twenty-five seconds separated him from the Harpoons' impacts.

"Take control of the ship and crash dive us now!" Cahill said. "And I mean now. Shift propulsion to the MESMA systems and get us under the Harpoons."

Working against the shifting deck, he reached for Walker's wrists and dragged him towards the stairs. Gravity assisted his gentle descent to the tactical control room, and he opened the door.

He stepped through, pulled Walker into the compartment,

and then latched the door shut.

From his chair, the supervisor looked to him.

"We've got about a minute before the helicopter's torpedo hits us. Maybe less. We need to run."

"Can't do it, mate. They dropped it right in our face, and those Harpoons are still up there."

"What are you saying?"

"I'm saying, give me the microphone and listen."

The man extended a handset, and Cahill spoke into it.

"We're going to take a hit by a lightweight torpedo. God willing, we've got a big enough ship to take it. I'm betting that it hits the port bow. All hands lay to the closest engine room. Carry all injured personnel back with you. Shut every watertight door on your way back. Get your arses moving. Now!"

He returned the microphone to the supervisor.

"You heard me. Get some guys on Liam, and let's get everyone back. I'm the last one to set foot in the engine room."

As the men cleared out of the room, Cahill gave it a parting glance before sealing the door behind him. As he turned into the berthing area, the supervisor ogled him.

"We're not going to make it, are we, Terry?"

"Maybe not. But don't count out the *Goliath* just yet."

## CHAPTER 12

Surrounded by men he trusted the most from his crew at the small table in a waterfront officer club in Karachi, Volkov tipped back a glass of vodka. Though his entourage was civilian, Renard had negotiated liberties for the *Wraith's* crew.

As his vision blurred, Volkov needed an extra second to focus on each man.

Sergei, the executive officer, Anatoly, the sonar expert, and Vasily, the trainer, tried keeping pace with his alcohol consumption. Wondering if he indulged beyond the wisdom of his years, Volkov waved his hand over his empty glass when offered a refill.

"That's enough for now," he said.

"You said you'd drink until you forgot about all the lives you took," Anatoly said.

"I've decided that such a goal is impossible. I give up. They'll haunt me forever."

He tried to forget the imagined visages of horror, but fictional faces gaped in frozen fear as his mind's faked memory recreated an exploding torpedo under a tanker.

"In fact," he said, "I think I'll just drink water for the rest of the night."

"But I bought you the best bottle of vodka I could find in this place. It's nothing like we can get at home, but it was quite expensive."

"Was it that expensive relative to your new salary?"

The sonar technician smiled and then giggled.

"No. I forgot how much you pay me now. But it wasn't a fair wager. You goaded me into betting against the dolphins when you knew they'd take action before I heard the Iranian submarine."

"I did goad you, because I knew I was right and that you were wrong. But what of it? Now, you've paid off your loss in the wager. Your debt is paid in full, whether I drink it all or not."

A Pakistani steward in a starched white shirt brought spiced meats from varied animals and grilled vegetables on long, thin sticks arrayed over a bed of saffron rice.

"Excellent," Volkov said.

"You like kebab?" the trainer asked.

"I like meat, and this platter smells delicious. I can't wait to taste the local cuisine."

"Maybe we should get some beer to replace the vodka and slow down our consumption of alcohol."

"I'm already committed to water," Volkov said. "But I agree that's a good idea for the table."

He looked around the room that his feasting crew filled, and then he looked to the steward.

"In fact, that's a good idea for all the tables. I don't want my men getting too drunk."

After the Pakistani waiter nodded and departed, the trainer took a jab at Volkov.

"You appear irritated, Dmitry."

"What makes you say that?"

"I have a sense about such things."

"Whether you're right or not, what business of it is yours?"

"I'm just trying to help."

While picking at a lamb kebab, Volkov softened his attitude.

"You may have a point. If you think I look irritated, then there's probably something irritating me."

"Do you know what it is?"

Fearing how deep the sensitive dolphin master could pry into his feelings, Volkov attempted to slow the inquisition.

"I'm sure it's nothing. Just a passing mood."

"No, I don't think so. I've noticed it for some time. There's something bothering you."

Volkov grunted and reached for a kebab.

"Talking it through always helps," the trainer said.

"Maybe with your dolphins."

"Nonsense. Well, yes, talking with my dolphins helps me and them, but I mean it's nonsense to think that it doesn't work with humans as well."

Volkov rolled his eyes and then gulped half a glass of water to rehydrate himself and wash down some lamb.

"Fine, you've proven that your captain admits to being human. Can you spare me the dissecting of my mind?"

"I'm sorry, Dmitry. It's just so obvious to me."

"For God's sake, man. You won't let it rest, will you? Okay, I'll blurt it out so you'll leave me in peace. I don't like that we were relegated to a secondary role in this mission. Jake and Terry get all the glory, and I'm just an afterthought."

The trainer furrowed his brow while digesting the confession, and then he wagged a finger.

"You can be bitter about it," he said. "Or you can be thankful that you're working your way onto a great team."

"What team? I was a distraction in the wrong ocean. We were a distraction. Renard can say all he wants about the psychological shock and awe benefit of a geographically-diverse attack on the Greeks, but I see it as a mere test he gave me that nearly got me killed. It nearly got us all killed."

"But we're here, and we survived. And we're all now wealthy men thanks to it. None of us would be so well off if it weren't for Pierre."

"Easy for you to say, Vasily. You didn't lose your commission."

The trainer frowned.

"I took my favorite dolphins with me, but I left a dozen of them behind for this job. You're not the only one who gave up something to work for Pierre. In fact, I could argue that you didn't give up anything. You had lost everything by the time he approached you."

Volkov pounded his fists into the table.

"That bastard took everything from me!"

The executive officer and the sonar technician cobbled together makeshift excuses of wanting to visit other crewmembers and escaped the table's tense talk.

"I didn't mean to offend them."

"They'll get over it," the trainer said.

Like a bursting balloon, the anger that had risen under the dolphin master's probing began to subside.

"I had everything I wanted before Renard took it from me."

"Did you really? I understand that command is one of the loneliest lots a man can have. I don't mean to be argumentative, but since we're alone now, I feel free to mention that I don't recall you having many friends."

Volkov chuckled.

"Mother of God, Vasily. Have you no discretion?"

"I spend most of my time with dolphins. It doesn't exactly exercise my diplomatic skills."

"I guess not. But I'll grant you that it exercises your intuition."

"Why do you say that?"

"Because you're right. I have no accursed friends or human relationships worth mentioning."

"I'm sorry to dig up wounds."

Volkov waved a hand.

"Don't worry about it. It takes a good deal of nagging to offend me."

"If it's any consolation, I don't really have any friends either, other than the animals."

"Is this the point where you ask me to be my friend or should I take the lead in this little dance?" Volkov asked.

The trainer blushed.

"I have no idea. But since I'm the lonely trainer and you're the lonely commander, I think we have to be friends by virtue of us each having nobody else.

"Hah! So be it. To you and me, Vasily."

Volkov lifted his glass, and the trainer clanked his against it. As the two departed men capitalized upon the calmness to return to the table, Volkov's phone rang, and he glanced at it.

"It's Pierre," he said. "Excuse me."

He stood and walked to a dark corner of the club. In solitude, he answered.

"This is Dmitry. What can I do for you, sir?"

"I know that your actions in this campaign are done," Renard said. "But it's come time where I would like your advice as a naval expert."

Renard's Russian was crude, and Volkov heard him getting help from a translator on the phone's far end every ten words.

In a dark instant, his resentment for losing his place in the Russian Navy battled his gratitude for his job in Renard's fleet. He disliked the Frenchman's control over him, but he liked his boss' salary structure and his promise of leadership and adventure.

Part of him wanted to tell Renard to go to hell while he returned the *Wraith* to Malaysia for an expected finder's reward, but he doubted he could succeed. Though the expected spies eluded his awareness, he suspected the Frenchman of employing surveillance over him as insurance.

Then, considering that any act of defiance against Renard, if it succeeded despite safeguards, would send him on a path of lonely isolation, he chose loyalty.

"I'm flattered," he said.

"No need to be. You're well qualified to offer advice. Terry is facing some hostilities that I failed to completely foresee, and it helps me to assess possible reactions with my commanders."

"I'll do whatever I can to help. My ship, your ship, rather, is far away from the action, but you have me and my crew at your disposal."

"I don't think I'll need anything except your genius."

"Tell me what's going on."

The Frenchman's voice sounded like he wrestled with despair and hope.

"I've lost communications with Terry while he's under duress. He's evading a heavyweight torpedo, avoiding several Harpoons from a frigate, and avoiding detection by helicopters."

"That sounds terrible. I thought he'd face less danger than this on his way out of the Aegean."

"As did I. Nonetheless, he's in the midst of it."

"Would you like me to get to the *Wraith* and evaluate the tactical feed?"

His boss' voice became pensive.

"No, I think not. Nothing so detailed. I just want to talk through generalities. If nothing else, I'd like to verify the advice and orders I've been giving and am planning to give while I have no choice but to wait for Terry to communicate again."

"I see. Waiting in silence is agony."

"Exactly."

Volkov felt less desired than he wished, but he played along as if he filled a vital need. Perhaps, he reckoned, such a simple chat held true value with the Frenchman.

"You've got him diving below the Harpoons, I assume?"

"Of course. Unfortunately, though, that slows him against the torpedo."

"But when he's surfaced, he's exposed to the Harpoons and the helicopters."

"Right. You see my dilemma–his dilemma."

"How's the Phalanx system faring?"

"It can safely handle one inbound Harpoon, two Harpoons when they circle back and expose broadsides to him after he dives under them and resurfaces. He's having some luck with his cannons against the Harpoons, too."

"That sounds logical to me, using the railguns against the Harpoons as a first defense, then the Phalanx as the last effort, for the times when he must be exposed."

After Volkov heard Renard's translator assist with elucidating the concepts, the Frenchman sounded unimpressed.

"We agree upon that. I appreciate your feedback."

"What about a hybrid state?" Volkov asked. "Can he put the *Goliath* on a downward angle with its head valves exposed to run gas turbines and keep enough evasion speed from the torpedo?"

"An excellent idea," Renard said. "He developed that tactic on his own to combat the Harpoons at distance, but with the exactness of the targeting against him, the missiles came back and appeared to have locked onto his exposed sterns. So that's a useful tactic, but imperfect."

A sick feeling of helplessness crept up Volkov's spine, compelling him to find a way to assist his teammates.

"I have a feeling Terry and Jake will need my help, but there's nothing I can do from this side of the Suez Canal."

"I don't fault you for being where you are," Renard said. "I put you there, and that burden is mine. Don't take it as yours."

"There must be something I can do."

"You did. I appreciate your tactical advice."

An epiphany hit Volkov, and he gasped as he hesitated to share it.

"Go on, man," Renard said. "You sound like you have an idea."

"No, I can't. It's silly. It's almost childish."

"Children are capable of great visions. I promise not to laugh if it's indeed silly."

Volkov mustered the courage to share his thought, and he felt lighter than air with the joy of having helped his colleagues when Renard dismissed him immediately to set it into motion.

## CHAPTER 13

Jake watched the toad-head shake.

"It's too far away for even me to hear," Remy said.

"Nothing, Pierre," Jake said. "We can't hear from here."

The Frenchman's face froze with its gaze angled away from the screen, and then his features fell into an ashen facade.

"Dear God," Renard said.

"What's wrong?"

"An undersea explosion on satellite infrared. The air-dropped torpedo just exploded."

The news punched Jake's stomach.

"Shit. Terry."

The anger Jake had hoped he'd imprisoned in his past escaped its bonds and flamed within him, and critical thoughts of his boss' hubris and selfishness swirled in his head. He clenched his jaw to silence his mouth while his mind screamed slurs at Renard. As he sensed the cauldron of insults bubbling beyond his control, he aimed his nose at the screen and drew breath to launch a tirade at the Frenchman for condemning the *Goliath* and its crew.

"Jake?" Henri said.

Jake turned and saw the mechanic beside him.

"What?"

"Perhaps a prayer?"

"Come on. Seriously?"

"For Terry, Liam, and everyone."

"Do you always do this when people die?"

"Yes, though usually silently. I assumed you could benefit from joining me this time, given your new belief."

"What would I pray for? A miracle to bring Terry back from the dead?"

"I'm not sure. We'll pray for whatever you want."

"Well, I want a miracle, but they're called miracles because God doesn't dish them out to every dumbass who begs for one. We screwed up, and our friends are dead."

"It's not your fault."

Jake turned, muted the console, and raised his voice.

"It sure as shit is my fault. It's your fault, and it's everyone's fault for being in Pierre's mercenary fleet. And most of all, it's Pierre's fault, but damn us all for buying into his sales pitch."

"Don't do this, Jake."

Sensing his voice had reached every ear in the *Specter's* control room, Jake lowered his volume.

"Do what? Speak the truth? We pushed too far in this mission, just like we did in Crimea. But this time our friends are dead. We play this stupid change-the-world game, and we think we're untouchable, but we're not."

"You still have a submarine to command."

"Command for what? We're skulking away to Israel, and then the game's over. Pierre's getting old, and he won't keep the fleet together after losing the *Goliath*. Especially not after losing Terry. I don't think he could take it. I'm not sure I can take it."

Jake noticed his hands shaking.

"Maybe you should retire to your stateroom," Henri said. "Like you said, we're just driving to Israel, and all the surface combatants that were chasing us have already reversed course. I can guide us from here."

"Yeah," Jake said. "Good idea."

He walked to his stateroom and sealed himself within it. Emotions stabbed him, and he flopped into his chair.

Reflecting upon pride as the worst sin, he judged himself guilty of arrogance in believing that he and Renard's small fleet could defeat Greece. Perhaps the mission had succeeded, but the cost weighed upon him–the loss of their capital ship and his friend, Terry Cahill.

Scanning the tiny room for a distraction, he saw his Bible. Lacking anything else to reach for, he grabbed it but then put it back on his table.

No passage could help, he decided.

He reached for it again and opened it to a random page, but he found dullness in the words of First Chronicles. Giving up on finding wisdom, he closed the book and returned it to his desk.

Instead of reading, he slipped headphones over his ears and pumped Christian rock music into his head. He tried doing push-ups to the Newsboys, but lyrics of praise and worship bounced off his angst. He switched to something angrier, selecting twenty-five-year old Soundgarden. While doing flutter kicks, he found himself in need of something older and darker, and he played forty-five-year-old Black Sabbath to indulge his rage.

After working himself into a quick exhaustion, he undressed and rolled into his rack. With frustration and sadness tormenting him, he expected to stare at the back of his eyelids, but sleep claimed him, and he slipped out of time.

Harsh knocking roused him from his slumber.

"What?" he asked.

"You have to hear this," Henri said.

"How long was I out?"

"You've been in your stateroom for about forty minutes."

"It feels like longer, or shorter. I'm not sure which."

"No matter. He launched a transmission buoy!"

"Who? Terry?"

"Yes! Renard just forwarded it. He's alive. The *Goliath* is seaworthy. Damage is limited to the port bow section. He has propulsion, and he thinks he can make nine knots but doesn't want to risk the speed and noise yet due to the damage."

As awareness supplanted a forgotten dream, a surge of relief overcame Jake.

"So he's okay? Terry's okay?"

"For the moment."

Then came realization and its subsequent anxiety.

"But he's trapped, surrounded by a task force."

"Unfortunately so."

"I need to help him. We need to rescue him."

Jake slid his feet to the deck and reached for his clothes.

"Agreed," Henri said. "I've already spoken to Pierre about it, but he's hesitant to let you."

"Hesitant? Is that a 'yes' or a 'no'?"

"He wants you to talk to him in private. I've routed his feed to your stateroom."

"Thanks."

"We're linked to him. I'll leave you to it."

Henri closed the door on his way out, leaving Jake with Cahill's fate at his fingertips. Alone, he noticed the gentle rocking of his room, reminding him of the *Specter's* shallow depth. He slid into his slacks, sat at his foldout table, and fired up his laptop.

The Frenchman's face appeared with fresh color masking his fatigue.

"Can you hear me, Pierre?"

"Yes, go ahead."

"I have nothing to say," Jake said. "I was hoping you'd have all the news."

"Indeed, I do. Terry's taken a hit from an air-dropped torpedo, but he's still in fighting shape and able to move while submerged. The problem is that half the Hellenic fleet is surrounding him."

"So him sneaking out without help would be tough?"

"Difficult, to say the least."

"Then I need to get up there and escort him out."

"Possibly," Renard said. "But I suspect the Greeks have considered this."

"What's the supposed to mean?"

The Frenchman's face darkened.

"It means that they likely left a wall of submarines between you and Terry. They've set up an ambush against you, betting that you've got the courage or arrogance to accept the challenge."

"They know me well."

"I suggest you take a longer look at the chart before you submit to such bravado. The natural choke points between the islands favor the Greeks. I've sent you my best estimate of the scenario and think you'll find it revealing."

"Sure, Pierre, I'll take a look. I'll reconnect with you from the control room."

"Jake."

"What?"

"Before you run off, I mean take a real hard look. The Greeks are licking their wounds and rethinking their approach with Terry, but I also suspect that they're delaying their hunt of him for the very purpose of enticing you to save him. I suspect a trap. If you don't think you can do this, consider that I have options available other than combat."

"Options like what?"

"Just don't plan on getting yourself killed for lack of alternatives. I'm a born negotiator, and there are always alternatives."

Jake freshened up in his sink and then walked to the *Specter's* central nerve compartment. He joined Henri at the navigation chart and leaned beside him.

Icons shaped like submarines dotted the few gaps between the smattering of islands that separated Jake from Cahill.

"He thinks six submarines are deployed?" he asked.

"It's the best estimate," Henri said. "Of the eleven Hellenic submarines, two are on distant patrols, two are undergoing refits, and one is tied to the pier with some apparent problem preventing it from deploying. That leaves six in the Aegean Sea that can stand between us and Terry."

Ten years ago, Jake would've made a haughty comment about his superiority over Greek submarines, but his wiser version knew to respect his adversary. He assessed with caution.

"Are these positions just estimates, or is there any data behind them?"

"Just estimates," Henri said. "But logical, don't you think?"

"Yeah. Heavy bias towards the direct routes to Terry. They're not going to make this easy."

"No, they're not."

"Come on," Jake said. "Let's talk to Pierre."

With the scenario memorized, he turned toward the elevated conning platform. Henri leaning beside him, he looked to the image of his boss on the display.

"What do you see, Jake?" Renard asked.

"I see a lot of hard work separating me from Terry."

"How long do you think he can survive alone?"

"Shit, Pierre, I was going to ask you the same thing."

"I need your perspective."

"It depends how brave the Greeks are. They must know enough about the *Goliath* to know that Terry can fight back against any attack they could mount. Nobody gets a free shot. Anyone who tries to take him down has to risk getting in range of at least one of his weapons."

"Correct," Renard said. "His port torpedo nest may be offline. He's not sure yet. But he has at least three heavyweight torpedoes in his starboard nest. That holds the surface combatants at bay and forces the submarines to think twice."

"Think twice enough that they're all avoiding him to instead set up ambushes between me and him."

Jake glanced over his shoulder at Henri for inspiration but received a dismissive shrug.

"Correct again," Renard said. "To hunt Terry, they either commit a submarine or commit surface combatants with helicopter protection, but not both. The mix would create the risk of attacking a friendly asset."

"Agreed. But I still haven't answered your question. If the Greeks are scared, the standoff could last a long time. Days, if they're super-cautious. Hours, if they force the issue."

"Right. Remind you of anything?"

Jake recalled his latest sea brawl with the Russians.

"You're not thinking about trying to declare it a standoff, are you?"

"It's an option to consider."

"I know it's not my area of expertise, but your leverage is weaker than it was with the Russians. Terry's in a worse position here than I was in the Black Sea."

"How so?"

The Frenchman's feigned interest in his opinion seemed patronizing, but Jake played along knowing his boss' ego needed stroking to resolve the conversation.

"I had six torpedoes aimed at six ships with a chance to have reloaded and shot a couple more. He's got three aimed at nothing."

"Go on."

"We never really hurt Russia when we attacked the lifelines to Crimea. In a way, we were doing the Russian mainland a favor by stopping its bleeding of resources into Crimea. But with Greece, we've attacked Greece and have hurt Greece. They have a right to be a lot angrier than the Russians were."

"True. But you and Terry were also both trapped in the Black Sea. In this case, there are multiple ways out of the Aegean."

Jake chewed on Renard's input and found a counterpoint.

"So that makes the Greeks more desperate to attack. They're angry, their pride's at stake, and Terry has a chance to slip away. And they have assets tied up in multiple places–the oil rig, around Terry, and standing guard against me. The clock is ticking for them, which can make them more aggressive than they want."

"Indeed," Renard said. "In fact, as the Greeks regroup, I would give Terry only twelve hours before they go after him. The Greeks want to be cool and sucker you in, but I doubt their patience will last. You need to do something drastic to catch their attention."

"Drastic, like me showing up and sinking something?"

"Yes. Sinking, or at least crippling with a slow-kill weapon."

"It would take me almost twelve hours at my best sustained speed to reach Terry, and that would include the exposure of snorkeling. Did you forget that I have at least two submarines between me and Terry on any path I could take? That's going to cut my speed in half."

"I did not forget. But you must attack. By defeating a Hellenic submarine, you'll be disrupting the Greek's plans, giving Terry hope, and signaling to Terry his direction to run."

"That would take me hours of prosecution to take down a

submarine that's waiting in ambush. They may be older submarines, but they have electronics upgrades and drones just like I do. They're dug in, and I can't just stampede through them like an idiot. You know damned well that beating them will take a slow, methodical approach."

"Indeed, I do know."

Jake eyed the Frenchman for signs of dismay.

"Then why do you look so smug?"

"Because I have a plan."

"Who could've imagined it? Pierre Renard has a plan. But you almost look ashamed of it. What's wrong?"

"There's nothing wrong with the plan itself. The only problem is that I didn't think of it. Dmitry did."

"Dmitry? Isn't he sipping vodka somewhere on a beach in Pakistan, or Burma, or wherever you stashed him?"

"Indeed he is on the beach, so to speak, but he's devised a way to help you help Terry nonetheless."

"This predicament's only an hour old. He didn't have much time to think about it."

"He didn't need much time. His idea was brilliant and nearly instantaneous."

"Let's hear it, then," Jake said.

"Get ready for a lengthy download to your Subtics system," Renard said. "And you may want to get me piped through to your main speakers so that I may explain matters. You've got a lot to learn, along with a few choice members of your crew."

"Okay. Can you at least give me a hint?"

"I'm delivering you a gift in six hours," Renard said. "I'll tell you the rest when you've gathered your tactical team."

## CHAPTER 14

Cahill heard the third starboard MESMA plant hiss to life.

"How are they doing on the port side?"

"Plant six is up," Walker said. "Plant four is still being restarted. They're waiting for your permission to enter plant two."

"Are you sure you're up for this?"

Walker placed his hand over the bruise on his forehead that had knocked him out.

"Just a bump. I was lucky to be unconscious when the helicopter's torpedo hit us. I can't imagine how scary that was."

"I don't care to live through that again," Cahill said. "As for MESMA plants, four are enough for now. When we're ready, we'll continue south at four knots while we get our bearings."

"I'll head to the port hull to manage the damage control."

"No," Cahill said. "Normally, I'd agree, but the Greeks are coming at us with surface and air assets. Our cannons are our best defense, and I trust you with those things by yourself."

"Are you sure you're not taking it easy on me just because I took a bump on the head?"

"Just follow me to the tactical control room and run things from there, and don't shoot any torpedoes without talking to me."

Cahill opened the watertight door to the berthing area and then continued to the tactical control room. Consoles showed the *Goliath* adapting to its recent amputation.

The torpedo had struck the port bow, and the heaviness of the lost buoyancy forced the ship to pump water from its port trim tanks.

"It's holding for now," Cahill said. "Stable on depth."

"The damage must be limited forward of port berthing," Walker said.

"Hopefully. I'll check on that soon enough. First, let's see who's watching us."

He studied the sonar display and exhaled when he noticed

silence in the surrounding water. Then a glance at Renard's low-frequency feed verified the Frenchman had received his distress call. Greek warships approached to encircle him, but the closest, the *Hydra*, kept its distance.

"If you were the Greeks, would you consider us dead and move on?" he asked.

"That would be wishful thinking," Walker said.

"True. But what's their next move? Come in guns blazing to finish us off? That would just force us to fight back out of desperation, if we're still alive. Come in quietly and see if we're still here? That leaves the risk that they miss us and declare us dead by accident while we sneak away. It's not as easy for them as you might think."

"I never said it was easy for them. But it's no laughing matter for us either."

"Let's see what we can see," Cahill said.

Switching between exterior cameras, he tried to examine the damage, but darkness enshrouded the depths. He then energized external lighting to illuminate the port hull.

"Bloody hell, it's gone," he said. "The bow section is completely missing."

"No kidding," Walker said. "At least it was a clean break."

"It may look clean, but I guarantee you there's jagged edges. We'll be noisy, mate. But I grant you we got lucky that there won't be large chunks of metal hanging around to resist our propulsion."

"I think we're solid up to the port tactical control room," Walker said. "The question is how long can we hold together and would we break apart if we have to sprint."

"Right. There might be invisible structural damage. But let's risk four knots and a turn to point our way out of here."

Cahill's tapping of a few icons set the *Goliath* crawling towards the south.

"Stay up here and get the normal watch sections going," he said. "I'm going to inspect the damage."

He walked sternward to the rear starboard MESMA plant and

turned athwartships towards the tunnel. Reaching through the circular doorway, he hoisted his torso into the cramped space and crawled. The stale air bothered him as he speculated upon possible invisible damage to the confining connection between the hulls.

Bowing his head under the air-intake cross-connect, he looked to the bilge and noted condensing water, free of leakage. Continuing on all fours, he followed hydraulic lines to the stern plane controller, scrunched his shoulders to his ears, and slipped past the oversized block of metal.

At the tunnel's end, he appreciated the access his prior order of relocating the spare railgun projectiles granted him. He opened the crawlspace's port hatch, performed his acrobatics, and set his sneakers on the deck.

His senior sailor on the port side entered the MESMA compartment.

"I thought I heard something," Johnson said.

"I came to check things out," Cahill said. "I'm sure you guys had it worse on this side."

"It was like an earthquake back here. Everything was shaking, but this ship's big enough to hack it."

"Back here, yes. I'm concerned about how far forward we can go and still be standing inside solid steel."

"Nobody's gone forward of plant four yet until you give the order. It's running hot now, ready to provide electrical load."

"Good to know. Let's have a look."

He walked forward into the number four plant. A man in coveralls confirmed what hissing steam told him—he had five working MESMA units.

"Let's check out plant two," he said. "You ready?"

"Ready," Johnson said.

Cahill opened the door, and the quiet, dry plant awaited. Emergency LEDs cast eerie shadows as he stepped through the doorway and turned on the overhead lighting.

"Ready to go for the recreational compartment?"

"Let's do it," Johnson said.

Another opened door presented a chamber of quiet shadows. After stepping between spare cannon projectiles and the Bowflex machine, Cahill reached the forward door.

He felt the metal for a temperature change and studied it for condensation, but it was dry.

"Ready to go into berthing?"

"Somebody has to," Johnson said.

"Here we go."

He cracked open the door and felt his blood pressure fall as low humidity and soft light greeted him.

"Dry as a bone," Johnson said. "I could've stayed in bed while the torpedo did its worst."

"Keep walking," Cahill said. "Our luck's about to end."

At berthing's forward door, he noticed condensation on it and ran the back of his hand against the cool metal. A glance through the small portal showed water droplets and fog blurring his view, but he discerned sloshing darkness.

"There's water rising in there," he said. "Go grab three men and come back here pronto with shoring kits."

Curiosity compelled him to crack the seal and reveal the damage, but wisdom allowed his patience.

To pass time, he walked to a hatch, opened it, and descended rungs into the bilge. He crawled under the deck plates and stopped an arm's distance from the watertight forward wall. Aiming a flashlight against the welds, he satisfied himself of the compartment's structural integrity.

After climbing and standing straight, he reached for a sound-powered phone and hailed the starboard hull's functioning tactical control center.

"Sonar supervisor."

"This is Terry. Any new contacts or word from Pierre?"

"Nothing," the supervisor said. "Pierre's orders are still to make four knots due south, which is what we're doing."

"Very well. Let me talk to Liam."

He heard a click as his executive officer lifted his phone.

"Liam here."

"I'm in the port berthing area surrounded by a bunch of dry racks. I see water in the port tactical control center, though."

"I don't think it's fully flooded," Walker said.

"The trim pump's keeping pace?"

"It's got to be. We're holding a neutral trim without an up angle."

Cahill considered the news as an option to leave the damage behind the door a mystery.

"That's encouraging," he said.

"Wait," Walker said. "I may have spoken too soon. We're about half a degree down now. The strain gauges on our cross-beams are also registering a torque."

"Keep watching. Be sure."

A few seconds of silence passed.

"I'm sure," Walker said. "It's slow, but the port bow is getting heavy. The pump isn't keeping up. If the compartment floods completely, we may lose control of the ship."

"Or lose the ship completely," Cahill said. "I'm sure this hasn't been modeled in our buoyancy calculations. You'd have a better sense of the impact of the damage if you slowed."

"How slow, then?"

"Come to all stop and see what happens when you drift to one knot."

Sailors with canvas bags entered the compartment and walked the center corridor to Cahill.

"Set down your bags, boys. Let's open this door and take a look. Depending what we see, we'll either fight a battle to shore up the flooding, or we'll declare the compartment a loss. I'm going to open it. Everyone else, stand by to close it if water rushes in."

With five men packed beside him pressing their palms against flat metal, Cahill grabbed and rotated a circular handle. The latches slipped free from their holds, and water pushed upon the door, against which he braced his shoulder.

"How high is it?" Cahill asked. "I can't see."

"About a foot and half above the deck," Johnson said.

"Take a look into the compartment. Can you see any flooding you can shore up?"

"Shit, Terry," Johnson said. "The front bulkhead is bent inward, and I mean the whole thing. It's like a wrecking ball hit it and bent it in. The watertight door held, but it's leaking all around."

"Close the door and latch it."

Cahill pushed and felt support from his crew overpowering the water.

"We'll head in there, Terry," Johnson said. "We can get to the door and shore it up. We can jam the leaks with some rubber and wedges, and we can brace the door to make sure it keeps holding."

"Sure," Cahill said. "If you don't mind drowning if the door pops off. No way, mate. You're not going in there, at least not until I make it a bit safer. Hold on."

He walked to the phone and hailed Walker.

"Liam here."

"How's our trim?"

"Not as good as I'd hoped," Walker said. "We're for sure heavy port forward. I'll need an up angle to hold depth with speed."

"Right. I'm going to head in there with a damage control party and shore the door. Take whatever up angle you need and keep us shallow at thirty meters."

"I'll take us to thirty meters with a ten-degree up angle."

"Very well. I'll wait while you get us there."

Cahill turned and froze when he faced five naked men. A hasty heap of clothes rested atop a high bunk.

"What?" Johnson asked. "You expect me to soak me skivvies in there?"

"No, mate. But I expected you to get into the water first before your willie shrank."

Ignoring muffled chuckles, Johnson marched away from the danger.

"Where are you going, Johnson? I was just playing around?"

"No offense taken. I just realized we need another person."

Moments later, the senior sailor returned with a younger man carrying towels.

"So we don't die of hypothermia when we're done."

"Good thinking," Cahill said. "You've obviously pictured this in your head already. What's on your mind?"

"Three men on the plank first to hold the door in place," Johnson said. "Two men will work on the damaged door only after the plank is in place. I don't want guys knocking the door off its hinges when they try to plug the leaks around it."

"Good thinking. But that's only five guys. Where's the sixth man going?"

"That's you, Terry. You close the door behind us."

"Bullshit."

"The ship can't lose the captain."

"Five of us are going in, and I'm one of them. I'm going in and will help wherever I'm needed. Look out for the drain in the bilge, too, since Liam has the trim pump sucking from the compartment. Don't get sucked under."

"Good point."

"I'm going in first, and I'm coming out last. Got it?"

Heads nodded.

"Good," Cahill said. "Grab your gear. Get your arses in there fast, and the last three men pull the door shut."

"Terry?"

"What?"

"Strip, unless you want to wear wet clothes."

Cahill made a rapid pile of his uniform and underwear, which he handed to Johnson. He then cracked open the door before letting the water push it wide enough for him to slip through.

His steps in the flowing stream reminded him of rolling river rapids. He waded forward against the slight incline and cringed in the coolness. The Aegean Sea's warmth fell short of the air temperature, and his body adjusted with a mild shiver.

A look forward showed the tactical control room's bulkhead with an artificial concavity. He stopped and realized how flimsy the wall of metal might be that separated him from infinite water. The flow and spray from cracks around the door exacerbated his fear.

"Come on, Terry," Johnson said.

The hefty veteran shouldered a plank and lowered it in the water. Turning, Cahill saw men closing the rear door and then fishing for a buttress against which they could secure the ten-foot-long beam Johnson had released.

A sailor lifted his hands from the fake lake that swirled around his knees and claimed victory in having found a good spot to prop the beam against a console's base.

The man waded upward, grabbed the board, and aimed it forward. Another sailor grabbed a shorter piece and held it against the door. A third pressed a wooden wedge into the gap between the pieces.

"Wrap the wedge in place," Johnson said.

As a sailor unraveled twine around the joint, Johnson lifted a rubber mat and stuffed it into a rift around the door. Water sprayed Cahill's face, and he tasted salt.

"Are you sure that's helping?" he asked.

"What?" Johnson asked.

Cahill yelled over the echoing water.

"Are you sure that helps?"

"Yes. Now drive a wedge in there gently to hold it in place. Don't hit too hard, or you could screw up the door."

Cahill tapped a rubber mallet against a wooden wedge until he felt snug resistance. Then Johnson removed his hands, and the rubber held.

"Other side," Johnson said.

The sailor ducked under the shored beam, half-swimming to the door's other side. Cahill followed, stifling a yelp as he dipped his chest into the water.

With his veteran, he repeated the tactic of wedging a rubberized mat into a rift.

"Now give me your mallet and a wedge," Johnson said.

Appreciative of the veteran's experience, Cahill obeyed. The sailor tapped bare wood into a smaller gap, and then he repeated the action on a final fissure between the door and the frame.

"That's good," Johnson said. "That should slow it down enough."

The flow and spray continued, though abated.

"That's it then," Cahill said. "Let's get to the back of the compartment and see if the pump can keep up."

The naked men began shivering but avoided touching each other as they grouped near the exit.

"You three, out," Cahill said. "I'll stay with Johnson in case we need to do more work."

A stream flowed out the open door, aiding the men's departure. As Johnson helped the men seal the exit behind them, Cahill reached for a sound-powered phone.

"Liam here."

"It's Terry. We've got shoring in place on the door and stuffed some wood and rubber into the gaps around the frame. Can you see anything yet about our weight getting lighter?"

"Not yet. Give it a few minutes."

"I'm standing naked in here with Johnson. Can you hurry?"

"Sorry, mate. It takes as long as it takes."

He started shivering as he hung up.

"Getting cold?" Johnson asked.

"A little. You know your way around flooding. Have you had to do this for real before?"

"No, but I taught damage control for three years."

"That explains it."

"Don't worry, Terry. We got ahead of this. The water level will go down. Give Liam time to verify it. Or you can just watch the water level for yourself against that weld line over there."

He pointed at the far wall.

"I noticed," Cahill said. "But there's an illusion of the water level dropping because we opened the door and a lot rushed out."

"Right, but it's gone down even further after that. Just a bit."

"I hope so."

"Call him and find out. I'm tired of standing here naked."

Cahill phoned Walker.

"Are we keeping pace?" he asked

"Yes," Walker said. "The trim pump's outpacing the flooding now. We have control of our buoyancy."

"Excellent."

"Do you want to send the rover out to inspect the damage?" Walker asked.

"Yes," Cahill said. "Send it while we're moving slow."

He replaced the phone to its cradle and reached for the door.

"You first," he said.

After following Johnson out of the room, he shut the door behind him. In the dryness of berthing, he reached for a towel and dried himself. Aware of his nakedness, he hurried to dress himself.

He walked the long distance to the port engine room where he leaned over a monitor, and he grabbed a phone.

"What can you see?" he asked.

"The rover's in position," Walker said. "I'll send the video feed to you."

The display showed underwater lights from a tethered submersible robot illuminating what invoked thoughts of a shipwreck. But the torn and twisted steel were the remnants of the bow section once attached to the watertight bulkhead of the *Goliath's* port tactical control center.

"That's a cleaner break than I'd thought," Cahill said.

"Agreed. The weight of whatever was left hanging after the explosion must have ripped it off rather neatly."

"I've seen enough. Stow the rover and get us back to four knots. Let's try to slip out of this sea unnoticed."

## CHAPTER 15

Floros raised his head and pressed his palms into the charting table. As he straightened his back, multiple thoughts dizzied him.

The *Hydra's* commander seemed to read his mind.

"It could be bottomed," he said. "The water's shallow enough."

"Or it could be destroyed," Floros said. "Or it could be sneaking away while its crew laughs at us. We won't know until we find the *Goliath*, whether it's broken in half or in fighting shape."

"We heard the weapon detonate. We hit it. What else could it have been?"

"Knowing the luck this pirate crew's supposedly seen, God himself may have protected them."

The commander leaned towards Floros.

"They're not giants, sir. They can be beaten. The evidence suggests that we already have."

"Perhaps we've beaten the *Goliath* and perhaps not. Regardless, I hold myself responsible to assure it pays its debt of justice. And if I had my way, I'd also take the same responsibility for the submarines that attacked our tankers. They attacked my nation, and I want them all."

"They attacked while you were busy defending the oil rig."

"Our activity around that rig is looking more like something these vandals keyed upon in the timing of their attacks. It's as if they knew our fleet would be focused on the oil rig before they planned their attacks."

"It's possible, sir. It's starting to look like several nations have conspired against us."

"Sadly so, but I believe we've weathered the worst."

"Perhaps, sir. What do you want to do next?"

Options buzzed in Floros' head, and he forced himself to pick one.

"I'm going to hunt the *Goliath* as if it still lives. I'll sink it twice if need be."

"The combatants of the old Task Force October Eighteen Two are still approaching from the south. They've reached eighty miles from the location of the *Goliath's* last known position."

"Expand the chart."

The Aegean Sea shrank, and a dozen Hellenic surface combatants appeared on the southern edge of the display. Floros grabbed a stylus and placed it on the icon of a frigate. He then dragged a line northward to define the base course he wanted the ship to follow. He repeated the motion with all sonar-equipped vessels in his new task force, fanning them out across his wounded enemy's possible exit routes.

"Set base speed at twelve knots," he said. "Begin anti-submarine evasion legs. I want all sonars in high-power search modes to block the *Goliath's* escape. Any ship that detects a submerged contact will attack it immediately. Pair gunships and vessels without sonar to those with sonar, and have them ready with cannons and missiles in case the *Goliath* surfaces."

"I'll see to it immediately, sir."

Reviewing the chart, Floros found himself hoping the southern combatants would drive his prey back into the *Hydra's* teeth so he could witness its destruction.

To distract himself from his bloodlust, he forced his focus on tactics and invoked a dossier of his adversary.

A wireframe three-dimensional model of the combat transport craft appeared with estimates of its makeup. The portions captured by photographs appeared with solid outlines, showing the domed bridge, the Phalanx close-in weapon system, and the elevated, stern-mounted railguns. Dotted lines shaped the questionable aspects of the vessel, showing outlines of a planar radar system around the guns and torpedo nests below each forecastle.

Considering his adversary's catamaran structure, he wondered if it could survive an air-dropped, lightweight torpedo. One half of the ship was guaranteed to survive, but he questioned the hydrodynamics of a twin-hulled vessel that had suffered a partial avulsion of its steel shell.

The damaged side would lose buoyancy and induce a torqueing stress over the cross members that united the halves. Designed to carry a naval submarine atop its connecting beams, the ship would be robust against this radial strain, but the strongest steel and stoutest welds had limits. Plus, the warhead's blast would have weakened joints and crossbeams.

"Sir?" the *Hydra's* commander asked.

"Yes. What is it?"

"Each ship in the task force acknowledges the new orders."

"Very well."

"What's on your mind, sir? You've been burning your eyes on that diagram."

"If the torpedo hit either side amidships, the *Goliath* is lost," Floros said. "There's no way it could be seaworthy if the torpedo hit anywhere near the middle of either hull. But if that did happen, then there'd be survivors inside the other hull, and they'd be on the seafloor right now."

"Are you considering a rescue mission?"

"I hadn't until I just mentioned it, to be honest. But if there were survivors, they'd be banging metal, and we'd hear it."

"If not yet, we would during our hunt."

True to the frigate commander's criticism, Floros blinked dryness from his eyes as he tightened his stare on the diagram.

"But what if instead the opposite happened?" he asked. "What if instead of a catastrophic hit amidships, it managed to show the torpedo one of its bow or stern sections?"

Seeking inspiration from the display, the commander leaned towards it.

"It could then still be seaworthy, sir."

"And if it's still seaworthy, a ship of its redundant design has at least one railgun and at least one torpedo nest available."

"Agreed, sir. If it's seaworthy, it can fight."

"Yes," Floros said. "So I need more helicopters."

He marched to a phone and hailed his boss.

"Are you having any luck getting me new helicopters, sir?"

"Sorry to disappoint you, captain," the vice admiral said. "The naval air boss is protesting. He said he's lost enough of his helicopters and airmen today. And I don't blame him. They're trained to hunt submarines, but that *Goliath* is something different, or was something different."

Floros wanted to label the aviators cowards, but he subdued his criticism and considered their perspective. He wondered if he could fly a flimsy tin can above an enemy that could surface without warning and fire shots at seven times the speed of sound.

"I understand, sir," he said. "I have enough firepower in my new task force to handle this."

"What's your intention?"

"I'm going to assume that the *Goliath* survived. I've got it fenced in with the combatants arriving from the south, and I'm going to hunt it down."

"I think you're wasting your time. A torpedo struck the *Goliath*, and it's probably resting on the sea bottom. I'm sending out a vessel with side-scan sonar to search for the wreckage."

"I'll have to respectfully disagree with you, sir."

"Duly noted. Go ahead and act on that disagreement. The task force is yours to do with as you wish. God forbid you're right and the *Goliath* slips away. I consider you the insurance policy against that embarrassment."

"I'll protect our dignity, sir."

Floros replaced the phone to its cradle and altered his tactics based upon his dearth of airpower.

"Get word to the task force helicopters," he said. "I want them close to the surface combatants protecting them, and I want the surface combatants protecting the helicopters with gunfire. We'll create a networked defense."

"I'll see to it, sir," the *Hydra's* commander said.

Floros sharpened his focus on the diagram of the *Goliath*. Ignoring the hypothesized power sources and propulsion train, he concentrated on the weapons.

"If it's in fighting condition, there are still two ways it can defeat us," he said. "Railguns can bring down our helicopters and cripple the propulsion equipment of our surface combatants."

"But you're pulling the helicopters back within protective range of our gunfire, sir. And we've shown that we can jam its guidance and evade its rounds."

"We must remain vigilant, but I grant you that the railguns are the secondary concern. But remember the other weapon system—the torpedoes. That ship has at least three heavyweight torpedoes available, possibly six or even eight."

"Not to be overly cavalier about it, sir, but we have more ships than that. At the very worst, we can survive a war of attrition until the *Goliath* is practically impotent."

Floros considered the comment, drew its logical but sickening conclusion, and mustered the strength to act upon it.

"Your statement is correct only if the frigates survive. If the *Goliath* defeats them, our best sonar systems are gone, and we'd have only deaf gunboats remaining. We need to protect the frigates even if it means sacrificing the others."

The *Hydra's* commander looked away while reflecting upon the new survival pecking order.

"Maybe not, sir. The helicopters can protect the gunboats and vice versa if the *Goliath* tries to surface. Like you said, we have a strong network penning in the *Goliath* from the south."

"That's a noble thought, but no," Floros said. "I want the three southern frigates protected from torpedoes at all costs. Place three gunboats in front of each frigate to absorb any hostile torpedoes. We must protect the frigates to optimize our sonar coverage and to keep their helicopters flying. Everything relies upon the frigates—hull-mounted sonar, variable-depth sonar, and flight operations."

The *Hydra's* commander canted his head and frowned.

"I understand, sir."

"Wait," Floros said. "Don't mention that they're going to be screens against torpedoes. They'll recognize that danger, but there's no need to be blatant about it. They'll also know that they need to be ahead of the frigates for their guns to be of any value. They'll understand the gravity of their duty, but they'll do it."

"Understood, sir. I'll pass the word."

Floros allowed himself minutes of mind-clearing inactivity while the droning of multiple conversations on the frigate's bridge became lulling background sounds.

On the display, icons shifted as he watched the warships maneuver per his will.

"The gunboat commanders have taken protective positions around the frigates," the *Hydra's* commander said.

"Very well," Floros said.

Moving his gaze to the larger scene of the Aegean Sea, he liked the view. The southern wall of his task force blocked the *Goliath's* escape, and the *Hydra* loomed to the north with freedom to hunt his trapped prey.

Guarding against hubris, he took several breaths to consider his next step. He thought about how to search for a unique and wounded animal, and the best solution he could ascertain was tightening a slow noose around the *Goliath*.

He judged his tactics simple but promising.

Then a new face entering the bridge through its rear door caught his attention, and the *Hydra's* commander turned to intercept the officer. Moving with a swagger, the new presence wore a confident and earnest look.

Floros recognized the frigate's helicopter pilot as he bent forward into a discussion with the commander. Unwilling to wait for the conversation to run its natural course, he walked to the men and interrupted them.

"What's the issue?" he asked.

"He wants to hunt the *Goliath*, sir."

Floros met the pilot's stare.

"More than one admiral has deemed that suicidal."

"They're wrong, sir," the pilot said. "They didn't rethink the tactics. I've been out there seeing my brothers get shot down. I want to avenge them, and I know what to do."

"Go on."

"It's all about keeping a low altitude during repositioning. For speed, we usually climb to pull the dipping sonars out of the water. If I instead use the winch, it will take me longer, but I won't have to make myself vulnerable to the railguns."

"The winches are slow, if I recollect correctly."

"You do recollect correctly, sir, but it's the only way I can take back control as a hunter. Given how we've got the *Goliath* penned in, I figure I can move just fast enough to give me a shot at rousting it, forcing its crew to make a mistake."

Floros nodded and turned to the display. As he walked to it, he felt the pilot follow him.

"Do you really hope to roust the *Goliath* alone?"

"It's a matter of probabilities. I'll be moving slowly, but it's a small area of water to search. Your guess is as good as mine."

"If I gave you another helicopter to join the search with you, is there a pilot in the task force you'd consider worthy?"

The aviator put his finger on the central southerly frigate.

"Papadakis. He's good."

"Very well, you can have him. Set up a search pattern accounting for your slowed repositioning, and take off as soon as your aircraft is ready."

"Thank you, sir."

"Don't thank me," Floros said. "It's I who'll be thanking you after you destroy the *Goliath*."

## CHAPTER 16

A small crowd formed around the *Specter's* central plotting table.

"I'm relying on dolphins to save the *Goliath*," Jake said. "This is ludicrous."

"I beg to differ," Renard said.

"You're on the loudspeaker now, and my tactical team is listening. You're facing a submarine full of doubters, except for maybe Antoine."

"Antoine is wise," Renard said. "I'm sure he remembers fighting against Andrei and Mikhail in the Black Sea."

"We all fought against them in the Black Sea," Jake said. "But I'm not sure we didn't give them too much credit."

"Ask Antoine about his respect for them," Renard said.

In a rare moment during which his sonar guru stood from his Subtics console during combat, Jake glanced across the table at the owner of the toad-shaped head. He noticed Remy was short and squat, likening his shape to an amphibian.

"I can't speak to their effectiveness," Remy said. "But I can verify that Dmitry communicated with them a lot in the Black Sea. He believed in them, and so did we, enough to the point of trying to kill them."

Jake recalled shooting torpedoes at the dolphins, and the clarity of hindsight caused him to doubt the tactical value of that attack. But the Frenchman's reply over the loudspeakers rescued him from wasting time on the historic analysis.

"And Dmitry still believes in them," Renard said. "They just assisted him greatly in his dealings in the Arabian Sea, and I credit him with our use of them now. Flying them to you was his idea, and I'm still stunned by how quickly he thought of it."

"And he could be laughing at me while I depend upon Flipper for the lives aboard this ship and the *Goliath*."

"Damn it, man," Renard said. "Stop doubting him. He proved his commitment in the Arabian Sea, and he cared enough about your fate and Terry's to open my mind to the dolphins' use."

"Maybe," Jake said "Call me a doubter. I need just a bit more evidence that these dolphins are going to help me and not send me down a suicidal path."

Jake recalled that his believing in Christ was an ongoing voyage of examining evidence. The study had unfillable holes, but he had the remainder of his life to explore all he could and nudge his belief towards the truth with each new step of discovery.

In contrast, Cahill's probability of survival ticked away as Jake assessed Volkov's recommendation of relying on dolphins. Complete trust would need to follow partial evidence, and the next statement from his French boss affirmed it.

"I respect your doubt," Renard said. "But you'll have to erase that doubt and test them while you use them."

The advice reminded Jake of the utility test his Christian colleagues proclaimed in assessing of Jesus' claims. His religious advisors had noted that knowledge's limits forced people into a parallel path of learning through study while also feeling the presence of their god through experiential exploration.

By attempting to follow the teachings, Jake expected to receive insights gained only by effort. So far, the incremental baby steps left him unconvinced but encouraged, as his attitude seemed to improve with a lessening of his chronic anger. Though sensing a deep, old cauldron of fury boiling within himself, he noted its temperature had lowered as his heart reached for a savior.

He committed to the same approach, albeit on a compressed timeline, with his faith in the Russian animals.

"I don't see that I have much choice," he said. "I can't power my way quickly through a half dozen submarines that are waiting for me with a perfect ambush. They probably even have drones, too. I'm good, but I'm only human. I need some magic help."

"Try the dolphins," Renard said. "I'm sure you'll find that they are magic."

"How much longer until they're ready?"

"Seven minutes from my recommended drop point," Renard said. "But I have communications with the Turks and can have the helicopter drop them wherever you want."

"No, just drop them where you planned. I'm still wondering how you got them to Izmir so fast."

"Dmitry and the *Wraith* are safely in Karachi. Admiral Khan may be retired, but he can still get me my choice of Pakistani military aircraft when needed, and in all reasonable haste–for a modest price."

"I won't even guess what you consider modest."

"To put it in perspective, transport for our two dolphins cost me less than a day's docking fee for the *Wraith* in Karachi. Stop trying to vilify this gift. Start embracing their tactical value and get your wits about the concept of using them."

Jake ran his head through his hair and raised his chin toward the overhead microphone.

"Shit, Pierre, you should expect me to challenge you at least once per mission on something, just to keep you honest."

The Frenchman's response was friendly.

"Indeed! Otherwise I should question your mental state."

"I'll give Flipper and his friend a chance."

"Thank you, my friend," Renard said. "I think you'll be pleasantly surprised. Their trainer spent seven years teaching them how to communicate and maneuver before they swam their first real mission, and he's been teaching them ever since. The trainer is excellent and devoted."

"We'll see."

"Careful not to be so cavalier about them, either," Renard said. "They're your assets to borrow, but you're obliged to bring them back unharmed."

Questioning his selfishness, Jake admitted to himself that he'd ignored the value of the dolphins beyond his immediate needs.

"How would I do that?" he asked.

"They'll follow you back to whatever port you achieve, provided you guide them properly."

"Okay, I'll deal with that when it's time," Jake said. "There's a lot of work between now and then."

"Agreed. But do remember that they are someone else's–dare I say–children. Dmitry said their trainer almost cried when he agreed to let you use them."

Jake suppressed his cynicism and tried to absorb the significance of such a loving bond. If the trainer cared that much, then he could bank on the quality of the training the dolphins had received.

But he considered their tactical value a separate concern.

"Okay, Pierre. I got it. I'll be careful with them."

"Thank you. I regret, however, that we shall now have to shift to low-bandwidth communications. With all the Greek submarines in the water, it's only a matter of time before they suspect that you're a mechanical dolphin. Best that you get into a habit of keeping your masts and antennas below the surface while you communicate with them."

"I'm as ready as I can be."

"You do recall Dmitry's detailed advice on how to make use of your new assets?"

"Yeah, yeah. Between all of us, I'm sure we've got it. Worst case, we'll read the operator's manual."

"As usual, I'd wish you luck, except I believe that you are charmed. I wish you only continued proof of my faith in you."

Jake nudged Henri's arm.

"Take us to fifty meters," he said.

As his French mechanic nodded and walked to his ship's control station, Jake shot his voice into the room.

"Back to your stations, everyone. We've talked through the details enough. I'm taking us deep to meet our new dolphin friends."

Jake returned his eyes on the chart, wondering where the line of Greek submarines awaited him. Accepting his guess was baseless, he sought his dubious mammalian tactical advantage.

As the deck dipped, he walked upward to his seat on the elevated conning station.

"Let me know when you hear them," he said.

The toad-head turned and offered a slight nod, and the side of Remy's face revealed his disdain in Jake's reminder of the obvious.

Leaving his sonar ace unperturbed, Jake studied the display by his chair and verified the *Specter's* position. Twenty miles separated him from the nearest location where he expected a Greek submarine. Safe–for now–but useless to help the *Goliath*, which was at least fifty miles away, pinned to the north behind a screen of Hellenic warships.

Time ticked away as Jake awaited his first connection with the Russian mammals. Pessimism for their usefulness grew as he watched Remy sit in stillness. Exercising patience, he stifled the urge to prod his sonar expert for a status.

"Got them," Remy said.

A glimmer of hope rose in Jake's heart.

"Seriously?"

"I'm listening on their bearing, and they're clearly calling out for a mothership, so to speak."

On Jake's display, the cetacean equivalent of a speech recognition algorithm generated a message number. He grabbed a printed sheet of paper that listed the possible messages the duo could transmit and receive.

"At least the software add-ons seem to work," he said. "If I believe it, that's message one, which is a request for a communication check with the host ship."

"Yes," Remy said. "Do you want it on the loudspeakers?"

"Yeah, pipe them through."

Aquatic sounds from a dolphin Jake assumed was Andrei chirped and whistled in the compartment

"They'll repeat the sequence until we answer," Remy said.

"Can't stress out the children," Jake said. "If I remember right, we're supposed to send out an acknowledgment message?"

"That's right," Henri said.

Jake glanced at his mechanic.

"You've committed this all to memory already?" he asked.

"Yes, Jake. Communications will govern our fate."

The chirps and whistles repeated.

"True enough," Jake said. "Antoine, are you ready to send the acknowledgement?"

"I have a menu open in front of me to send any message you want. You say it in English, and I'll send it out in 'dolphin'."

"Very well," Jake said. "Send the acknowledgement."

The *Specter's* sonar system played a recording of cetacean sounds, filling the compartment through the submarine's hydrophones. Seconds later, Jake recognized a different batch of chirps and whistles.

"They acknowledged our acknowledgement," Remy said.

Jake considered the animals' perspectives in his tactics to break through the hidden Hellenic wall of submarines. He accepted their view of the undersea world as a sonic painting, knowing their mental pictures eluded his grasp. He sought the limited, discrete information he could extract from them.

"Very well. Now let's figure out where the Turks dropped off our new pals. We already know the bearing of their incoming responses. So next is to determine their range. Pierre suggested that we do it three times to get an average. You ready to send out three range checks, Antoine?"

"I am ready to send out three range checks."

"Send out three range checks."

Three series of outgoing recordings followed by mammalian responses filled the control room.

"Based upon round-trip timing and the sound-velocity profile, the distance to Andrei is nine miles," Remy said.

"Very well," Jake said. "Send it to the chart."

On his commanding officer's display, an icon appeared that reminded him of a seafood menu.

"That's a shrimp bed," he said.

"It's the closest thing to a dolphin we've got, Jake."

"I don't like it. Change it to a friendly submarine. Let's give them credit for being warriors, at least while they keep doing their jobs."

The image changed to a blue submarine.

"Make it two submarines, co-located, just to be clear."

"Done," Remy said.

Jake stared at his dolphin-submarines while considering his next move. As the initial success in connecting with them and geo-locating them bolstered his confidence, he took his leap of faith.

"Let's see what they see," he said. "It's time to query them for submerged contacts."

"One query at a time, Jake," Antoine said. "And you have to ask them discrete questions about each contact."

"Right. Pierre said they'll likely see multiple contacts. They'll supposedly report any submerged contacts moving clockwise, considering us at twelve o'clock for reference. Start with querying for the bearing to a contact."

"I'm ready to query them for the bearing to a contact."

"Transmit the query."

An exchange of chirps and whistles.

"They say a submerged contact is at five o'clock."

"Very well," Jake said. "Now query for the range."

Another exchange of chirps and whistles.

"They say it's far away," Remy said. "Remember that they're trained only to say if a contact is close, far away, or between close and far. Near is within a nautical mile of their position, far is beyond ten, and in between is a random guess."

"Far away is fine for now," Jake said. "That means we've got time to drive the geometry, especially if they're stationary waiting to ambush us. Continue with the next query for range."

Three contacts later, Jake met Henri's stare.

"The dolphins must be seeing drones," Jake said. "If I assume two drones per submarine, they'll report a total of nine to twelve contacts."

"Indeed," Henri said. "They have excellent natural skill, and I'm sure they can tell a submarine from a drone."

"But they don't know how to tell us which are drones and which are submarines, unfortunately."

"Precisely the limitation I was beginning to lament."

"Well, let's exhaust the information they can tell us, and then we'll figure out how to figure out what's what."

Jake ordered Remy to continue the queries. Ten minutes later, he saw twelve submerged contacts outlining a barrier between him and Cahill. As the last one appeared in the *Specter's* Subtics system, he stepped down to the central chart and bent over it. He felt his mechanic appear beside him.

"Holy shit," he said. "That's four submarines, each with two drones covering a whole lot of water. There's no way to punch through that without..."

"Yes?" Henri asked. "Without what?"

"Shit," Jake said. "Without dolphins."

"Agreed, but be careful. There's nothing trivial about this. We can't attack twelve targets without risking the noise of reloads, even counting the two weapons the dolphins carry."

"But we can punch our way through six of them, including any drones we can't tell apart from submarines," Jake said. "And that's enough."

"I see what you mean," Henri said. "We're not defeating four submarines and eight drones, but we're only penetrating their wall. We only need to break through."

Jake blocked out the Frenchman's words while awaiting inspiration as he looked at the icons. The moment of clarity he needed arrived, and he saw his efficient path.

"We need to defeat only one," he said.

"Without telling a drone from a submarine?"

"Possibly. What we already know is useful information. Get a communication buoy loaded to tell Pierre what we know about the twelve contacts, and launch it with a ten-minute delay."

"Understood. I'll get it launched. But do you really think you already have a plan in mind to get us through the ambush?"

"Sort of."

"Even without being able to tell which of the twelve contacts are submarines and which are drones?"

"I think I know how to overcome the communication barrier we're facing with our newest hunters on the team," Jake said. "And I think we'll be able to discern a submarine from a drone just in time to make a difference for helping Terry."

## CHAPTER 17

Cahill stood in the *Goliath's* tactical control room, praying for the solitude of silence as he stared at several sonar displays. The hull arrays heard nothing, but he knew they were challenged against distant, quiet contacts.

The noises on the towed sonar array concerned him.

"I see a lot of contacts," he said. "But nothing crisp like the well-machined screws of a combatant. It's not just wishful thinking, is it, to think we're in the clear?"

His sonar supervisor shook his head and slid his earpiece behind his jaw.

"No, sir. I have all the surface combatants identified in our system based upon Renard's low-bandwidth input. With that advantage, it's easy to stay away from them. It's only the helicopters and submarines that scare me."

"You mean until we stop running in circles and try to break out of here," Cahill said.

"Yes. We're safe for now but trapped."

"And they're tightening the noose," Cahill said. "You can see them converging on us from the south. Our only saving grace is that they're moving slowly. I think they respect our firepower."

"Either that, or they take us for dead."

"That would be even better, but they're professionals, and I don't expect them to risk that conclusion untested. They're coming."

Cahill turned and stepped beside Walker, who leaned over the plotting table.

"I don't like it," Walker said. "The noose, as you said, is tightening. We may have to surface and fight our way out."

"Against that wall of combatants to the south alone, it would be risky. Given that they can jam and evade our rounds if we use only satellite guidance, we'd have to get within range of our phased array radar, and that would place us near the range of the frigates' cannons."

"Near their range, but still beyond it, if we're careful enough.

I've calculated that we've got about a three-mile advantage against them, based upon the height of our radar arrays detecting the frigates by their tallest masts. We can target their engineering spaces with certainty and cripple them."

Cahill absorbed the insight while expanding the chart.

"But look just a bit to the south, and you see a wall of submarines," he said. "As soon as we announce ourselves on the surface, we're easy prey for them."

"But we're well over twenty-five miles away, and possibly farther than that."

"The distance can be closed quickly by a sprinting submarine to within launch distance of us, and then a torpedo can find us with over-the-horizon guidance through a wire if we linger on the surface to attack multiple surface combatants."

"I'm trying to find us a way out of this, mate," Walker said.

"I know it, and it's good thinking. I'm afraid that there's just no obvious tactic. There's risk at every bloody turn and in every bloody direction."

A sailor stirred and called Cahill's attention to news from his boss. He thanked the man and invoked a train of text on the table.

"Check it out," he said. "Pierre's sent us data based upon Jake's work in identifying a lot of the submarines. I'm sending the new updates to the chart."

Ovals of uncertainty spread from north to south with thin axes across their east-west middles.

"These solutions are almost useless with their shitty guesses at the ranges," Walker said. "And they're incomplete. It says he assumes there are twice as many drones as submarines that he's detected, and that means there's at least two submarines unaccounted for by that math."

"Logical."

"Pardon my ignorance, but what's the big deal about a drone anyway?"

Cahill realized that despite Walker's fast learning, his undersea warfare lessons would continue over many missions.

"These drones are like remote-operating vehicles with sonar suites. Jake's used them many times to his advantage, but they're ineffective beyond slow speeds, unless you use them actively, which Jake can't while he's trying to be undetected."

"So now the tide is turned while he has to try to maneuver through submarines that are prepositioned against him."

"Right. Four Greek submarines have deployed two drones each, which almost triples the area of their acoustic coverage."

"Almost?" Walker asked. "Geometrically, it looks like a complete tripling."

"True, but drones don't have anywhere near as many hydrophones as their host submarines. Even when drifting in the water as part of an ambush, their coverage is good but not great."

Cahill watched Walker move his finger over the submerged icons, trying to fathom the makeup of the barrier between their ship and their cavalry, the *Specter*. He then rapped his knuckle against their colleague's submarine.

"If they're spread equally, and Jake's located here, why doesn't he just shoot one torpedo down the bearing of the four submerged targets in the middle of each group of three?"

"A good question, but you assume the one in the middle is the submarine. A careful commander might deploy two to the right and zero to the left, or vice versa. The range on these drones is respectable, and the Greeks have had plenty of time to prepare for Jake."

"I see."

"Or picture two submarines committed as listeners that have deployed four drones each from the center of the screen. Since they need their guidance wires to use the drones, those tubes are occupied and can't be used to launch torpedoes. But there would then be other submarines waiting. And remember that the entire submerged defensive geometry is still a guess until the dolphins get closer to the Greeks. There are submarines even they can't detect yet."

Walker straightened his back.

"We need to develop a plan and carry it out," he said. "If we're going to die, let's die using our wits and courage and every bloody asset we have on this ship."

"Easy, Liam. We don't have to die today."

Cahill half-believed his sentiment as it echoed in his head.

"Then what's your plan?"

"Let's remove the most immediate threat," Cahill said. "Since the helicopter pilots have figured out they'll die if they hunt for us, they're no longer the biggest problem. It's the frigates. We'll start in the west and see if we can cripple the first."

"You're not worried about the submarines then?"

"I'm always worried about submarines. That's why we'll be moving between surfaced and submerged operations the entire time."

He considered the chaos of combat and realized he'd need speed to maneuver–and possibly to dodge–incoming weapons.

"And the next thing we need to do is see what sort of speed we can maintain submerged."

"Would you like to make our best submerged speed towards the westerly frigate?"

"Yes. And when we surface, we'll see what sort of speed we can sustain surfaced. We'll figure out our limits with the damaged port bow and work within them."

Walker tapped the screen and invoked lines.

"I've assumed a best sustained submerged speed of nine knots and recommend course two-two-six to reach firing range of the westerly frigate."

"How much variance is in that solution if you account for the frigate's anti-submarine zigzag legs?"

"A lot. We'll have to wing it as we get close."

"So be it," Cahill said. "Come right to course two-two-six."

Walker tapped the command, and a display showed the indiscernible shift in the *Goliath's* heading. As Cahill pondered how to give speed commands to compensate for his damaged port bow, Walker offered a possible solution.

"I suggest you try turns for eleven knots on the port engine to compensate for the increased bow friction. Turns for nine on the starboard engine should be sufficient."

"Agreed. This may tax our present MESMA lineup, though. I want all plants on line."

"MESMA plant two is on standby."

"Bring up MESMA plant two, make turns for eleven knots on the port engine, turns for nine knots on the starboard engine."

Fearing his ship would protest the new speed by oscillating, Cahill discovered his concerns had merit as numbers representing the *Goliath's* speed ticked upward.

"The MESMA plant two team reports their plant is up and running, but now the deck is shaking," Walker said. "I recommend slowing back to four knots."

"Damn it. Slow to four knots."

"Slowing. This is bad, Terry."

Cahill pictured the damaged ship in his mind as he pondered the hydrodynamics.

"Bad but not hopeless," he said. "Place a five degree up angle on the ship."

Walker tapped keys, and the deck tilted.

"Let's try it again, only a bit more conservative," Cahill said. "Make turns for seven knots on the port engine, turns for six knots on the starboard engine."

The increased speed felt smooth under his feet, but the look on Walker's face as he held a phone to his ear signaled the port hull team's repeated report of unwanted undulations.

"The deck is shaking in MESMA plant two," Walker said.

"How bad, compared to last time?"

"About a quarter as bad."

"Increase the up angle to ten degrees."

His executive officer obeyed, and the deck inclined.

"Now how bad is it?"

"They say it's hardly noticeable," Walker said.

"Very well. Make turns for eight and a half knots on the port engine, turns for seven knots on the starboard engine."

"Light shaking, Terry."

"Increase the up angle to fifteen degrees."

He held a rail as the *Goliath* pointed upward.

"That seemed to calm it," Walker said. "I recommend seeing what we can do all out."

"Make turns for eleven knots on the port engine, turns for nine knots on the starboard engine."

A minute later, Cahill thought he had his ship under control, but then a report from Walker about the starboard weapons bay surprised him.

"Shit, Terry," Walker said. "The starboard weapons bay watchman was doing daily checks, and the inner diameter of the cannon is too large."

Cahill recalled that each shot from the railgun removed a thin layer of the barrel's metal, transformed it into a plasma cloud, and spurted it out the muzzle as a firestorm with each projectile. Time and random wear forced periodic replacement, and he carried several spares, but the swapping took half an hour–if rushed.

"That's why we check it. Get them started on replacing the barrel immediately. If they hurry, they'll be ready in time for our attack on the frigate."

Thinking himself lucky for having enough time to fix his railgun before needing it, Cahill disliked his next piece of news.

"Helicopter," the sonar supervisor said. "Moderate signal strength. Bearing zero-six-one."

"Very well," Cahill said. "I see that at least one pilot has the balls to hunt us. Either that, or he's suffering from delusions of grandeur."

"It's almost in our baffles," the supervisor said. "Probability of detection is small."

While driving from the airborne threat, Cahill kept his mind focused on the surface combatant targets as Renard's periodic, low-frequency updates shifted them about his chart.

But his lead sonar expert redirected his attention.

"Terry," the supervisor said.

"What?"

"The helicopter is making noises I haven't heard one make in a long time. I think it's lifting its sonar system with a winch."

Cahill assessed the anomaly.

"That's a patient pilot," he said. "Patient and wise. I also wonder if he knows how much danger he's in."

"What danger?" Walker asked. "He's minimizing his risk to our radar and cannons by staying at low altitude instead of lifting his sonar quickly by climbing. To me, that's cautious."

"The tactic is cautious, which is exactly why I have to kill him. If he thinks he's discovered a way to hunt us safely, his colleagues will draw the same conclusion, and then those helicopters hiding near the surface combatants will become our new worst enemy."

"Shit, mate. Good point. You mean to surface and attack?"

"I do. We've got one working cannon, and that helicopter's a sitting duck while its pilot thinks he's safe. And our position is still far enough away from the westerly frigate that our intent to attack it next won't be obvious when we surface. Now's the time, and I mean right now. I'm surfacing the ship."

Cahill tapped keys to slow and surface the *Goliath*. His stomach dropped to his knees with the rapid rise, and the deck rocked in the waves.

"Raising the port cannon," he said. "Bringing the phased array radar online."

"I've got it on radar already," Walker said. "Seven miles away. Altitude one hundred feet. A sitting duck like you said."

"Prepare to fire twenty splintering rounds from the port cannon at the helicopter."

"The port cannon is locked on the helicopter, ready to fire twenty splintering rounds."

"Fire."

After the first sonic crack, Cahill ordered a satellite connection to his boss. He turned to the row of Subtics system monitors behind him and saw an unfamiliar face materialize.

"Can you hear me?" he asked.

"Yes," the man said.

The accent was thick and French.

"Get me Renard. Now!"

"Right away."

The man disappeared, and five sonic cracks later, Cahill's boss appeared.

"Another smoke break?"

"Would you believe I was actually resting?" Renard asked.

"Did I wake you?"

"No," Renard said. "I was taking a two-hour nap while you and Jake appeared safe from harm, but the watch captain here had already summoned me when the helicopter from the *Hydra* braved a hunt for you. Your beckoning merely hastened my arrival."

"You look like shit, mate."

As another sonic boom shot from the port railgun, the Frenchman rubbed sleep from his eyes and turned his head to study monitors.

"I feel better than I look, I trust. I've got satellite coverage of you on the surface shooting at the helicopter. I see you're using just one cannon."

"The starboard barrel needed replacing. I'm taking care of it before I go after the frigates."

"Understood. I see your plan, and I admire your assertiveness."

After the next sonic crack, Walker confirmed the loss of radar return, and then the supervisor reported the splash.

"Cease fire." Cahill said. "I've removed that helicopter from me arse, and I've got to run, Pierre."

"Before you do, take note that there was a second helicopter assisting the first, but it's now retreating to the south."

"Good to know."

"Also, for your planning, you need to know that Jake is working from the east while you appear to be moving west."

"Bloody hell. Damn it then, I'll change my tactics. I'll head east. A little misdirection might help anyway."

"Good idea. I'll keep the low-bandwidth updates coming."

"They always help, Pierre."

He tapped keys to secure the radar, shut off his connection to Renard, lower the railgun, and inhale water into the *Goliath's* tanks.

The burden of having dealt death weighed on him, but he stuffed the load deep within him. He convinced himself he had no choice in killing the aircrew and topped off his therapy with a victorious declaration.

"I don't think any other pilots will be trying that again soon," he said. "We just got the message across."

"Agreed," Walker said. "But we also revealed our position. Even if nobody got active radar return off us, which I believe they did, they've got us triangulated off our emissions. We're now a known quantity."

"That's fine. Our next move is to get within radar range of our next target anyway. The worst those mongrels can do is make it easier for us by coming at us."

"They could all still swarm us, if they move together, coordinated. They could overwhelm us with all their firepower."

"Only if we sit still and let them," Cahill said. "Which we won't. We're holding nine knots submerged."

"But what if there's a submarine near us and we just gave it all the information it needs to target us?"

Submerged threats haunted Cahill's subconscious mind, and Walker's question raised his fears to the forefront of his focus.

"Since we have no idea how fast we can run, and since there's no safe direction to do so, then we're dead if a submarine was near us when we surfaced. So let's pray there wasn't."

## CHAPTER 18

Jake watched the toad-head turn.

"The dolphins announced a range shift," Remy said. "A target has moved from far range to in between near and far."

"Which target?"

"They can't say. You have to guess."

"Correction," Jake said. "You have to guess. I'm delegating to you since you know them better."

"I'll guess it's the one they're swimming towards," Remy said. "Submerged target eleven. But it could be any of five targets based upon the geometry."

"Assume it's target eleven since that aligns with our plans. Update target eleven's range to ten miles from the dolphins, and get a range check on them to be sure where they are."

As the *Specter* and the Russian mammals exchanged chirps and whistles, Jake envisioned the pending attack before issuing the order.

"It should work," Henri said.

The Frenchman stood below Jake, resting his forearms on the polished rail.

"Do you have any doubts in your ability to read my mind?"

"None whatsoever," Henri said. "In fact, I can read your body language and predict most of your thoughts before you have them. I am your unofficial therapist, after all."

"I don't have time now to consider how scary that is."

"Then do what you always do and focus on tactics."

"Yeah," Jake said. "This plan's got a lot of moving parts, and I wanted to think it through one more time. But you're right, it's going to work. Dolphins, camera shots, torpedoes. It'll be fine."

Jake stepped down and walked with Henri to the central table. The dolphin-submarine tandem icons moved towards the nearest submerged target.

"Camera range to take a picture that requires flash illumination is about what?" Jake asked. "Fifty feet?"

"Yes," Henri said. "They'll need to be on top of their mark."

"And they're limited to eleven knots sustained speed. So that means they'll reach target eleven in fifty-four minutes."

"Approximately."

Jake grabbed a stylus and drew a line from an icon of the *Specter* to the submerged contact.

"And a torpedo would reach it in about thirteen minutes."

"You'll need to allow at least two minutes to get some sort of readable image from the dolphins' cameras, as well."

"Then we're sitting tight on shooting a weapon at target eleven for another forty-one minutes. But I need to get the longer shots launched at targets ten and twelve before that."

He drew two more lines.

"Fifteen minutes and seventeen minutes of torpedo runs."

"If you believe the ranges," Henri said.

"They're just guesses at this point, but the torpedoes will handle what we need them to handle."

The Frenchman stiffened.

"Only if you use active seekers, and only if the targets are true submarines and not drones. You'll be giving away your element of surprise."

"You have a better idea? We're the aggressors working against time. There's no time to be delicate."

"Sadly, I do not. I just dislike giving up our advantage."

"You have to give up the element of surprise at some point to benefit from it," Jake said. "But maybe the dolphins can give us updates before we shoot."

He returned to his seat and oversaw his crew while the dolphin-submarine tandem icon inched toward an unidentified submerged contact, target eleven.

The toad-head stirred again.

"The dolphins just announced another range shift," Remy said. "A target has moved from far range to in between."

Jake glanced at his display and assumed one of two submerged targets could be within ten miles of the mammals.

"Any guess as to which one?" he asked.

"I'll guess it's the one to their immediate left. It feels closer than the one on the right."

"You can't hear it, can you?"

"No," Remy said. "I can't hear anything because all the Greek submarines and drones are drifting silently with the current. They've created an impenetrable wall except for the help from the dolphins allowing us to see them."

"Then why do you think it's the one on the left?"

"Because you're going to force me to guess. So I guessed."

"So be it," Jake said. "Give target ten a range of ten miles from the dolphins and get a range check on them again."

The loudspeaker played aquatic sounds in rapid succession.

"What was all that?" Jake asked.

"Range checks and another range shift report," Remy said. "They just passed from far range to in between on another contact, and I'll guess it's target twelve. The geometry now precludes targets nine and lower from being ten miles from them."

"Good," Jake said. "Set the range to target twelve at ten miles from the dolphins. Even if we got targets ten, eleven, and twelve screwed up, we're wrong by no more than three miles on any one of them."

"Three miles is enough to throw off a surgical torpedo shot."

"I'm not going surgical," Jake said. "I'll turn on the seekers with plenty of advanced time to absorb the slop."

"The submarines will hear the weapons through the drones."

"True, but then what? If I heard a torpedo coming for one of my drones, I'd sit tight and wait while I generated a solution on that torpedo backwards like a tracer bullet going the wrong way. If these guys are smart, they won't give up their ambush positions just because they hear a torpedo attacking a drone."

"Thank God you're in charge," Remy said. "I hate these sort of decisions."

"I've made my decision. Assign tubes one through three to targets ten through twelve respectively. Have the seekers wake up nine miles away from us."

The sonar expert turned his head to the technician beside him and talked him through the presets for each weapon.

"Tubes one through three, all slow-kill weapons, are assigned to targets ten through twelve respectively," Remy said.

Chirps and whistles arrived every ten minutes as the dolphins offered their unsolicited range checks. After thirty minutes of low-intensity analysis, Jake stood and reached for the overhead piping to flush fatigue from his flesh.

"It's time," he said.

"To launch weapons?" Henri asked.

"Tubes three, one, and then two, in that order, two minutes apart, starting with tube three."

The French mechanic repeated the sequence and walked about the room to verify the preparations. When ready, he looked to Jake.

"Antoine is ready for your orders."

"Tube three is ready," Remy said.

"Presets?"

"Medium-speed run. Anti-submarine mode. The active seeker will turn on after nine miles of running."

"Very well. Shoot tube three."

The soft whine and pressure change hit Jake's ears.

"Tube three indicates normal launch," Remy said. "I have wire control. I hear its propeller."

Six minutes passed as Jake launched two more weapons from the *Specter's* tubes.

"And now, ten minutes of patient waiting, hoping nobody heard any of that launching noise," Jake said.

"Nobody heard," Henri said. "They're all to the north, waiting for you sprint by. They have no idea we've used nature's sonar experts against them."

As the minutes ticked away, Jake was restless in his chair until Remy brought his focus to his next move.

"The dolphins announced a range shift," Remy said. "A target has just moved from in between to near range."

A glance at his display encouraged Jake as the Russian animals demonstrated their merit.

"That's a mile sooner than expected," he said. "But I'll take it.

Set the range to target eleven at one mile from the dolphins, and get a range check from them."

Remy announced a slight update to the cetaceans' position.

"They're five minutes from camera range," Henri said.

Jake expected cameras atop their body harnesses to capture images of target eleven to confirm its identity. Five minutes later, he ordered the image.

The *Specter's* recorded chirp told Andrei to point his nose at the contact for three seconds while the apparatus atop his head snapped a picture of the dark depths.

Jake recognized the new incoming sound of crackling shrimp, the camera's signal that simulated the sea's biological noises, pulsing through the loudspeakers. Given the low baud rate, he expected five minutes to form the full image, but less than two minutes to discern a tiny drone from a *Type-209* submarine.

"Order the dolphins to hold their position," he said.

Remy complied.

As the synthetic shrimp symphony sounded, a grainy picture took form on Jake's display. He noticed Henri glaring at the same image evolving at his control station.

The synthetic shrimp crackles continued building the resolution, and the subject's form had become discernable.

"That's no drone," he said. "That's a submarine."

"Agreed," Henri said. "A little common sense guessing and a little luck led us to the right assumptions."

"Keep weapon two on track," Jake said. "Weapon two is properly seeking a submarine."

"Where to send the dolphins next?" Henri asked.

"Target nine," Jake said. "We've got torpedoes investigating targets ten and twelve."

"If ten and twelve are indeed drones, you'll be unable to verify it. A lack of return from a torpedo seeker fails to prove the existence of a drone. It only verifies that a submarine doesn't exist where you thought."

"I'll take my chances on the implied logic," Jake said. "Antoine, can you send the dolphins to check out target nine, if you query them on all contacts and send them to number nine right after they report on it?"

"Yes, Jake. I'm proud of you for actually reading their operating manual and understanding my convoluted path to give that order to them."

"Query them for all contacts. If for some reason I get distracted while they're reporting on number nine, send them to number nine."

"I'll have them swimming for target nine in five minutes."

The loudspeakers broadcasted chirps and whistles as the dolphins started their report with the first submerged contact on their *Specter*-centric clock, target one. Jake trusted his sonar expert to guide the cetaceans where he wanted.

"Weapon one is on top of target ten," Remy said. "No return."

"I declare target ten to be a drone. Mark it as such in the system and steer weapon one towards target eight."

"You believe target eight to be a submarine?" Henri asked.

"I'll assume the center of each group of three submerged contacts to be a submarine until proven wrong. They didn't expect us to have our advantage with the dolphins, and they're not thinking in terms of complex drone geometries. They're just covering as much water as they can, as simply as they can."

"I've steered weapon one towards target eight," Remy said. "The weapon's battery reserve is only three percent."

"Three percent is fine."

"The range is still suspect, Jake," Remy said. "And on this angle of approach with our weapon already out there, it could be off a lot on the bearing. It could be a complete miss."

"Irrelevant. It's a free weapon, and it'll do nothing worse than confuse our enemy."

Remy shrugged and then turned as the technician beside him offered an update, which he relayed.

"Weapon three is on top of target twelve," Remy said. "No return."

"I declare target twelve to be a drone. Mark it as such in the system and steer weapon three on course two-six-zero."

"Two-six-zero?" Remy asked. "No target given?"

"No target given," Jake said. "Let weapons one and three bracket target eight, and let our weapons also serve as de facto drones. Let them push back our enemy, or, with a little luck, acquire a submarine."

"I've steered weapon three to course two-six-zero," Remy said. "The seeker from weapon three has gone active. Target eight has just accelerated and is making turns for twenty-two knots based upon the blade rate for a Greek *Type-209*."

Jake looked at his display.

"Our weapon is two miles away," he said. "We've got target eight. It's ours."

"Weapon two has acquired target eleven and is accelerating to attack speed. Range is confirmed as fourteen miles from us."

"Very well," Jake said. "No way it's getting away."

With the Greek submarine trying to sprint away after being dead in the water, Jake expected most of the twenty-four undersea limpet bombs of his slow-kill weapon to attach.

"Target eleven is accelerating and turning, but it's no use," Remy said. "Impact is in ninety seconds."

"Is anything else out there accelerating?" Jake asked. "There's a complex dance about to start, and I just kicked it off."

"Nothing yet," Remy said. "But I'll hand off monitoring of our weapons to our other technicians and listen."

"Very well," Jake said.

A junior sailor announced the detonation of weapon three underneath the fleeing Greek submarine. Although unaccustomed to listening to submunitions breaking from the *Specter's* custom warhead and attaching to a submarine's hull, the youngster thought he heard most of them find their mark.

"We'll know soon enough, lad," Jake said.

Unsure if six or seven of the first third of bomblets detonated, the young sailor gave his enthusiastic report. The Hellenic submarine was flooding and fighting its way to the surface. When the next third of minor detonations pierced the target's skin, it was already rising like a cork.

"That's enough for target eleven," Jake said. "Henri, backhaul tube two and reload it with a drone."

"A drone? Do you really think it's necessary with the abilities you've seen the dolphins demonstrate?"

"That's a good point. It depends if I'm playing offense or defense in the next few hours, which depends on what Terry does. So, I'll take your advice and change my mind. Load tube two with a slow-kill weapon."

Jake suspected the explosion of the final third of the bomblets compelled the flooding vessel's commander to feel gratitude for being alive and to excuse himself from the battle while fighting the sea's inrush into his ship.

"Target eight is now accelerating," Remy said. "You were right, Jake. It's also a *Type-209* submarine. It's making turns for eight knots and heading east to investigate what we just did to its colleague."

"And it just turned into weapon one, didn't it?"

"Yes. I'm using the bearings to target eight to confirm the range. We were off by three miles, but since it turned towards our torpedo, it will hit with a small steer. I recommend a steer to the right of ten degrees."

"Steer weapon three ten degrees to the right."

Remy spoke to a junior technician seated next to him and shot periodic glances over his shoulder to verify the sailor's work.

"Weapon three has accepted a ten-degree steer to the right," Remy said. "Battery remaining is now nine percent with the increased rate of closure."

"Turn off weapon three's seeker," Jake said.

"Weapon three's seeker is off," Remy said.

"Turn the seeker back on when the weapon's a mile from target eight. Hopefully target eight's crew didn't hear our torpedo while they were outside its search cone, and I don't want to announce that it's coming until it's too late."

Jake stepped down to the central plotting chart and studied

the chaos. He'd forced one submarine out of the battle, and he expected to banish a second from the fray. He'd identified two targets as drones, both now severed from their host as it had tried to sprint and then emergency blow to the surface.

He had broken the wall, inserted himself within it, and taken control of a corridor to freedom he hoped Cahill could reach.

## CHAPTER 19

Floros stared at his chart and squinted against the sun's glare.

"Two submarines forced to surface," he said. "They'd all be dead if it weren't for this mercenary navy's self-righteous indulgence in less-than-lethal torpedoes. This is disgusting."

"I can't fault the undersea warfare team," the *Hydra's* commander said. "The ambush was set up well."

Floros agreed but hesitated to admit it.

"Well enough that a lone *Scorpène*-class submarine defeated two of our best submarines that had prime waiting positions in their home waters."

"I can't explain it, sir."

Grunting, Floros looked at the important icons to guide his thoughts towards action. He blocked out the submarines as a distraction beyond his influence and retained his clarity on the surface combatants and aircraft.

"Neither can I," he said. "But it's irrelevant. The mercenary submarine is beyond our reach and vice versa, if we move quickly against the *Goliath*. I'm putting that ship on the bottom before its rescue submarine can interfere."

"We have its last known position, and it's been submerged since shooting down our helicopter. The area of water in which it could be hiding has grown small, and we know it's damaged."

As he watched the line of his task force's combatants curl around the *Goliath*, Floros lamented the loss of the latest aircrew, having met their leader and respected his dedication.

"Damaged, but deadly against a pilot who thought he could confront it."

"That was a helicopter, sir. You have a task force of cannons heading for it aboard ships that can survive its railgun rounds."

"One shot," Floros said. "One round from a seventy-six-millimeter cannon will end this. That's all I need."

"You'll get it, sir. The *Goliath* must surface to fight since it can't avoid the sonar systems you have encircling it."

"Let's make sure the circle forms smartly."

He grabbed a stylus and dragged lines from the southerly combatants and drew them forward in a clamping formation around his enemy's last surfaced location.

"This is what I want," he said. "Twenty-five knots speed."

"Twenty-five, even with anti-submarine zigzag legs?"

"No more anti-submarine legs. This is a race against a clock with that enemy submarine breaking through the southerly line."

"I will relay the order to the task force, sir."

Floros leaned over the chart as the chokehold began to subdue his enemy. As the radius of uncertainty to the vandal vessel shrank to less than twenty-five miles, he sought a new perspective of the waters.

"Show me the gunfire coverage for the cannon of each ship in the task force."

Colored arcs extended from his frigates and gunboats to overlay half the area under which the transport ship hid.

"In an hour, I'll have the *Goliath* under complete coverage."

An icon appeared in a gap between his ships' gunfire reach.

"Multiple ships have just detected the *Goliath's* radar," the *Hydra's* commander said. "We have it located outside of gunfire range of our nearest ship, but I'm receiving several requests to launch anti-ship missiles."

Floros saw red.

"Have these idiots learned nothing? Offensive missile attacks are feeble unless paired with torpedoes, and nobody's within torpedo range. Defensive strikes are optimized at three missiles only–no more, no less. I won't allow an uncoordinated wasting of our anti-ship missiles!"

"I'll tell them to hold their fire, sir."

Icons representing supersonic railgun shots peppered the display, and recalling his knowledge about defenses against railguns, Floros grabbed a microphone and sent his voice to his entire task force.

"To all ships," he said. "This is the task force commander. When targeted by railguns, use evasive maneuvers, pop chaff, energize point defense systems, and combine your shipboard efforts with the support from our early warning and control craft to jam the railgun guidance. The *Goliath* can be overcome. We have the firepower and the will. Continue driving towards it with all your weapons ready."

As he lowered the microphone towards its cradle, the images of his enemy's projectiles flying towards his task force's easternmost frigate stopped him. He hailed the targeted combatant's commanding officer and heard the proper amount of fear and tension in the man's voice.

"I'm under fire, sir."

Through the radio circuit, he heard the rapid chainsaw rounds of the frigate's close-in weapon system and the sonic booms of two simultaneous incoming shots. He was relieved that the riot of ripping metal failed to materialize.

"I know, commander. Stay calm. As your first measure of defense, launch three Harpoon missiles at your enemy. Three is the perfect amount to push those railguns back underwater."

"Three Harpoons. Give me a moment to launch them, sir."

Floros watched three traces appear on his display.

"Good. You'll have only two more minutes to deal with incoming railgun rounds."

"I'm sure you understand that two minutes is a deceptively long time when you're under fire, sir."

"I do. Again, stay calm. I think the *Goliath's* commanding officer has access to satellite infrared to target you. I recommend that you generate black smoke and circle back underneath the hot cloud to conceal your thermal signature."

"But that will prevent me from closing range, sir."

"That's fine, commander. The rest of the task force will close in while you dodge the incoming rounds."

"Understood, sir."

More chainsaw sabots and sonic booms.

"I also recommend you temporarily abandon your engineering spaces. Your propulsion equipment is the *Goliath's* preferred target."

"That's a negative, sir."

The next volley of chainsaw sabots and sonic cracks preceded the howling screech of punctured metallic flesh.

"What's been hit, commander?"

"My bow, sir. The rounds are targeting my bow. I just lost part of my sonar system with that hit. Damage assessment is underway. I'm generating black smoke, but I'll be exposed for several minutes while I turn back under the cloud."

"Why isn't your jamming working? You're using your organic systems and getting assistance from an electronic warfare aircraft. The *Goliath* can't guide its rounds throughout their entire flights. You must be creating some jamming effect."

"I am, sir, but the accursed rounds are moving at Mach 7. Even when I jam their last miles of flight, I can't move my ship out of the way fast enough. Until I get under my smoke screen, I'm exposed, and the *Goliath* will hit what it targets."

"How's your close-in weapon system doing?"

"As well as yours, sir. It can take down one incoming round but not the second of a salvo."

"Very well, commander. You may take a few more rounds before you're under your smoke screen, but I trust you'll control any damage you may take."

Returning his gaze to the overhead view of the battle, Floros dwelled on the *Goliath's* new goal–sonar. The enemy commander was proving shrewd and adaptive.

"He's developed a new tactic," he said.

"What tactic?" the *Hydra's* commander asked.

"He's attacking our bow-mounted sonar. Get the undersea warfare officer up here."

Twenty seconds elapsed, and then Floros saw a tall, thin officer enter the bridge. He gestured the man to his side.

"What advantage does the *Goliath* gain by destroying the bow-mounted sonar systems on the frigates?"

"That would eliminate the most powerful sonar systems we have for transmitting active acoustic energy," the officer said.

"What's the disadvantage of losing those systems while

keeping our towed systems or our variable-depth systems?"

The officer frowned in thought before answering.

"I'm not entirely sure, sir. The variable-depth systems can transmit actively as well."

"Think, man. The *Goliath's* commander has the ability to strike whatever part of our ships he wants–propulsion, cannons, missiles, or sonar. Why sonar?"

"He obviously intends to evade submerged, sir."

The railgun projectiles shifted direction, spraying their destruction towards another of the task force's frigates. As Floros wondered if his adversary sought another sonar system, he overheard a report that the railguns had rendered the first frigate's bow-mounted array useless.

"I see that. But can he hope to think that taking away three hull-mounted systems will deafen our entire task force?"

"No, sir. He may simply be playing the odds of weakening our sonar coverage and thinking he can take his chances against the helicopters and the towed systems."

"He doesn't strike me as a commander who plays with uncertain odds," Floros said. "He's calculating something."

"He must know that our missile load among the task force is enough to force him to submerge while we close in on him. He also knows that he'd need some luck to cripple all the propulsion systems on every ship to prevent cannons from getting into range against him. So, he knows his best odds of escape are while submerged."

"Perhaps," Floros said. "Perhaps he's just shifting the odds in his favor, or is he doing something cleverer."

The officer stared through the bridge windows at the clear sunny seas while calculating odds. Then his face flushed.

"Maybe, sir. There's a fundamental difference between a bow-mounted sonar system and towed systems."

"Yes," Floros said. "He can shoot holes in one kind and not the other, as he's proving on his third frigate now."

"Not just that, sir. The bow-mounted systems must search in the shallow surface channels because that's where they're located. If I were him, and I just deafened the task force in the surface channel, that's where I'd evade."

"Shallow. Where he can also surface rapidly and shoot down helicopters if needed, or shoot at our cannons or propulsion systems or missiles or any other accursed target he wants."

"Yes, sir. I think he's going to try to evade in the surface channel, just beneath the waves."

Floros recognized his opportunity to outthink his enemy.

"We'll have to keep our helicopter dipping systems and trailed sonar systems in the surface channel to find him. Get this advice to all undersea assets."

As he issued the order, the *Hydra's* Phalanx system protested the *Goliath's* incoming shots, and sonic cracks pounded the bridge windows. Floros held a railing as the seasoned ship-handling lieutenant barked orders to wiggle the frigate out of the way of projectiles that slipped by the close-in weapon system, but a projectile found its way into the bow.

Screeching metal howled.

"That took out fifteen percent of our bow-mounted sonar system's hydrophones," the *Hydra's* commander said. "Shall I generate a smoke screen and attempt to circle back, sir?"

"No," Floros said. "Grant him the inevitable. The bow-mounted sonar systems will soon be useless, but we know what he's doing, and we're twenty-five minutes from having him blanketed with gunfire coverage."

The radar return from the combat transport ship disappeared, and its icon shifted to a submerged target.

"The *Goliath* just dove below the three Harpoons, sir."

"Slowed. Silenced. Disadvantaged. Have all ships move in at flank speed."

The *Hydra's* commander tapped a command into the display, sending the order through a tactical data system. Floros watched his eyes flit across the screen absorbing incoming reports.

"All commanders acknowledge the order of flank speed, sir. We'll have two ships within gunfire range in twenty-two minutes."

"Good. Let us turn this unprovoked attack against our homeland into our glory. Let us be the nation that silences this international menace."

Floros realized the absurdity of events that had started with his defense of an oil rig but had seen hostile vandalism transform him into an instrument of vengeance. He thought he'd slipped beyond the bounds of reality, watching some other man in his captain's uniform lead his nation's hunt.

As airborne graphics of anti-ship missiles traced arcs around the dive point of the now-hated vessel, the radar return came back, signifying his adversary's skill in timing his exposure above the waves.

"He's taken down two Harpoons already," the *Hydra's* commander said. "And he has a broadside shot at the third. He's using his Phalanx system and railguns well, sir."

"I can see that. This challenges my working theory that he intends to evade in the surface channel. Send three more Harpoons at him, this time one each from the south, west, and east, timed for simultaneous arrival. Make sure he follows his own damned plan and keeps his damned railguns submerged while we move into gunfire range."

As the *Hydra's* commander extended his fingers towards the display to coordinate the strike, a bridge officer scurried to his side. Animated, the man shouted his news, and Floros overheard it.

The *Goliath* was hailing him.

"In Greek?" Floros asked.

"Yes, sir! A translator I assume. Perfect Greek. He's speaking on high-frequency voice."

"Is he still on the line?"

"Yes, sir!"

"Put him on the speaker."

He raised his nose upward towards a microphone and projected his voice.

"This is Captain Nicos Floros of the Hellenic Navy. I'm the

commander of the Hellenic task force you've been illegally attacking. With whom am I speaking?"

"Through a translator, you are speaking with the commanding officer of the combat transport ship, *Goliath*."

The *Hydra's* commander stepped in Floros' view and begat a low-volume discussion.

"Should I launch the Harpoons, sir?"

"No, not yet. Stand by."

Floros raised his voice again.

"You claim no country's flag? Then you admit to your piracy? You also demonstrate your cowardice by withholding your personal name."

"Both omissions are matters of practicality for my mission. Another matter of practicality, your safety and that of your sailors, is the reason I contacted you."

"You have great audacity to think that I'd even speak to you," Floros said.

"But you've proven yourself wise enough to listen. I offer you a truce. I will withhold my weapons and drive away in peace if you withhold yours, and you will never again have to deal with me in your waters."

"You call that a truce?" Floros asked. "You skulk into my homeland, attack my people's energy infrastructure, kill innocent people, and expect me to let you go? You are truly insane."

"I have six torpedoes targeted at your four largest ships and two other ships of my random choosing. By my reckoning, that includes the one you're standing on. Note that I don't have the luxury of humane warheads like my colleagues. All my weapons are heavyweight torpedoes that will crack six keels and vaporize flesh. I wish I could offer you a less violent threat, but such are my constraints."

Unsure why, the verbal exchange shifted Floros' thought patterns about how he would finish the *Goliath*. He redefined the enigma hybrid catamaran as a classical submarine for the duration of the battle and drew conclusions based upon this epiphany.

Knowing he would have the support of his vice admiral, he expected to take control of the Greek submarines that patrolled nearby. A *Scorpène*-class vessel had broken their wall, and he would transform the broken screen into hunters of the inferior submarine, *Goliath*. Including the *Pipinos*, which had forced the *Goliath* to flee from its well-placed torpedo, he would dedicate four submarines to chasing the wounded combat transport ship.

He recognized the folly of expecting four submarines to hunt as a unit, but he could commit three to setting up a perimeter around the *Goliath* while the fourth hunted. The surface combatants and helicopters would also join the perimeter, which they had drawn during their efforts to encircle their adversary.

In a flash of awareness, he stood in mesmerized awe of the simplicity of his decision. Having feared railguns, he'd countered with missiles and cannons. But the enemy sought to intimidate with torpedoes, and Floros would retaliate within the realm his nemesis had declared as the new battlespace.

But first, he wanted to challenge his enemy's bluff.

"Six torpedoes?" he asked. "I notice that you took damage to your port bow, right where your port torpedo nest is located. Why should I believe you have six torpedoes when I suspect you have only three?"

Bluffing or not, the intruder upon his nation's sovereignty fired back with respectable zeal, leaving Floros to hope that his submarine commanders could match their enemy's mettle as he planned to place the yoke of responsibility upon them to obliterate the upstart fleet's flagship.

"Because you can't know the effects of the damage I took. But I promise you one thing, Captain Floros of the Hellenic Navy. The first torpedo I launch will be aimed at you. If you continue this battle, I will crush the *Hydra* first."

## CHAPTER 20

Cahill shared a thought he considered strange.

"What if he agrees to the truce?"

"Then we'd know he's a liar," Walker said.

"Come on, I made a good argument, and maybe he doesn't give a damn about defending the old regime. Maybe he just wants to get home to his family and restart his life under the new puppet government."

"Then we'd go home, too, I guess," Walker said. "Or, as long as you're living in a fairy tale, we could first see if the new prime minister will let us tour the islands as his personal guest. We could visit tourist sites in the Aegean Sea on his yacht, and when we go ashore to dance with elves, you can ride his pet unicorn."

The Frenchman's voice issued from the console.

"Neither sarcasm nor fantasies become you, Liam," Renard said. "And he's not the prime minister yet, although I'm doing all I can to accelerate that."

"Even if you do push things along, it won't be in time for him to make this blasted task force stand down against me, will it?" Cahill asked.

"No, it won't. He's proven that he can negotiate peace about the oil rig with the Turks, but he's not entrenched enough yet to order his navy to let a criminal run free."

Cahill looked to his translator for a reply from the Greek captain, but a shaking head suggested a delay. While he assumed the task force commander digested his offer, he watched for signs of weapons launches and continued talking with his boss.

"Now you call me a criminal? You make it sound like I deserve to be sunk. Should I just give in to guilt and surrender?"

"When you signed up with my fleet, you agreed to be vilified by those we prosecute. However, the praises from my clients for your actions are lofty, and I'm more energized than ever to negotiate your exit."

Cahill reflected upon his narrow escape from the Russian Navy at the bottleneck exit from the Black Sea.

"More energized than when you saved us from the Russians? I thought you were pretty well energized back then, and you barely got us out in time to keep the Black Sea from being our tomb."

"I was more desperate then than energized," Renard said. "What I mean now is that I expect a positive outcome. The political movement in Greece has been more favorable than I had expected, and I anticipate the ultimate approval of our actions from all major stakeholders in our mission."

Cahill realized his French boss let ambition blind him to the immediacy of the real crisis.

"We're still out here exposed and vulnerable, but you sound like you're already declaring victory."

"I'm declaring a victory for that which we've already won," Renard said. "Credibility. We've all won it together as a growing team. After proving our efficacy and our reliability in the Black Sea, we piqued the interest of many wealthy nations. Now, in this campaign, we've shown our abilities firsthand to the richest client base. We have a very bright and profitable future."

Cahill looked again to his translator for a reply to his offer of peace, but the Greek task force's commander remained silent.

"All well and good for repeat business, mate, assuming you get me arse out of here to repeat it for you."

"Therein lies the challenge," Renard said.

"Too bad you can't just throw down cash on the table and make the problem go away."

"Never discount bribery when I'm negotiating, but that option's not available to me quite yet. However, I must admit I overheard you doing a fine job of negotiating with the Hellenic task force commander in your own right. What inspired you to suggest that you have six torpedoes available?"

"I have no idea what made me think about it. I know bloody well they were torn away when we lost our port bow, but I just wanted to sound convincing when I told me translator I had six torpedoes. The truth is, I don't know why I didn't flinch. Thankfully, me translator didn't know enough about the damage to call me bluff on it, and he delivered the message like a champion."

"But I suspect our adversary saw through the charade," Renard said. "Just be ready to run when your offer is rejected."

"Don't worry, Pierre. I'm ready to slip away as soon as this verbal jousting is done. I have to admit, I hate waiting for the man to flinch. I much prefer action to talking."

As if prompted by fate's irony, Captain Floros' answer issued from the loudspeaker, and Cahill understood its tone before the translator confirmed the Greek officer's declining of the offer.

"That was gracious of him to finally answer," Cahill said.

"Despite his delay, I agree," Renard said. "I think he respected you for offering him the peace, and he's paying you a gesture of respect by giving you a direct answer. As expected, however, he cannot accept your terms. I suggest that you also respond now with a gesture of respect, but be firm."

Cahill looked to his translator.

"Tell him that the next time I offer him a peaceful solution, my terms will be less flexible."

The translator spoke the message, garnering no response.

"I see one missile each departing from three ships," Renard said. "I missed the launches due to degradation of the thermal imagery under the smoke clouds, but I've verified that missiles are flying at you. Check for them on your tactical system and take note that your time on the surface is now limited."

"Understood," Cahill said.

He glanced at his boss' face and saw him looking down from his camera while hearing the audio report flowing through his headset. While Renard's thoughts drifted away, Cahill set the *Goliath* into action.

"Find me a target to shoot before I submerge us, Liam. I want to make use of the time up here."

"The helicopters are still too far away," Walker said. "I recommend propulsion equipment, starting with the frigate to the east. The return is spotty under chaff and the smoke screen, but we can get some decent shots into its engine room. I recommend ten splintering rounds before we submerge."

Cahill ordered the suggested attack, and while Walker oversaw the railguns, the Frenchman offered his parting update.

"Interesting," Renard said. "Jake just reported movement of the Hellenic submarines. It may mean nothing, but I shall forward you the information on the low-bandwidth channel as I receive it."

"Thanks, Pierre."

"I've also ordered Jake north to assist you," Renard said. "He's grown quite fond of his new Russian friends and believes he can use them to protect you when you're within reach of his aid. God willing, that will be soon."

"Great to know, mate."

"Ah, and I believe your railgun rounds just hit something incendiary on your targeted frigate. I saw a fire blooming through the smoke cloud from the satellite's infrared."

"No more time for talking," Cahill said. "Got to go."

He submerged the *Goliath* below the incoming Harpoon missiles, grasping a rail as the deck dipped. Then he reversed the floor beneath his feet and invoked a fifteen-degree up angle to overcome the port bow's hydrodynamic disadvantage.

As his ship settled, he checked his tactical display and noticed a surprise. Renard's update showed the Greek surface combatants turning away from him, and he pointed at their icons.

"What do you think that's all about?"

"Not sure yet." Walker said. "It could be them taking your torpedo threat seriously, but we know bloody well they're aware that we only have three torpedoes."

"That's still three cracked keels. That could be enough to scare them all off," Cahill said.

He suspected his adversary's turning away was more involved than his bravado suggested, but he let his optimistic declaration linger to invite his executive officer's feedback.

"Maybe," Walker said. "But we need to think there's more to it than a defensive posturing. The latest volley of Harpoons proves that this Captain Floros isn't afraid to shoot weapons."

Cahill kept his subconscious mind working on the riddle while using the conversation to assess the new geometry.

"No matter the reason, it gives us breathing room," he said. "All those anti-ship missiles stay farther away, those cannons stay out of range, and the helicopters will be staying back, too."

"Agreed. But you look like there's something you don't like about it."

Curling his shoulders over the plot, Cahill rested his weight on his forearms and thought through the transforming battlespace. A monumental shift in the Greek strategy came into focus.

"Pierre said Jake heard some submarine movement," he said. "If subs are moving and surface combatants are keeping their distance, that means something. In fact, I think it means everything."

He pushed his torso vertical and enunciated his logic for Walker's benefit while he reached for a stylus.

"Jake pushed through the submarine defenses too easily–too quickly. He did it so fast that they gave up trying to stop him and turned their entire focus on us."

"I was afraid you'd say that," Walker said.

"Yeah, mate. They're coming for us. The entire Greek submarine fleet that's anywhere near us is now hunting. The wall to the south that was trying to keep Jake out lost two of its subs from the order of battle, but that leaves three subs from that wall plus the one that already shot at us."

"This ship's a marvel of technology," Walker said. "But beating a wolf pack isn't our specialty. We're not built for it."

Cahill drew ovular estimates of the surface ships, helicopters, and submarines tightening around him. His prison became clear, and he assumed that simplicity and fear of friendly fire dictated having one submarine–whichever the Greek Navy deemed the most capable–enter the enclosed arena to kill him.

Then a spark of optimism let him consider an alternate scenario in which politics dictated the identity of his foe, and he hoped the most arrogant commanding officer would use his personal connections to gain entrance into the duel. Perhaps, Cahill hoped, even with a wounded ship that was inferior in a straight undersea battle, he could outwit a halfwit.

Then a deeper burning optimism rose within him as he considered Jake. His colleague, his friend, his cavalry. Time worked in Cahill's favor as the *Specter* raced north to intercede.

But he wondered what Jake could do to help him. He suspected the Greek submarines had started north of his colleague and had headed northward first, enjoying a two-hour head start.

Having planned to slip past a semi-deafened frigate, Cahill rethought his egress. A submarine now supported each wounded surface combatant, and with the task force's curling around him, the south, west, and east were blocked. To the north, the *Hydra* remained, taunting him to attempt passage to dead end shorelines of the nation he'd attacked.

All doors seemed closed. All doors were closed–until a burst of brilliance graced his awareness.

"You're right," he said. "We can't beat a wolf pack. But I see a way out of this predicament."

"That's mighty clever of you, given that you're the only one who's certain what our predicament is."

"I am. And I could use a distraction to help get out of it."

"The Harpoons are still circling above us, I believe."

Walker looked towards the sonar supervisor, who nodded.

"Then get a communications buoy ready for Pierre," Cahill said. "I want Jake to put some slow-kill weapons into the eastern-most frigate and its escorts."

"You want him to blow a hole for us to exit?"

"Yes, that's exactly what I want him to do."

"But you expect there's a submarine in that area, or at least there'll be one by the time Jake could get there."

"Right. I do expect that, but I didn't say I was going use the exit. I just want Jake to create it."

Walker slid across the chart, pulled out a keyboard, and started clicking its keys. His typing speed impressed Cahill.

"The message is loaded," Walker said. "I assume you want it

set to transmit as soon as it hits the surface?"

"Yes, set the buoy for immediate transmission. Time is critical."

"The buoy is ready."

"Launch it."

The executive officer tapped a key and confirmed the buoy's ascent.

"What orders now?" Walker asked. "Do you want to wait for Renard to confirm receipt of the buoy's message?"

"No need. Whether or not Jake and Pierre help me, I know what I'm doing next."

"Shall I make ready another communications buoy to let Pierre know your plans?"

"Yes," Cahill said. "And get ready for a decisive move you won't soon forget."

## CHAPTER 21

Jake checked the *Specter's* speed.

"Eleven knots," he said. "How long do I have on the battery?"

"Three hours until you need to recharge, another ten minutes until cell reversal," Henri said. "We can't catch any hostile surface combatants before needing to snorkel, but we can reach torpedo range of the nearest frigate and its gunboat escorts."

"True, assuming they stay away from Terry. But that's not what's bothering me. It's this eleven-knot chase that's bothering me. We're half deaf at this speed."

"The Greek submarines are moving equally fast."

Jake stepped down to the chart and looked at clouds of doubt and inaccuracy.

"We don't know what the heck they're doing," he said. "It's all guesses, all conjecture."

"But informed conjecture," Henri said. "Need I remind you that Antoine heard two submarines turning north after you damaged two others and sent them to the surface?"

"Yes, I remember. But that doesn't mean they all headed north. And even if they did, one could have turned back."

"The most likely scenario is that they're all chasing Terry. You demoralized them when you broke their ranks, and they're likely chasing the weaker and more valuable prey."

Disliking the ambiguity of facing hidden hostile submarines, Jake chose caution.

"Slow to four knots."

"Four, Jake?" Henri asked. "We'll be delayed in aiding the *Goliath*."

"You heard me."

The Frenchman relayed the order to the engineering spaces and joined Jake by the charting table where he lowered his voice.

"I think you're being paranoid. All the Hellenic submarines must be heading north after Terry. He needs our speed of intercession, not our caution."

"What if one sub stayed behind in ambush waiting for me to speed by with that nice high bearing rate that torpedoes love? If they're smart, that's what they're doing. They're baiting me into a race to the north and leaving one sub behind to spring the trap."

"But you trust the dolphins now, don't you?" Henri asked. "They're insurance against such an attack."

"I trust them only as well as they can communicate. And even they have limits on what they can hear."

"You may as well find out what they hear now."

"Okay. I can do at least that much."

Jake ordered Remy to query the dolphins for all contacts. While listening for enemy vessels, his sonar expert oversaw a younger technician in interfacing with the mammals. As the clicks and whistles fed information into the Subtics system, large ovals of range uncertainty overlaid the submarines.

All submerged contacts were distant from the cetaceans, making their data useless for tracking the hostile threats, but it gave Jake relief that none were close to him. After stepping around the table, he crouched beside his sonar expert, who slid an earpiece to his jaw to listen.

"The range data says we're safe," Jake said. "But I want to do a secure active search to be sure."

"I understand what you're thinking, but keep in mind that the Greek submarine crews have probably figured out we're using the dolphins against them. The exchanges we just had with the dolphins for our updates might have given away an idea of where we are."

"All the more reason for a secure active search to make sure we're alone."

"But the more chance that any nearby submarine is alerted and listening."

"Do it. Five millisecond pulse, one-quarter power, three hundred and sixty degrees."

Remy called up a command screen, tapped an icon, and invoked a display showing the thin outgoing sonic pulse. Holding his breath, Jake watched the sound expand outward without a returning echo.

"Okay," he said. "We're alone."

He stood.

"Henri, bring us back to eleven knots."

"With pleasure."

An hour later, Jake stood from his captain's chair to stretch his legs. He wished the icon of the nearest frigate to get closer to the central crosshair representing the *Specter* on his display so that he could attack it, but physics constrained the rate of closure.

While he lamented his submarine's speed limits, he watched his sonar expert exchange words with a junior technician.

"The dolphins announced a range shift," Remy said. "A target has just moved from far range to in between near and far."

Jake stepped down to the central table to see it.

"There's only one contact it could be," he said.

"Yes," Remy said. "Target five."

"That's a gift," Jake said. "Set the range to ten miles and assign tube one to target five. Medium-speed run. Anti-submarine mode. Set the active seeker to turn on at six miles."

"Tube one is ready," Remy said.

"Very well. Shoot tube one."

Jake felt the pressure change in his ears.

"Tube one indicates normal launch," Remy said. "I have wire control. I hear its propeller."

As the icon of this weapon extended towards Jake's intended victim, Henri stood and walked to the table.

"The dolphins will reach their recommended rest time in three hours and their mandatory rest in six hours. They'll need to rest and feed in six hours, no matter how hard you push them."

"This mess should be resolved by then," Jake said. "Set an alarm for four and five hours from now and remind me of the dolphins' rest requirements at each interval."

Henri returned to his station, and Jake saw something on the display he disliked.

"Antoine, slow weapon one to slow search speed. I don't want it catching target five too soon."

"I've set weapon one to slow search speed," Remy said.

"Very well, Antoine."

The French mechanic approached Jake.

"What's your concern?" Henri asked.

"Giving away our position to the easternmost frigate and its escorts. It would give away only blunt data, but no need to broadcast it early. I intend to have weapons in the water heading for the surface ships before weapon one detonates."

"Understood. I support it," Henri said.

"Let's plan it out, then," Jake said.

"I'm listening."

"We have two gunboats and one frigate to the east. I'll launch weapons at the gunboats first since they're three and five miles farther away than the frigate. I'm going to double up weapons since they're slow-kills. I won't sink anything, but I'll cripple the gunboats and distract the frigate's captain while he tries to plug forty or so small holes in his ship. Make sense?"

"Of course, but only if you're sure Terry's going to come this way. Isn't that speculative, given that he'd be a fool to try to push through the submarines that now hunt him?"

Jake reflected upon the prison break, and for a moment it seemed absurd in its impossibility. Then he remembered his dolphins–his advantage. They could enable his quest to sanitize the waters of hidden Hellenic hunters.

"Agreed there's a lot of submarines out there to clear away before we can spring him free, but we need to do this one step at a time."

"What's the first step then?"

"We hamper the surface ships from long range since we have Pierre sending us their targeting data and since they're driving back and forth across their patrol areas predictably."

"Despite the long-range shots, you make good points. The

surface combatants are vulnerable."

"And it gives me time to reload all my tubes while still approaching the area."

"Then you'll be giving up wire guidance and leaving the torpedoes to their own random fates. Six torpedoes may hit the same ship, and they may all miss completely."

Jake recalled the unusual guidance his boss had rendered prior to his departure for the mission. Renard had encouraged liberal use of weapons despite the chance of wasted ordnance, convincing him that the Frenchman had negotiated a monumental payment from his European clients.

"I'll take my chances. It may waste torpedoes, but Pierre's not too particular about the operational costs of this mission.

After Henri agreed, Jake aimed his voice at Remy.

"How's weapon one looking?"

"Fine, Jake."

"Can I cut the wire?"

"I recommend against it," Remy said.

"You always recommend against it. But do I really need to guide weapon one?"

"Only if target five tries to evade in the next–I'd say–three minutes."

"Cut the wire to tube one," Jake said. "Henri, have tube one backhauled and reloaded with a slow-kill weapon."

As the French mechanic relayed orders to the torpedo technicians and managed their efforts, Jake addressed Remy.

"Assign tubes one and two to gunboat five, tubes three and four to gunboat six, and tubes five and six to frigate three. Have the seekers wake up eleven miles away, medium-speed run, anti-surface mode."

Remy acknowledged the order and turned to the technician beside him to verify he adjusted the presets to each weapon. But an unsolicited burst of chirps and whistles froze him.

"That's a new one," Jake said. "What's it mean?"

"I'm not sure," Remy said. "I'm waiting for the system to finish its voice recognition."

"So, it is a new message we haven't heard?"

The sonar expert delayed his answer while pressing his muffs into his ears.

"Yes," Remy said. "It's a new message. But now I hear a Doppler shift on target five. Target five is turning away."

Jake slid around the navigation table and stood behind his sonar guru. He slapped the shoulders of the technicians seated on either side of him.

"You–torpedo presets. You–dolphin communications. Figure out what they said and send them a confirmation."

Jake then leaned into Remy's ear.

"And you tell me what hostile sounds are out there and what they're doing. Then get me updates from the kids on either side of you and let me know what's going on."

As the veteran nodded and curled his chin towards his chest to listen to the water's acoustic clues, the dolphins surprised Jake with another report of a new undersea contact.

Then they reported again.

Then they reported a fourth time.

"What the heck?" Jake asked. "Are they stuttering?"

The fury of conversations in front of him prompted his patience, and he folded his arms while waiting.

"Torpedoes in the water," Remy said. "At least four, all coming from the bearing of target five. Target five just launched a salvo at us."

"Shit. Right full rudder, steady course one-zero-zero."

The deck angled.

"I'm analyzing how good the shots are now," Remy said.

"Damn it," Jake said. "There's a good shot in that salvo since I fed them our bearing by talking to the dolphins. That crew figured out the big fake dolphin that kept talking too much was us."

"They have no idea of our range, other than the blunt estimate wave-front analysis of our transmissions may have granted them," Henri said.

The torpedo seeker alarm wailed, piercing Jake's ears.

"Silence it!" he said.

As a technician stopped the electronic howling, Jake looked at the torpedo seeker's bearing and recognized the danger.

"Their ignorance of our range may be the only reason we can get out of this alive," Jake said. "The first torpedo has a near-zero bearing rate, but they have it running slow and searching for us too early."

"Understood," Henri said. "Countermeasures?"

"No. Not yet. Maybe never."

"We're steady on course one-zero-zero. The rudder is amidships. Do you wish to accelerate?"

"No. Let's make sense of what we hear first. Antoine?"

"The other three torpedo seekers just went active," Remy said. "But I'd still like you to slow to hear what target five and the surface ships are doing."

"That's risky."

"Your turn to the right already has the closest torpedo on the left drawing slight left. All the other torpedoes are also on the left drawing slight left."

Jake twisted his torso to the tactical scene on the table and saw lines fanning out every fifteen seconds with raw bearings to the four incoming torpedoes.

"Two of them may draw slight right if I slow. That means they'd be overtaking us on possible intercept courses."

"We'll be fine once you speed up again."

"Unless target five still has a wire and steers them towards us," Jake said.

"I need you to slow to tell you what target five is doing."

"Fine. Shit. I'll give you five knots for thirty seconds. Henri, slow to five knots."

While the *Specter* slowed, Jake addressed the technician seated to Remy's left. The sailor confirmed the assignments of all six loaded slow-kill weapons to the proper three surface ships.

When the ship's speed fell to five knots, Jake began a silent countdown and burned his eyes on Remy, hoping for insight. Before thirty mental seconds elapsed, the guru slid his listening equipment behind his neck and looked up at Jake.

"Target five is making twenty-two knots and will evade. It's already slipped outside weapon one's seeker cone. The good news is that it probably lost the wires to all its weapons while turning and sprinting away."

"I don't like it, but I can live with it. What else have you got?"

"The surface combatants you assigned our torpedoes to aren't turning back where you'd expect them to turn back. They've broken from their repeated patrol patterns and are continuing to the east."

"But that's outside the battlespace," Jake said. "It's like they're quitting the battle and walking away."

"Or it's like target five told them about us, and they rightly assumed we were getting ready to shoot torpedoes at them."

"I see. It's been thirty seconds. Can I speed up now?"

"Yes, I recommend that you do, or else the first torpedo may become a threat."

"Henri, make turns for eleven knots."

Jake turned from his sonar ace and watched Renard's low-baud data trickle across the tactical display. Updates to the easterly frigate and its gunboat escorts aligned with Remy's observations.

"Shit," he said.

He made a rare trip to Henri's station to solicit the Frenchman's advice. His unofficial therapist and tactical sounding board swiveled in his chair and faced him.

"A lot just happened to us. What's your first thought?"

"Great question," Jake said. "Forcing me to prioritize the noise in my head. Let's start with why target five made one good shot at me and three shitty ones. It could easily instead have been two or three good ones to increase the probability of hitting me."

"Do what you always do, and start with the geometry."

"Yeah. Good thinking. Hold on."

Jake visualized the data, played with it in his mind, and

sought significance in the multitude of objects in motion.

"There's a large bearing separation in the three bad shots," he said. "I assume that's because they had three different running speeds, like target five shot them at fast speed, medium speed, and slow speed to spread them out in front of us."

"In front, like a wall to the north."

"Shit, Henri, those three torpedoes are a temporary version of the wall the Greek submarines set up between Terry and us the first time. But I can't shoot torpedoes out of the way, and I need to run from the good shot coming at us."

"And even the good shot erred to the north," Henri said. "All four torpedoes had either a primary or secondary goal of forcing us away from the *Goliath*."

After a moment to ponder the insight, Jake felt his heart plummet into his stomach.

"I can't help Terry," he said.

"I'm afraid I agree," Henri said. "At least I agree for the short term. Have faith that he'll find a way to survive a bit longer than you hope, and think through the long-term options."

Jake's mind raced into a temporary panic, but then he assessed the factors governing his situation, and he drew calmness from the methodical analysis.

"Let's next get the dolphins into a holding pattern before they slip out of range. We can't keep up with them anymore. Antoine, order them to hold their position."

Remy sent the order, receiving silence as the response.

"They were only eight miles ahead of us," Jake said. "They should still be in range. Try them again. Jack up the power to full."

Again, the sonar guru issued the command and the dolphins ignored it. Jake struggled to recall if there was a mitigation for letting the Russian animals swim beyond communications range, but he wanted to avoid the situation.

"One more time," he said.

The response of chirps and whistles relieved Jake.

"They acknowledge the order to hold their position," Remy

said. "They may have lingered near the surface during their last breath, but they're back underwater now."

"Very well, Antoine. Henri, get a communications buoy ready for Pierre to update him on all the submerged contacts, including our course and speed and the position of our dolphins."

"I shall see to it. Do you have any recommendations for him, or for Terry?"

Having considered Cahill's fate dire, Jake appreciated Henri's subtle challenge. He leaned his hips into the navigation table and forced himself to brainstorm a positive outcome for his colleague.

The constraints of submarines to the south of Cahill narrowed and accelerated his thoughts. He conjured up one idea he found risky and desperate, and he hoped he could get it to Cahill in time to act upon it–or reject it for a better option.

"Yeah," he said. "I've got a recommendation for you to type into that buoy. It's ugly, but if Terry or Pierre can't think of anything better, it's all we've got."

## CHAPTER 22

After inspecting the space for structural integrity, Cahill had relocated his command to the *Goliath's* bridge. A glance above him confirmed the distant daylight, which he welcomed.

As he approached his target, he groped for optimism and lofted encouraging words to his executive officer in hopes that an uplifting response might raise his spirits.

"This can work, Liam."

"I thought it was crazy when you first said it," Walker said.

Feeling no positive energy, he tried again to coax a spark of enthusiasm.

"Pierre's data feed said Jake recommended the same plan. That's two smart blokes thinking of it independently, if you'll humor me on calling meself smart."

"You're smart enough, alright. But I've never accused you of being sane. Given the two blokes who managed to concoct the idea, independently or not, now I'm certain it's crazy."

"Any better ideas?"

Walker offered a blank stare.

"None. But it doesn't mean I have to like yours."

"We can't just sit here and hope that four submarines happen to miss us while they scour waters the size of a postage stamp."

"I'd like to think that we can, actually. Things that are hidden have tendencies to stay hidden if they don't do drastic things to make themselves discoverable."

Cahill glared.

"You're thinking like a surface warfare officer again."

"Just telling you how I see it, and I don't like it."

"We've done this before. Why do you think it's so crazy?"

"Because we've never done anything like this before."

"The *Krasnodar*, mate," Cahill said. "What's wrong with your memory? That was only three months ago."

"Oh, that *Krasnodar*," Walker said. "Silly me. I completely missed the parallels between a stranded and crippled Russian submarine and a fully healthy *MEKO-200* frigate that's already used its weapons and helicopters to blow twenty percent of our ship off."

Cahill clenched his jaw and vented his frustrations through gritted teeth.

"Again, mate. Do you have any better ideas?"

"None. Should I shut up now and start following orders?"

"I'm always open to your ideas, but if you're out of them, you're out of them."

"I guess I just needed to bitch about it."

"Very well, then. Now would be a good time to shut up and follow orders."

"Let me get into character then."

Cahill scoffed.

"You need to act to be me executive officer?"

"Rarely. Sometimes. Okay, more often than I care to admit. If I didn't detach me mind from me body with all the shit you make me do, I'd soil me britches every other day."

"I'm doing the same thing now, mate. I'm getting me head around this insanity before I share it with the gang. Here goes."

He tapped an icon and aimed his nose at a microphone.

"Listen up, lads. If you're not scared, you're either braindead or lying. So keep your mind focused on your job, do it right, and trust your shipmate to do the same. We're the best crew money can buy, and we're the best combat-tested band of mates on the high seas. We're going to sneak up on the *Hydra*, surface beside it, and cripple it. Once that's done, I'll deliver me terms to the Greek task force commander and have you all drinking beer in Toulon by tomorrow night. That's all."

"Sounds great," Walker said. "Now how do you propose to do it?"

Cahill reflected upon the defenses that opposed him. The *Hydra* had sacrificed its helicopter in a failed hunt, and the submarines remained to his south. His railguns had silenced the hostile bow sonar, leaving a variable-depth sonar pinging for him below the surface channel in which he hid.

The frigate relied on speed as its primary advantage, but

Renard's updates simplified the tracking. To survive, Cahill needed to predict his target's future location and maneuver to it.

Facing a nineteen-knot speed disadvantage, he feared the impossibility of his task except for one fact–the Greek task force commander mistook the hunter for the hunted and the predator for the prey.

"We need only help Captain Floros achieve his intent," Cahill said. "He's looking for us, and he will find us."

"His intent is to find us with a cannon round or a torpedo," Walker said. "You'll have to be a bit more specific on how you intend to throw a wrinkle into his plans."

Cahill tested his second-in-command.

"What do you fear the most about that ship?" he asked.

"The cannon."

"Why the cannon?"

"Even if there were any Harpoons left, we could dive below them. But you can't dive below cannon rounds because they penetrate the water far enough to hit us if we submerge too slow or too shallow."

"What about the torpedoes?"

"They have half the range of the cannon."

"But with our damage, we're slowed if we need to evade."

"That's only relevant if we get close enough for torpedoes to matter."

Cahill raised his eyebrow at Walker.

"And?"

"Shit, Terry. You want to get within six miles of that thing?"

"No, mate. I want to get within six inches."

Though alone with him on the bridge, Walker stepped to Cahill and lowered his voice.

"Have you really thought this through, or are you making this up as you go along?"

"I have a plan, and I'm trying to explain it to you."

"I thought you were quizzing my knowledge of the *MEKO-200*-class to prove how insane you are. I'm changing me answer to torpedoes, by the way, since you plan on getting so close."

"And therein lies me point," Cahill said. "We'll be too close for torpedoes due to anti-circular run safeguards. You were right the first time. The cannons are the concern."

Walker's eyes narrowed.

"Until we're within six miles. Then we're torpedo fodder."

"Unless we're within half a mile when we surface. That's too close for a Mark 46 torpedo to launch and acquire us."

"It's actually a bit farther out than that, if you're feeling like a superhero. May as well test the limits with our lives."

"Pierre was right," Cahill said. "Cynicism doesn't become you."

"That was sarcasm, mate, but my point still stands. I thought your idea was crazy when you suggested it. Now that you're spitting out the details, I'm convinced you're trying to kill us."

"But if I can get us that close to the *Hydra*, the only concern would be the cannons, don't you agree?"

"Well, yeah. But how do you propose to sneak up on something doing anti-submarine zigzag legs at twenty-eight knots when we're limited to nine?"

Cahill pointed to the screen.

"It stopped doing zigzag legs five minutes ago. It's on a predictable track, and our last turn placed us on an intercept course."

"Perhaps for the time being. What if it veers?"

"If it veers, I'll send a torpedo on either side of it to entice it to come back to the middle."

"It's too deaf to hear us launch torpedoes."

"But its friendly submarines aren't. I'd turn on our torpedoes' seekers early to make tracking them easy, and the subs would provide the warning."

"Our gunners are going to have to be perfect," Walker said.

"The Mark 45 cannon is a big target, and it's sitting right there on the forecastle in plain sight. Even if they hit low, they'll hit the magazine or its loading and maneuvering components.

As a system, it's a big and complex target with moving parts, and one well-placed splintering round can take it down."

"Or it could take ten rounds or more, in which case, it'll have time to spit hell back on us from point-blank range."

"But we'll have the element of surprise and be attacking from point-blank range as well. And I'm also going to place us on the side so the cannon would have to rotate a good forty-five degrees to target us. That would give us an extra volley."

As Walker stepped away, placed his hands on a railing, and tensed his shoulders, Cahill braced for more objections. Knowing the crew trusted his executive officer's opinion, he needed his agreement for the risky plan.

"What about the close-in weapon systems?" Walker asked. "There's two on that ship, and that's three thousand holes in us."

"We'll take them out after we hit the cannon."

"Why not before the cannon? They could cripple our cannons before we take them out."

"You're discounting the element of surprise."

"And I have to be honest that I think you've placed an undue premium on the element of surprise," Walker said. "This is an alerted crew."

Cahill reconsidered.

"Very well. You make a good point. They can react much faster than the cannon. We'll take out the Phalanxes first."

Walker shook his head.

"Why all this fuss about how to outgun the *Hydra*? Why not continue north beyond it and try to escape to Turkish water?"

"Renard took that option off the table while the new prime minister is negotiating the oil rig's future with the Turks. We can't risk putting pressure on Turkish diplomacy by being found in Turkish water, or we'd screw over one of our major supporters. That would ruin everything we've been working for. But don't worry, I'll get us out of here in style with the *Hydra's* help."

"Then we've got nothing left to do but deftly move ourselves into spitting range of it."

"And then surface just our cannons, of course, and win a punching match."

"According to Pierre's data, we've got about forty minutes."

"Agreed. Get our best two gunners into the tactical control room with our A-team sonar techs for a briefing."

Thirty minutes later, his team knew their roles, and his gunners knew the vulnerable locations of the American-made Greek weapons to aim for.

As Cahill watched the sounds of the *Hydra* grow in strength, Renard's feed verified the proximity of his target.

"Five miles," he said.

The deck rolled and pitched in the shallows, and a report from the sonar supervisor brought a surprise.

"The *Hydra's* variable-depth sonar is now in the surface channel. I recommend going deep to avoid counter-detection."

"Very well," Cahill said. "Taking us to seventy meters."

He tapped several icons, ordering the *Goliath* deeper while maintaining the fifteen-degree up angle to combat the damage.

"Even with an up angle, we can descend smartly," he said. "I thought Pierre had overdone the size on the pumps, but the water management on this beast is amazing."

"Going deep makes it harder to surface at the right spot for our attack," Walker said. "Maybe we should delay our approach a bit and make sure we're dead ahead of the *Hydra*. That'll give us more time to maneuver, and it'll make us harder to be detected on the sonar, with a bow-on aspect."

"Now you're thinking like a submarine officer. We'll do it. Coming right to course zero-eight-zero. Slowing to four knots. Time to intercept is now fifteen minutes."

Cahill watched the crosshair of the *Goliath* reach the future track of the *Hydra*.

"Bringing the rudder to left full to point at the *Hydra*," he said. "I'm also reversing our angle to fifteen degrees down to elevate the cannons."

As the deck brought him steady and then rolled him forwards, he pressed an icon to hail his gunners.

"You ready, boys?"

Two voices responded over the loudspeaker.

"Sure, Terry."

"Damned right we are."

"Given our new position in front of the *Hydra*, you won't see the rear Phalanx when you hit the surface. Your firing order will be the forward Phalanx, then the cannon, then the rear Phalanx."

"Got it."

"Yeah, we both got it."

"If you can't see the cannon clearly, shoot through the bow. There's enough working parts to that thing below the forecastle that you can damage it without even seeing it."

"I'm ready."

"Me, too."

"Keep the communication line open, boys. It's all up to you now. I'm giving you both manual fire control. Raise your cannons when you're at minimum depth to do so, and start shooting the instant you're clear. Don't wait for me."

As he looked back to his display, he noticed the *Hydra* remained on course two miles away. He tapped graphics to give his ship a gentle rise in depth and to accelerate.

"I'm staging us shallow at fifteen meters," he said. "Bringing us up slowly. I'm also going to force this to happen a little to the right to give us a better field of fire and to give us maneuverability at three knots."

Daylight illuminated the bluish water above the dome.

"One mile," Cahill said.

"You're tempted to go early?" Walker asked.

"Yes, but I won't. Remember the torpedoes."

He tapped a key to bring the weapons bay camera images onto his monitors. They each showed dark blue murkiness.

"Sixteen hundred yards," he said.

"We're technically inside the minimum range of a Mark 46 torpedo now," Walker said.

"Agreed, but consider how fast that ship can maneuver beyond that minimum range and then launch at us. That's a good reminder for me to assign torpedoes to the *Hydra*, though."

Cahill tapped several graphics to open the outer doors to his surviving torpedoes and to set their aim at the frigate.

"Our weapons are ready," he said. "Twelve hundred yards."

"It's time, Terry."

"Get the translator up here while I raise the stern sections."

The monitors showed the sky as the weapons bays breached the surface. After a second, his eyes focused on the approaching frigate, and a pair of sonic booms told him his gunners were obeying his orders to fire when possible.

The warship appeared unaffected as the second pair of cracks echoed over Cahill's head, but then he saw smoke rising from the white dome of the *Hydra's* forward Phalanx system as another pair of booms raced by.

Unsure if the Phalanx could return fire, he hedged his bet.

"Port gunner, shift to the main cannon!" he said. "Starboard gunner stay on the Phalanx!"

With rounds covering the distance in less than half a second, Cahill's gunners proved capable at hitting their marks. Though the shots had little time to splinter, their small diameters of buckshot bore holes where needed.

The forward Phalanx looked like a used small arms target, and pockmarks riddled the cannon, but intelligent movement of the frigate exposed its rear Phalanx.

"Port gunner, stay on the main cannon!" he said. "Starboard gunner move to the after Phalanx!"

Below, Cahill heard the door open and the steps of the translator joining him on the bridge. Keeping his eyes on the monitors, he saw the Mark 45 cannon rotate towards the *Goliath*, but its barrel froze in a harmless direction while clouds of smoke rose from its punctured housing.

"Port gunner, shift to the after Phalanx!" he said. "Starboard gunner stay on the after Phalanx!"

As Cahill thought he'd bested the *Hydra*, its rear close-in weapon system erupted, and he heard echoes of shredded metal inside his ship. To his relief, he saw a solitary railgun shot puncture and silence the final threat to his ship.

Then his railguns fell silent.

"Weapons bays, report status!"

He heard a high-pitched voice.

"This is starboard weapons bay. My life just flashed in front of me. I'm unharmed, but I think a hundred rounds hit the cannon."

"I'm glad you're okay. How bad's your cannon?"

"It's out of commission. I don't know what all's been hit yet, but a lot of rounds came through and hit a lot of shit, Terry."

"Very well. What about the port weapon?"

The next voice sounded more calm.

"I'm out of commission, too, but I don't think I got hit as bad. One of us hit that Phalanx and stopped it as it was swinging at me. All the damage on the port cannon is on the capacitor."

"Can it be repaired?" Cahill asked.

"No way. It's Swiss cheese."

"This is going to make negotiations with the *Hydra* rough," Walker said. "Do you think you can bluff your way through?"

"Maybe. But maybe I don't have to."

He projected his voice to the microphone.

"Starboard weapons bay, how's your capacitor?"

"Untouched. All damage is to the cannon."

Cahill turned to Walker.

"Head aft, grab the biggest spare cables you can find, and cross-connect the capacitors. Get guys working on both sides of the ship and have them mate the connection in the tunnel."

"That could work. Each cannon has a spare cable, and they're long. I think we've also got some battery cables that can bear the load and close the gap."

"Get going."

"How long do I have?"

"As long as I can stall His Majesty, Captain Floros of the Hellenic Navy. He may need a demonstration at some point to verify that I'm the only one left with a usable cannon."

As Walker sprang down the stairs, Cahill reached for several icons. First, he energized his phased-array radar system to give him a view of nearby threats, and he was relieved to find none. He then opened a satellite communication to Renard, who offered a quick greeting and then promised to remain silent until needed. Finally, he opened a high-frequency voice line to the *Hydra*.

As the frigate sailed by him, he told his translator to hail it, and he heard an extended, angered response.

"If you can get a word in edgewise, tell the *Hydra* to stop or else I'll test how far me cannons can bore holes from its engine room to its bow."

When the Greek rant ceased, the translator relayed the message. After a hesitation, the voice Cahill recognized as belonging to Floros took on a suspicious tone.

"He says he destroyed your cannons with his Phalanx."

"Tell him, I concede damage to me starboard cannon, but I would prefer to avoid inflicting further damage upon him to prove him wrong about the port cannon. I have one cannon to his zero."

During another challenging Greek exchange, Cahill surfaced the entire ship and shifted his propulsion to the gas turbines. Huge volumes of air swooshed through the ducts that fed the engines. Unsure how the damage to his bow would slow him, he was ready to test his speed against that of the frigate.

The translator updated him.

"He says your ship is damaged and he can outrun you until he is outside minimum range for his torpedoes."

Cahill tapped a key to bring the *Goliath* to fifteen knots. He watched his port bow undulate in the swells and ignored the warnings from the port MESMA plant that complained of shaking.

"Tell him I have good enough speed to make that a difficult endeavor and that even if he succeeds, my torpedoes are bigger than his. Much bigger. Emphasize that."

A Greek exchange.

"He says that you only have three torpedoes, and he has a task force that will come and kill you if you attack him."

"Tell him I agree and might even let him choose which ships I sink in addition to the *Hydra*, which will enjoy the first cracked keel and bone-crushing shockwave through its decks."

While awaiting the translation, Cahill heard Walker's voice over the loudspeaker.

"Go ahead, Liam. What's your status?"

"I need at least fifteen more minutes. This is laborious work just connecting the cables, and then I've got men trying to override the charging circuit logic to let the starboard capacitor power the port cannon. We're just as apt to blow up our capacitor as we are to use it to power the starboard cannon, changing things this fast."

"Keep working," Cahill said. "I'll let you know if we need to risk firing. Don't try anything risky until I order it."

The response and translation came.

"Captain Floros has ordered the entire task force to surround our position, but he's agreed to slow while you state your intent."

"Tell him I intend to tie up to him and have him tow me out of the Aegean Sea."

Another Greek exchange.

"He wants to know why he has to tie you and tow you."

"It's so that his mates don't launch any weapons at me. They'll have as much chance as hitting him with missiles or torpedoes if they do."

A final Greek exchange.

"He's not promising you an escort out of the Aegean until he hears from his admiralty, but he agrees to begin towing you away. He says he agrees to tie you up since it's the only way he's guaranteed to know where your rotten ship's located at all times. He said to come to five knots, and he'll tie you to his stern."

Slowing the *Goliath* to five knots, Cahill wondered if he'd missed a detail. Renard would have to finalize the negotiated exit, but he trusted his boss in that element.

Just as he considered the Frenchman's role, he heard his voice from the console.

"That was well executed," Renard said.

Cahill verified the high-frequency voice line was off.

"You know that I don't have me port cannon up yet."

"I heard. Still, you will eventually, while he won't have anything to shoot at you. However, the rest of the task force will as soon as the assets move into position."

"But I've got me choice of three ships I can sink, and when Liam has the port cannon working, I can cripple the engine rooms of any combatant that tries to get in cannon range of me. I believe that gives you enough leverage to talk me out of this mess?"

The Frenchman's face lit up.

"Indeed it does," Renard said. "And I'm almost saddened that you made it too easy for me."

## CHAPTER 23

Jake leaned his hips against the plotting table.

"I love happy endings."

"Don't we all," Henri said.

"I don't like this eight-knot escort speed, though. It's too fast for my tastes. I can't hear everything I want, and we still don't know where all the Greek submarines are."

"Pierre had to concede their staying submerged to get his other demands met. I'd call it a minor detail in an otherwise resounding victory."

Jake reached for a railing as the deck pitched.

"How much longer until I can secure snorkeling?"

"Another twenty minutes," Henri said. "Then you'll have enough battery energy to maintain eight knots until we're safely out of Greek waters."

"How long until I can wake Andrei and Mikhail?"

"You're using their first names now?"

"They're hard not to like. How long until nap time is over?"

"Another hour and twenty minutes recommended. But you can roust them whenever you want. The manual says their trainer has made them flexible in this area, and they supposedly slept and ate a meal during their flight out here. So I expect that they're refreshed enough and fed."

"As long as we're in the surface channel, we'll wake them before we come down from snorkeling."

He turned to the navigation table and verified the dolphins' positions two miles behind him and two miles ahead of the *Hydra-Goliath* tandem. Realizing they'd drift behind the Greek ship if he waited to wake them, he changed his mind.

"On second thought, I think I'll wake them now. I want to keep them ahead of Terry."

"Good idea," Henri said.

"Antoine, send the wakeup message."

Chirps and whistles played over the loudspeaker, but the cetaceans remained silent.

"Try again," Jake said.

"Maybe they're groggy from too short a nap," Remy said. "Here goes another try."

This time, the dolphins responded with a wakeup acknowledgement and more.

"That seemed long for a wakeup message," Jake said. "And some of that sounded familiar, like we've heard it before."

"The second half of it was familiar," Remy said. "It was the new submerged contact message."

"Do they normally do that when they wake up?"

"That answer's not in the manual," Henri said.

Jake offered a quizzical look to his mechanic.

"You really memorized that thing?"

"I did. My assumption for the lack of such clarity is that you can't predict which contacts are old or new when you can't predict what changes around the dolphins while they sleep."

"But they can tell one submarine from another, can't they?"

"It depends. They can only tell the difference if there's a distinguishing feature between them. But if the submarines are outwardly equivalent, they can't tell. For example, they'd be challenged to distinguish the *Specter* from the *Wraith*."

Jake intensified his inquisitive stare, and the Frenchman reached for the printed manual on his console.

"It's all in the appendices," Henri said.

"I just thought that was meaningless theory behind the commands, but you're proving me wrong."

"You're quite welcome."

"Anyway, then we have no choice but to walk them through a complete report of submerged contacts."

"Agreed," Henri said. "We may as well verify that their worldview corresponds with ours."

"Antoine, order a range check and then query Andrei and Mikhail on all contacts."

The recorded orders played over the loudspeakers, and the mammals responded as commanded. Jake knew he offered the Greek submarines an idea of his location by issuing the orders, but during a ceasefire he accepted the risk in exchange for information.

He also expected that his secret role in escorting the *Goliath* to safety was a needless insurance policy. Renard had done what the Frenchman excelled at, and the negotiations were complete. With the threat of annihilation of the task force, the puppet prime minister had the leverage he needed to order the naval forces to honor the truce.

As part of creating the leverage, Jake had reloaded four of his tubes with heavyweight torpedoes, and each one targeted a different ship than Cahill's three weapons. Though not guaranteed to hit all seven ships, the combined threat of torpedoes from the *Specter* and the *Goliath* provided enough fear to motivate peace.

Despite his outward mannerisms and his attempts at inward assurance, Jake wondered why he felt like something was about to break.

He counted the submerged contacts as the dolphins reported. The sloppiness of the range information bothered him, and he made a mental note to ask the trainer to improve that feature. But the summation of data aligned with possible locations where his historic data suggested submarines and their drones would be.

Then came the new submarine, the one from the west that had fired at the *Goliath* and had escaped the dolphins' detection–until now. Jake heard the mammals report the first drone from that vessel but thought he missed something when the chirps and whistles stopped short of calling out a second drone.

"Every submerged submarine still has its drones out," he said. "These guys aren't making any pretense about lowering their guard."

"True," Henri said. "Nor should they. Pierre couldn't push for any special behavior of the submarines. It was too much to ask of the Greeks. How would you feel if he forced you to surface in the face of an adversary?"

"Like shit. Like a failed submariner. But that's not what's

bothering me. What's bothering me is why this new submarine to the west has only one drone."

"Because it's a torpedo," Remy said. "Torpedo in the water, bearing three-three-one."

Jake's adrenaline spiked.

"Can you hear its seeker?" he asked.

"No, just its high-speed screws, and barely. I would have needed another minute or two to hear it if not for the dolphins."

"Can you estimate the speed based upon blade rate?"

"Forty-five knots."

Jake watched lines of bearing fan out on his display.

"It's on our right drawing right. No concern to us, but track it against its bearing rate. Let's see if these Greeks have done what I hope they haven't."

"Shot at Terry?" Henri asked.

"Yeah," Jake said. "And it's time to let Pierre know. Secure snorkeling and raise the radio mast."

As Jake stepped to his chair, the ship stopped rumbling, and he saw Renard's face on his display.

"What's wrong, Jake?"

"Hold on, Pierre. Antoine, assign tube six to the new submarine."

"That's a heavyweight, Jake," Remy said.

"I know. Assign tube two as well. I'm planning to shoot a slow-kill and a heavyweight and shut one or both off depending how these bastards react."

"Tubes two and six are assigned to the new submarine, designated as target thirteen."

"Jake, what's going on?" Renard asked.

"I just picked up a new submarine to the northwest, and it shot a torpedo towards Terry."

"Mother of God," Renard said. "I was clear in my negotiations and resolute in my threats. Now this is escalating into another Black Sea crisis."

"May I shoot?"

"Absolutely not. The last thing we need is you letting anger get the better of you."

"I'm not angry," Jake said. "Well, okay, I am, but this is warranted anger."

"You're preparing to kill men for carrying out orders," Renard said. "I'm sure the fault lies with some inane mid-level admiral. Let me use diplomacy to rid us of this stupidity."

"Antoine," Jake said, "assign tube six back to the surface ship it was aimed at. Keep tube two assigned to target thirteen."

"Good move," Renard said. "Give me time to warn Terry and contact my diplomatic channels. I recommend you lower your radio mast to avoid detection. I'll hail you on the low-frequency feed if I need you."

"Thanks, Pierre. Henri, lower the radio mast. Take us to thirty meters."

The deck dipped and then leveled.

"Slow us to three knots," Jake said.

"Three?" Henri asked. "We'll be overrun by the *Hydra-Goliath* tandem in an hour at that speed."

"I don't think we'll stay slow that long. I just want to let Antoine get a better sense of what's out there."

He heard the French mechanic stand and cringed as he felt him move beside him.

"Why do you have this nasty habit of getting close to me when I don't want to hear from you?" Jake asked.

"Because I know when you don't want to hear from me," Henri said. "Can't you tell I know when you're hiding something?"

"It's like you're my living conscience. It's spooky. Yes, I'm hiding something."

"Well?"

"If that torpedo hits Terry, I am shooting a heavyweight at the submarine that launched it."

"I think that's what Pierre would want. That's not really a secret you need to guard."

Jake waited for the Frenchman to walk away, but he lingered.

"Okay, I'm also planning on sending Mikhail and Andrei to

lay explosive charges on it, and I'm not waiting to hear if the weapon gets shut down or not. That's the real reason I slowed. It's so I could stay in contact with them and bring them home when they're done."

"I see," Henri said. "A sort of retaliatory spanking for violating our ceasefire."

"Yeah, call it what you want. But that crew deserves a good scare for giving us a good scare."

"I can't say that I disagree.

Jake stood up straight.

"Seriously? You wouldn't think of me as a spoiled brat or an angry child if I sent them in now?"

"I think it's a fine punishment for shooting a torpedo at Terry, assuming they do indeed reconsider and shut it down."

"Thanks, Henri. Antoine, order the dolphins to lay explosive charges on target thirteen."

"That's a thirty-two-minute swim," Remy said. "I suggest you first make them approach the target and have them prepare to lay explosive charges when they get there."

"Fine. Send them on an approach to target thirteen."

Chirps and whistles signified the order and the obeying.

"Is the hostile torpedo still running?" Jake asked.

"Yes. Six minutes to impact," Remy said.

"Shit. How the heck do they expect to hit the *Goliath* without damaging the *Hydra*?"

"I'm seeing a possible answer here," Henri said. "Pierre's feed says he talked to Terry, and there are spotters on the back of the *Hydra* looking at the water to the west, probably for the torpedo's surface hump. It's likely they were going to talk it in to the *Goliath* with last-second steering orders."

"That's ballsy," Jake said. "And desperate."

"And at this point, highly risky," Henri said. "We can provide intelligence on the torpedo that Terry can merge with his organic systems, and he'll have a good idea of its location. He can break the tow line and slip beside the *Hydra* at the last second. That would make the ultimate target a coin toss."

Jake looked to the data feed on the tactical chart.

"Pierre wants me to come shallow," he said. "Take us to periscope depth, Henri."

As the deck angled upwards, Jake heard Remy's enthusiastic voice.

"The hostile torpedo has shut down."

The ship bounced with the surface swells, and Jake watched his boss' face appear on a display.

"The submarine admiral who ordered the last attack is now on his way to the brig," Renard said. "Prime Minister Daskalakis has taken care of the matter and sends his apologies."

"He's the official prime minister now?" Jake asked.

"Interim, but I'm sure he'll hold the position."

"I heard the torpedo shut down. He must have some real power already."

"He does. Take a look at the scenario as I send you updates. You'll start to see new surfaced contacts."

"No shit. You made the submarines surface."

"Surface and head home. These warships are staffed by men who have been wronged, but they're rightfully shifting their anger from you to the men who used greed and corruption to drive their country to economic ruin. They want to head home and be part of the new regime's punishment of the old more than they want to sink a foreign ship they'll never have to see again."

"Then it's over."

"Indeed, it is."

"Antoine, call Andrei and Mikhail back," Jake said. "We're really going home."

# CHAPTER 24

Cahill watched the sun set over the remnants of his port hull.

"You're sure we're completely safe now?" he asked.

"Yes," Renard said. "That last torpedo was the bitter bite of an old admiral who thought he'd earn an extra star with vigilante heroism. It rightfully instead earned him a trip to the brig, a demotion, and a forced retirement, in that order."

"Good to hear an update about the justice. I haven't heard much from this supposed task force commander, Captain Floros."

"That's because the task force is disbanded, and Floros flew off the *Hydra* with the last transport helicopter."

A combination of nostalgia and respect tickled Cahill's heart as he watched torn and ugly metal generate an oversized bow wave.

"He fought well. He nearly won."

"His admiralty agrees with you, and he'll be rewarded," Renard said. "He could have destroyed you and declared victory at the loss of hundreds of lives and over a billion dollars' worth of hardware, but he chose the proper course of sparing lives within his task force and our fleet."

"Yeah, he did."

"I must also commend you on keeping the *Goliath* in fighting shape. That was a bit of excellent combat leadership. I'm not sure that even the great Jake Slate could have done as well."

On a monitor above the Frenchman's face, Cahill saw Jake's smile turn into an indignant frown.

"I would've figured out in time that I needed to use the bow to protect the rest of the ship, too," Jake said. "At least I'm pretty sure I would have."

"Not to worry, Jake," Cahill said. "I've forgotten how to command a true submarine now that I'm accustomed to this beauty. You command the same ship long enough, and you think of it as part of yourself. That's one advantage we have over the supposed 'real' navies of the world. Too many officers in the pipeline are looking for command jobs, and you need to rotate through them so quickly. But I get to command the *Goliath* as long as Pierre lets me, and I wouldn't change this job for the world."

"Then you need to stop getting its port bow, or should I say your left hand, blown off. That's twice now per my count."

"Right, mate. It beats being dead, though."

Beside Cahill, Walker lowered his optics.

"I see the Italian frigate on the horizon. *Bergamini*-class, based upon the Selex radar dome atop the forward mast."

"You surface warfare officers have great eyes. It looks like a speck of dust to me."

"It would help if you ever put one of these magnifying contraptions to your face. They're called 'binoculars'."

"Why bother when I can trust your younger and better-trained eyes? Anyway, that's our escort into international waters. If our friends on the *Hydra* have any intention of reneging on the ceasefire like their renegade submarine, they're running out of time to do it."

"Indeed," Renard said. "I'm quite proud that I was able to garner support from the Italians. That frigate, which is specifically the *Alpino*, mind you, will escort you through international waters, into Italian waters, and all the way to French waters to dissuade any of the remaining Greek submarines on distant patrols from attempting independent hostilities."

Cahill intensified his focus on Renard.

"The Italians were major supporters of this effort from the beginning, weren't they?" he asked.

"I'm never going to reveal the details of any of my business arrangements, as a matter of protecting you from the information. However, I think it's obvious that the Italians were involved deeply and early, given their commitment now to escort you."

Reflecting upon the European Union countries struggling with debt management, Cahill identified a conflict.

"Italy's suffering from a poor debt structure and economic

performance, too. Why would they be so quick to help push Greece out of the EU? Isn't that creating a bad precedence from the Italian perspective?"

"Not really. Think of Greece as a sacrificial anode instead of the first domino. Only one nation needed to be removed from the union to provide adequate relief. That removal, by the way, isn't a guaranteed outcome, but it's highly probable with the new sentiment I believe is rising in the Greek leadership and with the European reaction to it. Once it does happen, the stronger nations can shoulder the burden without having to oust other weak nations."

"Got it," Cahill said. "And I don't know enough about such dealings to argue otherwise. It's just good to know that me ally is really me ally."

"After the independent hostile decision of the Greek submarine admiral, I shall take nothing for granted about my influence over your safety after such rapid shifts in government power. Thankfully, the Italians agreed to be your insurance policy covering you to French waters for a modest cost, and I'll remember such insurance policies for our future egresses."

Checking the tow lines between the *Hydra* and his starboard bow, Cahill looked ahead and saw long shadows stretching over the frigate's wake. Though the Hellenic combatant had escaped without deaths, he knew the Greek aviators, tanker crews, and workers at the re-gasification terminal fared worse.

"Nobody's asked yet," he said. "So I will. How many lives did we take in this mission?"

He glanced at the monitors and saw faces looking downward. Jake remained silent as the Frenchman looked up and forced an answer.

"The last estimate is twenty-four," Renard said. "A lot of the aircrews you shot down survived. It could have been much worse."

"Yeah," Jake said. "Imagine if we were stuck using heavyweight torpedoes. We'd be counting over a hundred."

"Indeed," Renard said. "The deaths are regrettable, but consider how many lives you have saved."

"That's the problem," Cahill said. "I'm not seeing it. It's too abstract."

"We ousted a corrupt leader and established a new, better government. Think of the first twenty-four children who will be spared from death because they'll receive proper medical care. It may not be today, tomorrow, or even a year from now, but you helped beget the necessary change to allow it. Then think of the first twenty-four elderly people spared by healthcare, or the first twenty-four citizens spared from death by squalor in slums, by traffic accidents averted by improved roads, or by riots averted by improved economic hope."

"By putting a puppet in charge?"

The Frenchman's face hardened.

"Yes, man. Don't let the derogatory nature of the metaphor fool you. A puppet who agrees to being controlled by nations that have proven their fiscal responsibility to their people will fulfill his fiscal responsibility to his people."

Jake waved his hand across the screen.

"Chill out, guys," he said. "We go through this gut check every time. We all know it's the right thing to do when we analyze it ahead of time, but when it finally happens, we feel sick and need to talk about it. It's okay. We did the right thing."

"You've been doing this a bit longer than me, mate," Cahill said. "I need a few more missions to toughen me skin to it."

"That's right," Renard said. "I even remember one of Jake's so-called gut checks taking place on the *Specter* back when it was called the *Hai Ming*."

Jake rolled his eyes.

"Oh shit, don't remind me. Can't we just let that die?"

"Not when you so cavalierly tried to placate us with platitudes and hand-waving. You created the opening in the conversation."

"Is this the one where Pierre had to lead the submarine into battle by a telematics link because Jake didn't feel like fighting that day?" Cahill asked.

"Come on, it wasn't like that at all," Jake said. "Pierre and I talked it through, and he told me to leave. I would've stayed if I was needed, and I even came back when I was."

The Frenchman blushed.

"I did release you, indeed. It's amusing, however, to entice your guilt about it because you make it so damned easy to do so."

"Bite me."

After a brief delay and a murmured translation that had become a background drone, Cahill heard a laugh from his loudspeaker. He looked to a third monitor at a man with a thick, graying beard that was trimmed short.

"I'd almost forgotten about you Dmitry," he said. "I see you like the story about Jake."

Cahill awaited the two-way translation while hearing the *Wraith's* commanding officer respond in Russian.

"Dmitry says he will learn English if for no other reason than to hear the embarrassing stories you tell each other," the *Wraith's* English translator said.

"Great idea," Cahill said. "When is the *Wraith's* crew going to join us for our celebration?"

"I'll answer that," Renard said. "Tomorrow night."

"But we're days from Toulon," Cahill said.

"I've decided that we deserve a vacation now," Renard said. "I trust you'll agree with a port call in Sicily?"

"Sure do, mate," Cahill said. "I can't argue with that."

"Excellent," Renard said. "I've already invited the wives of the crews. So I'd be in dire straits if you disagreed."

Silence overtook the multi-way conversation while Cahill enjoyed daydreams of Italian food and drink. He assumed his colleagues entertained the same visions.

Shadows reached across from the frigate to the *Goliath* as his executive officer snatched him from his thoughts.

"We're leaving Greek waters," Walker said.

"Very well. Any word from the *Hydra* yet?"

"None. Shall I hail the commanding officer and request that

lines be cast off?"

"No, not until the *Alpino* is within half a mile and ready to mate to us. Hail our Italian friends first."

Cahill trusted Walker to handle the niceties and formalities of communication that surface warriors considered second nature but which managed to challenge submarine officers.

With nods and grunts, he gave Walker permission to let the Greek frigate cast off its lines and turn back to its home waters while having the Italian frigate take the *Goliath* as its towed cargo.

"The commanding officer of the *Hydra* didn't even say 'good-bye'," Walker said.

"Some partings are so sweet they don't need words."

"Right, Terry. I think we've seen enough of each other."

"Hey guys," Jake said. "I don't want to spoil the group hug, but there's still some business we need to talk about."

"I thought that's what tomorrow night was for," Cahill said.

"Are you kidding?" Jake asked. "I've seen you drink. You won't have a coherent thought after eight o'clock."

Cahill chuckled.

"Good point, mate. What's on your mind?"

"The dolphins."

"I love them," Cahill said. "Can't get enough of them lads. They're trailing your ship just fine, aren't they?"

"They are for now," Jake said.

The Frenchman became animated.

"I haven't forgotten them," Renard said. "I have a helicopter ordered to pick them up in five hours. I needed to get their trainer to the area before I could schedule the logistics. The trainer assures me they'll be able to keep pace with the *Specter* until then."

"That's great to know," Jake said. "But that's not what I meant. What I meant was their future use."

"I think they've earned their way onto this team," Renard said. "In fact, I can only see brighter and more useful futures for them in our coming missions."

"Exactly," Jake said. "But do some quick math. The dolphins work in pairs, and we have only one pair to go with our three ships."

The Frenchman frowned.

"I admit to a rare moment where you're thinking ahead of me strategically. I hadn't taken any action on our Russian mammalian assets yet, but as long as you've broached the subject, we may as well speak about one pair of dolphins supporting four ships."

"Four ships," Cahill said. "Don't tease us."

"I'm not. I won't tell you the details, but I ask you to trust me on the progress of the construction of the *Goliath's* sister ship."

"That strengthens my point," Jake said. "One pair of dolphins and four ships. Seems we're a bit thin in dolphins."

Shrugging, the Frenchman sounded dismissive.

"You speak as if they're free."

"Okay then, how much do the extra dolphins cost?" Jake asked.

"Do you truly expect me to share one of my significant cost structures with you? Secrecy in such matters is paramount for my negotiation strategies."

"Yeah," Jake said. "For me, I expect you to share."

The Frenchman scoffed.

"Very well, then. For you, for Terry, for Dmitry. And why not for Mikhail and Andrei, too? I negotiated a price of ten million dollars for each dolphin."

Jake's eyebrows rose.

"Ten million dollars per dolphin," he said. "Are there others in the training pipeline?"

"Of course, there are. The Russians take them very seriously, as all evolved navies do—or at least should."

"And it's still ten million each, even if you buy in bulk?"

"Yes, Jake," Renard said. "I know of no frequent flier or rewards programs for purchasing military dolphins. They're expensive little fellows, are they not?"

"Expensive?" Jake asked. "For these little fellows, ten million each sounds like a bargain to me."

"Easy for you to say since it's not your money."

"No, but it's my ass out here in the battle. And if you want my ass, Terry's ass, and Dmitry's ass to come back in one piece from the next mission, I suggest you buy six more of them."

Cahill smiled.

"I agree."

After a two-way translation through Russian, Volkov agreed.

"Very well," Renard said. "I know when I'm outnumbered. I'll see what I can do. Just don't mutiny before you arrive in Sicily."

"Wouldn't think of it, mate."

"Never crossed my mind, either," Jake said.

"Don't patronize me, gentlemen. I know you've each thought of it at least once in your dealings with me. But for God's sake, if you ever do turn on me, don't let it be over a handful of dolphins."

## CHAPTER 25

Dmitry Volkov took a last look into the dry dock basin at the second ship he'd led in battle. He knew few modern submarine captains saw real combat, and he considered himself privileged to have commanded two different ships into hostile action within a three-month window–and to have survived.

In the Black Sea, the Russian submarine *Krasnodar* had proven its survivability with its rugged dual-hull construction. Then in the Arabian Sea, the mercenary *Wraith*, born of French design, sold to the Malaysians, and then reborn under piracy into Renard's fleet, had proven its elusiveness with its anti-air missiles.

He loved both submarines and found sorrow in leaving each. However, he held hopes of rejoining the *Wraith* for a future mission.

First, he needed to unite with the team that owned the mercenary vessel, but the thought of their company intimidated him.

To him, they were elite. If he counted the *Goliath* in the reckoning, then two of its members had commanded multiple submarines in battle. Even the retired leader, Pierre Renard, had demonstrated more combat leadership in his career than Volkov had in his two battles. Worst of all, Renard, Slate, and Cahill had united to defeat him in the Black Sea. In their midst, Volkov felt vulnerable.

His actions on the *Krasnodar* had impressed Renard enough to earn an invitation to the fleet, but Volkov doubted himself. He wondered if Renard were testing him against a gap in his command structure. The Frenchman needed a leader and crew, and Volkov considered himself a mere candidate for a job.

Renard told him he'd earned the position as the *Wraith's* commander, but the true test–acceptance by his colleagues–awaited. Over recent missions, Slate and Cahill had risked their lives for each other and had developed a rare bond. Volkov needed to break into their ranks if he wanted to lead a submarine into combat again.

Bright lights bathed the mercenary vessel in its concealed concrete pen. Atop the ship, one of the commandoes Renard had sent to secure his property spoke with one of the technicians the Frenchman had sent to babysit it. Pakistani naval security personnel guarded, patrolled, and controlled access to the compound's perimeter.

Volkov turned from the *Wraith* and stepped into the limousine with a Pakistani admiral.

"Come on," the admiral said in English. "It's time. Your crew is already aboard the aircraft waiting for you."

From the vehicle's cabin, the translator repeated the words in Russian.

"Thank you, admiral," Volkov said. "To verify, how long can I keep the submarine here?"

After a volley of translations, the answer came.

"I told Mister Renard two months, but I would much prefer fifty days. I have a ship awaiting an overhaul that I'd like to get started sooner than later."

Given the speed at which his French boss found clients, Volkov suspected the *Wraith* would leave Karachi long before the Pakistani admiral needed the dry dock.

"I'm sure that will be fine," he said. "But I'll also verify that Mister Renard is aware of your needs."

Fifteen hours, a short nap, and a shower later, Volkov felt like a square peg in a restaurant for round holes.

In Catania, Italy, his boss had reserved a large room in the most expensive restaurant he could find. Though some men were absent, most of the three crews crammed themselves into tables to enjoy local beers, house wines, and a family-style array of salad pasta, and fish.

As alcohol loosened lips, the men of his crew tested their English with Cahill's Australians and Slate's bilingual Frenchmen. Their efforts earned them strange looks as their English faltered and as the overwhelmed translators struggled to bridge the frequent misunderstandings.

The snippets he heard bothered him as he realized the crews ignored tales of the week's campaign against Greece in favor of arguing their past battle against each other in the Black Sea. The animated talk grew lively, and he sensed arguments forming.

Unskilled at social gatherings, Volkov avoided his normal refuge of alcohol so he could try to prevent the disaster unfolding before him. He found ironic solace in the counsel of a man he'd once doubted, the dolphin trainer.

"Vasily?" he asked.

Lasagna hanging from his mouth, the trainer offered a blank stare, lifted his napkin over his face, and accelerated his chewing. After washing down a mouthful with wine, he spoke.

"Yes, Dmitry. You look troubled."

"Doesn't this bother you?" he asked.

He aimed his arm at one of his sailors with his foot on a chair hovering over an Australian technician. The young Russian's eyes bulged as he used poor English and a translator to convince the *Goliath's* sailor of the Russian crew's superiority.

"Not really. From what I can tell, this is how submarine crews behave."

"I don't share your optimism," Volkov said.

"I think you should," the trainer said. "Look over there. Isn't that the same sort of conversation taking place between members of the *Goliath* and the *Specter*? Doesn't it look like the groups are comparing notes to prove which crew is superior?"

"They could be arguing sporting team abilities or swimsuit model attractiveness for all I know."

"Regardless, my point is that they're arguing. That's what young, proud submarine sailors do. Let them do it."

"But I am responsible for their behavior. I fear an argument will become a push, a push will become a shove, a shove will become a–"

"You're overreacting, Dmitry."

The definitiveness of the statement and the trainer's courage to cut off his speech caught Volkov's attention. Their friendship was new and untested beyond the confines of a submarine, and he needed a second opinion—one he considered wiser.

"Perhaps you're right, Vasily. I appreciate your counsel, but I should get advice from an older man who's seen this sort of thing many times before. Please, excuse me."

To avoid appearing cheerless, he grabbed his full wine glass as he stood. As he pushed his wooden chair back under the draped tablecloth, he had to lean away from a bustling waitress who scurried by him with clanking beer glasses.

Scanning the room, he found his boss standing at the bar with his wife and men he recognized as Renard's countrymen and long-term friends. He braved the walk into the crowd.

The Frenchman exercised his crude Russian.

"How are you, Dmitry?" Renard asked.

"I'm fine. Can we talk alone?"

With a gesture, Volkov guided the Frenchman out of the pack and to a translator who was trying to defuse a debate between sailors from the *Goliath* and the *Wraith*.

"Tell Pierre that I'm concerned about this growing intensity among the different crews. Their arguments appear to be gaining momentum towards hostilities."

"Yes, sir. The words are becoming harsh. I'm having trouble inserting my own soft words into the exchanges. I'll tell him."

During the translation, the Frenchman gave a dismissive wave.

"Pierre says this is normal for submarine crews."

"Tell him I know what's normal for submarine crews," Volkov said. "This is excessive. Has he forgotten that these two crews tried to kill each other three months ago?"

During the next translation, the Frenchman's face hardened.

"Pierre wants you to follow him outside with me."

On the restaurant's patio, Volkov felt the sultry air and faced ivy-covered walls of stone. His boss faced him and attempted communications in Russian, asking for help from the translator when words escaped him.

"There's nothing wrong with your crew's behavior," Renard said. "Only your behavior."

"My behavior? What do you mean?"

"This is supposed to be a celebration, but you appear as if you're looking for a fight."

"Do I?"

"Yes."

Volkov swallowed his reactive anger and tried to give credence to his boss' opinion.

"Really? I had no idea."

The Frenchman's face softened.

"I think I know what's wrong," Renard said.

"Please, if you know, share."

"You're still fighting the lost battle of the Black Sea."

The words stung.

"I don't understand."

"I had hoped that one outcome of your success with the *Wraith* in the Arabian Sea would have been solace for your defeat in the Black Sea, but I see now that I'm wrong."

Volkov scratched his beard while pondering the concept.

"So you're a psychologist now?"

"No, I'm just stating what I see."

"But what you see is from the perspective of a psychologist."

"I can only ask you to ignore me as the source of the observation and to consider the observation on its own merits."

"Perhaps," Volkov said. "Let's say for the sake of argument that you're right. Then what?"

"Then you must grieve your losses and move on. You lost your battle, you lost your commission, and you lost your submarine. That's a lot of suffering, and I should have had this conversation with you before putting you in command of the *Wraith*. In one respect, it's a testimony to your strength of character that you led the *Wraith* successfully with this burden still on your soul."

The insights made Volkov uncomfortable.

"You are a psychologist. At least this is how I imagine one speaks."

"It is how they talk, indeed. But you needn't worry about

paying me two hundred dollars per hour. I'll give you my findings free of charge to keep you as my commanding officer."

Renard smiled, and Volkov chuckled.

"You may have a point," Volkov said. "But even if you're right, even if all this insight is true, what would you have me do?"

"Fake it for tonight and see how it goes."

"How would I fake it?"

"Approach Jake and Terry as if you had defeated them."

"But I didn't, and I don't see how to fake confidence. Confidence is earned by achievement, not by fantasy."

"But I have every confidence in you. You were ambushed in the Black Sea, and you lost because you fell into a trap. But after surviving that trap, you fought as brilliantly as any commander could. I know it, and they know it. If there was any doubt, it's been erased by your performance in the Arabian Sea."

"It's hard enough just trying to talk through a translator," Volkov said. "Now you want me to play a mental game as well?"

"Do what you must to convince yourself you belong here."

The words swam laps around Volkov's head as the Frenchman asked him to wait outside while he went back into the restaurant. A minute later, he held his breath as Renard reappeared with the other two commanders behind him.

Having already shaken hands with them that evening, he restricted his salutation to a nod.

Renard spoke English, and Volkov awaited the translation.

"Jake and Terry both wish to thank you."

"For what?" Volkov asked.

"For the idea of sending the dolphins to them."

"It was the least I could do. It was the only way I could think to help them from the other side of the Suez Canal."

"Terry says it may seem simple in retrospect, but it was nonetheless brilliant. Jake says he agrees and doesn't think they could have survived without them."

"Please tell them both they are too kind. I was glad to help."

Both commanders nodded and appeared reverent as they

spoke in English, the American first, then the Australian.

"They both just emphasized that they are glad you are with them, and they look forward to more missions with you."

The respect warmed Volkov's heart and loosened his tongue.

"Please tell them I respect them not just for their abilities as combat leaders, which are remarkable. Also let them know that I admire their bond. What I've heard of their work together is commendable in the way they've risked their lives for each other. I can only wish to earn my way into their ranks by proving my bravery for their sakes in our future missions."

The translator uttered half the sentiment, sought a reminder from Volkov for the second half, and then continued. After the American and the Australian digested the words, Jake replied through the translator.

"Jake says he welcomes you to the team and looks forward to the opportunity to build that bond of trust."

The Frenchman interjected through the translator.

"Pierre says the next time he plans a mission, he'll do his best to get you deeper into the action."

The offer quenched a deep thirst.

"Please let him know that I appreciate that," Volkov said. "Now that I've had a taste of working for this team, I'll do whatever it takes to become a permanent member."

THE END

## About the Author

*After graduating from the Naval Academy in 1991, John Monteith served on a nuclear ballistic missile submarine and as a top-rated instructor of combat tactics at the U.S. Naval Submarine School. He now works as an engineer when not writing.*

Join the Rogue Submarine fleet to get news, free audiobook promo codes, discounts, and your FREE Rogue Avenger bonus chapter!

# Rogue Submarine Series:

*ROGUE AVENGER (2005)*
*ROGUE BETRAYER (2007)*
*ROGUE CRUSADER (2010)*
*ROGUE DEFENDER (2013)*
*ROGUE ENFORCER (2014)*
*ROGUE FORTRESS (2015)*
*ROGUE GOLIATH (2015)*
*ROGUE HUNTER (2016)*
*ROGUE INVADER (2017)*
*ROGUE JUSTICE (2017)*
*ROGUE KINGDOM (2018)*

# Wraith Hunter Chronicles:

*PROPHECY OF ASHES (2018)*
*PROPHECY OF BLOOD (2018)*
*PROPHECY OF CHAOS (2018)*
*PROPHECY OF DUST (2018)*

John Monteith recommends his talented colleagues:

Graham Brown, author of The Gods of War.

Jeff Edwards, author of Steel Wind.

Thomas Mays, author of A Sword into Darkness.

Kevin Miller, author of Declared Hostile.

Ted Nulty, author of The Locker.

ROGUE INVADER

Copyright © 2017 by John R. Monteith

## Braveship Books

www.braveshipbooks.com

The tactics described in this book do not represent actual U.S. Navy or NATO tactics past or present. Also, many of the code words and some of the equipment have been altered to prevent unauthorized disclosure of classified material.

ISBN-13: 978-1-939398-82-6
Published in the United States of America

69049834R00138

Made in the USA
Columbia, SC
12 August 2019